BURNING UNDER

A Novel

by

TOM BENNITT

Tom Bennitt (signature)

STEPHEN F. AUSTIN STATE UNIVERSITY PRESS

Managing Editor: Lauren M. McDaniel
Cover Design: Joshua J. Hines

COPYRIGHT © 2018 Stephen F. Austin State University Press

PUBLISHED BY STEPHEN F. AUSTIN UNIVERSITY PRESS
414 Aikman Drive, LAN 203
P.O. BOX 13007
NACOGDOCHES, TEXAS 75962
sfapress@sfasu.edu
sfasu.edu/sfapress
936-468-1078

ISBN: 978-1-62288-224-3
First Edition

Dedicated to
my wife, Rebecca,
my son, Harrison,
and in loving memory
of my mother,
Sue Riley Bennitt.

CONTENTS

PART FOUR

PROLOGUE

Larry walked from his truck to the mine entrance. The rain fell in sheets. Lightning flashed like a strobe. Thunder rattled around the ridge. He considered running but it seemed futile since he was already drenched.

The mantrip rattled and bounced as it shuttled his crew deep underground.

Larry was first up on the continuous miner, the big coal-cutting machine resembling a scorpion. With no rock or shale to bust through, the steel claws hummed through the seam, tearing off big chunks. He finished the first cut in solid time.

He stopped and walked over to Section Two, where Luke and Tree were bolting the roof. Tree kept yelling fuck as he tried to drill a steel rod into the narrow hole above. The glue-covered rod was supposed to bind into the hole and stabilize the roof, but something was wrong.

Larry heard a loud noise, like a dynamite blast, followed by a long, low rumble. The dirt floor buckled. The power cut out. The machines went dead.

"Was that from the storm?" Tree asked.

"Too loud for thunder," Larry said. "Came from inside."

"Methane explosion." Luke paused. "We need to haul ass."

PART ONE

COAL VEINS

One week earlier.

Larry's truck snaked along the valley road, the bald tires sliding in slush. Steep ridges flanked the road, concealing this bastard land from the modern world. A thick fog oozed off the river and swallowed the light from his truck's one good headlamp. He stopped on the shoulder, left it running, and jumped out. He scooped a handful of snow and spread it across the muddy front windshield. All around him, chunks of wet snow dropped from burdened branches of spruces and hemlocks. Late March thaw. First glimmer of spring.

He reached behind the driver's seat and felt around the cab floor – pushing aside the twelve-gauge and coffee can full of buckshot – until his fingers gripped the deer spotter. When he pulled back on the road, he steered with his right hand and held the spotter with his left. The strong beam of light knifed through the haze and pointed the way forward. He downshifted at the base of a steep grade. As he rounded a switchback he swerved to avoid a coal truck, screaming downhill. *Assholes,* he thought, *always going Mach Three, trying to squeeze in more runs.* Soon, the road narrowed and turned to gravel. The rotten-egg stench of sulfur draped the air. He passed the two bony piles of coal, like black pyramids, beside the tipple, and the company sign – COMMONWEALTH ENERGY, SARVER MINE – and, finally, the security booth, nodding to the guard who had beady eyes that made Larry think of Charles Bronson.

He parked beside an old Tacoma, owned by his buddy, Tree. He got out and circled the truck. Dented quarter panel. Rust spots on the hood. Exhaust pipe rigged to the back bumper with a coat hanger. The truck bed held a fishing pole, a crossbow, and a case of Iron City beer. He brought his face up to the driver's side window. Tree was passed out: sprawled across the bench seat, mouth agape, blanketed by his Carhartt jacket.

Larry tapped the window. No response. He opened the door.

Tree shot up, rubbing his bloodshot eyes. "What time is it?"

"About seven. You sleep here?"

Tree cracked his neck. "Got a little banged up. If I went home, would've slept in."

A tall black man, the tallest miner Larry knew, Tree's real name was Calvin but no one called him that. During his second Iraq tour, shrapnel from a roadside bomb caught the artery behind his knee. Now, three surgeries later, he walked with a slight limp.

Larry climbed the warped wooden steps to the miners' change room, an old trailer. He punched his time card and opened his locker, removed his coat and Steelers cap, and threw a sweatshirt over his overalls and faded THIN LIZZY t-shirt. He laced up his steel toes and clipped the mining hammer and self-rescuer device, a small oxygen canister, onto his belt. He pulled his gray hair into a pony tail and adjusted his hardhat. Completing his morning ritual, he rubbed his forearm tattoo – a pikaxe and shovel, intersecting to form an X – for safety.

As the mantrip rattled through the cool damp darkness, Tree talked about the dog races and how he'd won on a longshot greyhound named Phantom. "Looked like a runt," he said. "But that sucker was flying. Almost caught the rabbit." They reached their workstation and got out. The top of Larry's helmet barely cleared the tunnel's roof.

The Sarver Mine was one of the last underground mines in Pennsylvania. Most companies had switched over to strip mining, using machines – rippers and hydraulic shovels – instead of human labor. Sometimes the land above would subside, and some old farmer would have to be compensated for the damage, but this method was still cheaper than underground mining. And while strip mining could not be considered eco-friendly, it was child's play compared to the mountaintop removal mining – scalping the tops of mountains with gigantic dozers and front-loaders – done in West Virginia and Kentucky. Down there, nothing was sacred.

You needed good hands to run the continuous miner. You had to know when to hold back, and when to push the ripper head deeper into the coal seam. It was the best paying job, but also the hardest. You couldn't show up drunk or high and expect to make six cuts of coal in a shift. But Larry's hands were rusty. He'd just started two weeks ago, his first mining job in five years. He'd quit on the doctor's advice, after he started coughing up flecks of blood. That was just a month after learning of his son Josh's death in Afghanistan. Could the world get any crueler than that? His son had been everything, his only family. Josh's mom, Kelly, had divorced him long before when Josh was fourteen.

Larry decided to pack up and leave home. He figured a change of venue might do some good. He traveled around the country, picking up jobs when he needed money. Worked in a meatpacking plant in Nebraska. Hung drywall in Mississippi. Drove a forklift in a Kentucky. But after a few years of drifting he returned home. With a pile of debt and a house he couldn't sell, he started mining again. He did it for the money, and thanks to the recent coal boom, the money was pretty damn good. If that made him a greedy old redneck, he was fine with it.

"Larry, hold up!" Tree yelled, after the power went out. "You tripped the generator." Tree's face was caked with soot. His teeth gleamed like pearls.

"Did I break the cable?" Larry asked.

"No dog, it ain't that bad."

He'd pushed the miner too hard. It sumped up the generator and killed the power. Common in smaller mines, not a major fuckup. Jerry the electrician would have them up and running soon. Luke, a roof bolter, walked over. He opened his tin of Copenhagen, took a fat pinch, and worked it under his lip. He had a beard and a scar under his right eye. He reminded Larry of Josh. Smart, funny, confident. Seemed he was wasting his talent down here.

"Hey old man," Luke said. "You havin' fun yet?"

"That's why I came back. The fun."

"You missed the flood last month," Tree added.

On Larry's first day, the foreman had mentioned it. He said two men had quit.

Tree laughed. "Water was up to my waist, no joke. Thought I might drown."

"Save the drama for your mama," Luke said, spitting a wad of tobacco juice.

"Your mother loves my drama." Tree grabbed his crotch.

They discussed tonight's boxing match at the Mountaineer Casino, featuring Donny Russo. Luke and Donny had played football together, from the midget leagues to varsity.

"Great linebacker," Luke said. "A Tasmanian devil. He'd smear that eyeblack all over his face. One game, he ripped the helmet off a three hundred-pound lineman."

"What for?"

"The dude tried to chop block him on the previous play."

Larry asked if he ever played college ball.

"Youngstown State. The Browns invited him to training camp, but they cut him."

Luke summarized the past ten years of Donny's life: returning to Millburg, marriage, kids, laying brick on construction crews. He began sparring with pro fighters in Pittsburgh, then hired a trainer and manager. Started at Cruiserweight but jumped to Heavyweight, where the real money could be made. Now he was ranked in the top ten.

"Hey Larry, you want to come with us tonight?" Tree asked.

Larry rubbed his goatee. "Let me think on it."

"Don't think too hard," said Tree. "That's the key to life."

Larry took the long way home. Past the power plant, the road began to rise high above the valley. He lowered his window. The warm breeze felt clean on his face. At the road's apex, he pulled onto the shoulder and cut the engine. He grabbed his one-hitter from the glove box and fired it up. He surveyed the Allegheny Mountains, rolling and blue like the ocean. But also like skin, covering veins of coal. The fading horn of a train issued from a distant valley. His grandfather used to take him hunting up here. The land had changed since then. Scanning the ridges, he counted four fracking towers – natural gas wells – sticking out of the land like heroin needles. Big chunks of forest had been cleared by mining or gas companies. State law required them to backfill the land – reclamation was the industry term – but it was never the same. Backfilled land was like a bad hairpiece: far away it looked fine, but up close you knew something wasn't right.

Sometimes, Larry felt he'd been born too late. Sure, life was harder back then. His granddad's family had lived in a one-room shack with a dirt floor, owned by the Frick Coal Company. But simpler, too. Today, you couldn't take pride in your work. Not miners. The tree huggers shamed you, and the rich snobs called you white trash. Maybe that explained why miners never stayed in one place. Many traversed the country for short-term work, from the bituminous mines in Appalachia to open-pit mines out west. They lived in motels or campgrounds, like the roughnecks who'd moved from Texas to the oilfields in North Dakota.

Once he stepped foot inside his house, Larry stripped and jumped in the shower. He'd forgotten how grimy you got from mining. He used Lava soap and steel wool on his hands and face, but coal stains were like tattoos. Walking into the kitchen, he found a note from Tina, his girlfriend, on the counter. She was going out tonight – "clubbing with friends" – in Pittsburgh. He smiled, realizing this left his evening free. He was eager to go see a heavyweight fight with his buddies, even though the location of the fight, a casino, gave him a moment's pause. In a past life, gambling and drugs had nearly buried him.

After nuking some leftover meatloaf, he drove to Tree's place. On Route 422, he got stuck behind a truck hauling gravel, which kept spilling out and pelting his windshield. Once he passed on a flat stretch, he felt more relaxed. Soon the blood orange sun faded behind the hills, leaving pink and violet strands. The kind of sunset that artist on PBS – the hippie with the afro and his "happy trees" – used to paint. He whiffed the loamy musk of rich soil and manure coming from the hillside dairy farms. Then he drove past a sign that read 'BUCK RUB: Taxidermy and Massage Therapy.' Owned by a hunter and his wife, a masseuse. Same building, but separate businesses. The left door opened to soothing music, massage beds, the smell of ointments. And behind the right door was a room full of animal heads and skins – deer, elk, bear –

with old country music playing on the stereo.

He crossed the river into Millburg, past the abandoned steel mill, and parked in front of Tree's house, a one-story rectangle of brick. When the mill shut down, drifters and bums would sift through the rubble for copper wire and scrap metal. But now the half-crumbled walls were overgrown with goutweed and creeping jenny, and the only signs of life were deer and coyote prints. He honked a few times, then waited.

Tree and Luke and PJ, a bartender, came out together and piled into his truck.

Luke, in a Carhartt jacket and a black Pirates cap, sat up front.

"Who's Donny fighting tonight, anyway?" asked PJ.

"Some big German dude," said Tree. "Used to fight mixed martial arts."

"That shit inside the cage? Man, those guys fuck each other up."

Luke saw Donny fight in junior high. "He was fighting some older kid over this girl named Jenny Hutchens."

Larry smiled. "There's always a girl."

"Donny's right hand broke the kid's jaw. Sounded like an axe splitting wood."

Tree tapped him on the shoulder. "So, what made you start mining again?"

"Same reason y'uns are down there. Money."

That was Larry's fallback answer but, truthfully, he also missed the fraternal bond that miners shared. Despite being old enough to be everyone's dad, tonight he felt like a kid. He'd forgotten how young men interacted, how they told stories to entertain rather than provide information, how they fictionalized details, and how the storyteller's audience cared more about tone and style than veracity.

They paralleled the Ohio River through a series of dingy towns that all looked the same: churches, bars, tattoo parlor, dollar stores, funeral homes, old factories. The river was the color of brushed steel. Crossing the state line, a giant billboard greeted them: 'WEST VIRGINIA – WILD AND WONDERFUL!' Below the slogan were pictures of healthy, attractive people hiking and rafting, and a shot of the mountains at sunset.

"At least they're half right," PJ quipped.

They passed the White Pony, a strip joint. Christmas lights framed the outside. The statue of a chrome horse stood beside the road. Then the casino, with its massive size and bright lights, came into view. Larry thought it looked absurdly out of place, like some cruise ship in the middle of the desert.

They bought tickets outside the boxing arena and shuffled in. Their seats were close to the ring, twenty rows back. They caught the last two rounds of the undercard, a welterweight bout between a veteran Irishman and a young black fighter from Cleveland. The Cleveland kid dominated the final round and won by split decision.

When the emcee announced the main event, the sellout crowd roared.

Donny entered the ring first. His gray cutoff hoodie revealed his giant pipes. A barbwire tattoo circled his right bicep. He had a shaved mohawk and his nickname, The Dagger, was etched on the front of his black satin shorts. His opponent, Axel Bleier, had the cauliflower ears of a wrester. He was bigger and taller than Donny but had shorter arms. He looked like a Tyrannosaurus Rex.

"That fucker's huge," Luke said.

"He's a fascist," said Tree, leaning back.

As the first round began, Donny sprang out of his corner, his gloves guarding his chin. He danced in half-circles around his opponent. Near the end of the round he threw a combination, but he left himself exposed. Bleier planted a straight right on his jaw. Donny hit the canvas. The ref began his count, but Donny got up after a few seconds. He escaped the round without further damage. The crowd buzzed, lusting for blood.

"Donny's toast," said PJ. "He walked into that punch."

"He's got a tough chin," said Tree.

During the middle rounds the pace slowed, as both fighters tried to find their rhythm. In the fifth, Donny landed several jabs. Two rounds later, Bleier punched Donny in the kidney. Must've hurt, the way he grimaced. A cut formed over Donny's left eye. His corner man would treat it between rounds, but it kept opening back up.

When the final-round bell rang, Donny was behind on points and needed a knockout to win. But he looked tired, throwing wild punches. The German should have played it safe, but he wanted the knockout, too. When he missed with a left hook and exposed his chin, Donny tagged him with an uppercut. Donny kept punching, his hands firing like pistons. Bleier wobbled and then collapsed, his face hitting the canvas first. When the ref's count reached eight, he still hadn't moved. Two seconds later the fight was over. Somehow, Donny had won. Tree started chanting "Dag-ger" and high-fiving everyone around him.

They filed out of the arena toward the casino and found the blackjack tables. Larry grabbed a seat at a ten-dollar table. He broke even for several hands, until the next dealer rotation. The new dealer, a laconic Asian woman, started feeding him terrible cards. He busted three times in a row. On his final hand he doubled down. He prayed for a face card, but instead was dealt a three. The cocktail waitress served his Rum-and-Coke. Larry tipped her with his last dollar chip and left the table. He passed a woman in an electric wheelchair playing the slots. A tube ran from her nose to an oxygen tank behind the chair. He found his buddies at one of the fifty-dollar tables.

"Larry, how'd you end up?" Tree asked.

"Lost a hundred."

"Not me." Tree pointed to his big stacks of chips.

"Hey man," Luke said. "Let's wrap this puppy up."

"Dude, I'm hot right now." Tree swigged his beer.

Sometimes, Luke and Tree conversed like a pair of old gay bachelors who'd been together so long, there were no secrets or surprises.

They got back to Millburg around midnight. Tree asked Larry if he was sticking around.

"I thought the night was over."

Tree wagged a finger. "Just getting started, old man."

Luke nodded. "Yeah, I got a hall pass tonight. Denise works night shift."

Larry rubbed his goatee. Tina would be pissed, but fuck it. She stayed out late every weekend, and besides, they were near the end of their road together, he could tell. She'd leave, once she found a younger victim, or a richer one.

So, he followed the guys inside and grabbed a Yuengling from the fridge.

Tree sat on the couch, smoking meth from a homemade pipe: a test tube duct-taped to the base of a light bulb. His tiny pupils jumped around like black marbles as he scratched his neck. If Tree wasn't totally batshit, then his toes were touching the line.

Tree smiled and took another hit. "No matter where you're going," he said, "with God's grace you can enjoy the ride. Heard that on the Christian radio station this morning."

He offered Larry the pipe.

"No thanks," Larry said, holding his hand out like a stop sign.

"Suit yourself, man."

Larry wondered how much more of this he could take. Not just tonight, every night and every day. There was nothing left, nothing new to discover. He was just retracing his steps in a vast maze. He drank a shot of Wild Turkey and let it burn. He walked to the window and peered out, shifting his gaze between the moon and its reflection off the river.

He made it home around two. A Millburg cop had tailed him for a couple miles, but he turned around at the county line. His bulldog, Fred, greeted him at the door. Tina was asleep on the couch. She wore a Bon Jovi t-shirt, a blanket covering her legs. A pizza box, empty Busch Light cans, and a bottle of Oxy on the coffee table. The television played that same George Clooney movie she'd seen a hundred times.

He and Tina had started out hot. She'd wear those tight shirts and jeans that made her tits and ass pop when she walked. But now she sat on the couch all day, drinking beer and smoking weed and watching her soaps. Of course, he wasn't exactly the poster-boy of good health, with his bad lungs. Their relationship had grown toxic. They hardly made love anymore, and he refused to take those pecker pills. Even worse, they were ugly to each other, trading insults like it was some perverse game. Still, he feared being alone. He feared dying alone.

As he walked past, Tina sat up and yawned. "Where you been?"

"Out," he said. "Listen, I'm working tomorrow."

"So what?"

"I need to get some sleep. Can you turn the TV down?" In the movie, Clooney was seducing a gorgeous Italian woman.

"Just close the bedroom door," she said.

"How many times have you seen this movie, anyway?"

"Why do you care?"

"If you like that guy so much, then go to Hollywood and find him."

"Trust me, I'd rock his world."

He chuckled. "Oh, I bet you would."

She threw a beer can at his head, but he ducked. "You got a broken dick and a mountain of debt. That's a low batting average, asshole. You're lucky I'm still here. You don't watch your mouth, you can find someone else to change your diapers."

His eyes widened. That was the most passionate thing she'd said in a long while.

John Simon Yoder had never warmed up to his first name. He considered it too generic, too forgettable. In college, he started going by his middle name, Simon, which seemed to bestow intelligence and wit. Men named Simon were secret service agents, or Nobel Prize-winning scientists who studied wormholes and string theory.

At times, Simon's imagination consumed him. This morning while checking the weather forecast, he imagined that Television and The Internet were two men from the same gentrified neighborhood. Two residents of a gated, artfully landscaped subdivision with a name like Chapel Glen or The Sanctuary at Brittany Plantation. The Internet, an advertising man, flaunted his thick hair and square jawline. He read literary fiction, spoke four languages, drove a Range Rover. Even The Internet's name had more gravitas, because it included a definite article. Meanwhile, Television had a turkey neck, receding hairline, and pear-shaped body. Instead of reading novels, he'd wait for the movie to come out on cable. A Chevrolet man, he refused to drive foreign cars. Finally, Television suspected that his wife was having an affair with The Internet.

As a child of the eighties with two working parents, Simon had been raised by television. The Price Is Right. Saturday morning cartoons. Mr. Rogers. He learned math from the Count on Sesame Street. He learned music from MTV. HBO and Cinemax taught him sex education. He knew the "Cheers" theme song, word for word. He loved sports, especially women's tennis. He got hooked on reality shows, even if they repeated the same script every season.

When he hit rock bottom, infomercials — mother's milk for insomniacs — became his new obsession. He'd smoke a bowl and watch thirty minutes of hyperbole and bad acting. He loved every format. The faux interview of the product's inventor. The exuberant pitchman's wacky demonstrations. Even the creepy doctor with the soul patch and black vest, selling his latest version of snake oil: *Rub my amazing product, Frontal Lobe Lube, on your forehead every night,* the doctor said. *Soon, it will seep into your brain and make you charming and brilliant.* Infomercial products were displayed throughout Simon's apartment. He clapped his lights on with the Clapper. He grilled chicken on the Foreman Grill. His Snuggie kept him warm on winter nights. Blood stains vanished with Oxy Clean. The Sham-Wow Towel soaked up minor floods. He watched his Chia-Pet grow!

Simon lived in a ketchup factory: the old Heinz plant on Pittsburgh's North Side, converted into loft apartments. This morning, like most, he made the reverse commute to his Millburg office. The parkway was bottled up by construction, orange cones squeezing two lanes into one. He drove a practical sedan with good gas mileage, but some days he imagined driving a black Cadillac hearse. He tuned the radio to WDVE. (Pittsburghers still valued classic rock.) He enjoyed singing in the car, the simple freedom it offered. Right now, "Lady" by Styx was testing his range. He followed the horseshoe exit into the business park and pulled in beside his building, The Commonwealth Energy Corporate Office.

He swiped his key fob and opened the side door. The head secretary, Deb, waved while continuing her phone conversation. A portrait of Deb's grandchild hung on the wall behind her desk. The baby was smirking, and its head was freakishly large. Simon had a theory: simple people – those who lacked curiosity or imagination – were happier, because they had lower expectations. Take his coworkers. Deb listened to country music and *shit happens* was her favorite expression. Bob jet-skied on Conneaut Lake. Scott took annual trips to Pocono Speedway, drinking Busch Light on top of his RV and watching cars whiz past. Sheila rode a motorcycle with a sidecar. Okay, Sheila was a badass.

The building had the ambiance of a typical corporate office, devoid of charm or warmth. Fluorescent lights. Landscape photographs on cream-colored walls. A few of Simon's college friends worked for tech companies in Silicon Valley. Their offices had cafes, gyms, movie theaters. They had flexible hours and played frisbee on the quad. Our best and brightest, Simon thought, now writing code for video games.

He filled his mug with stale coffee and strolled to his desk, waving to Julie and Hippie Jim. He set down his leather satchel – insecure men might call it a purse – and surveyed his stack of unfinished work. On top was a letter from the EPA, issuing a warning about coal sludge from the Sarver Mine polluting a nearby creek. He powered up his computer and checked his email. The one from Richard, his boss, read: "See me when you get in." He walked the plank down to Richard's office and knocked on the half-open door.

"Come in," Richard said. "Have a seat." Richard Blount, the CFO, had a nasally voice and curved spine. His office had a distinct maritime theme, replica Navy battleships sat on the side table and a picture of a sailing yacht with the caption "INSPIRATION" hung on the wall. But Richard had never served in the Navy and was not a sailor. He didn't even own a kayak.

"This conveyor belt problem isn't going away," Richard said.

"Since the belt was defective, why can't we sue the company that made it?"

"German company. We'd have to sue in Europe. Different laws. We'd lose."

"But they assured us the belts would hold two tons of coal. I've got the emails."

"And that's our back door," Richard said. "But we still have exposure."

"Because of Kevin?" Simon was referring to the company's in-house engineer.

"No, Simon. Because of the contract you wrote. There's no language anywhere regarding liability for a manufacturing defect."

"I thought liability was implied in these contracts."

"Nothing is implied," Richard said. "Ever."

Simon imagined torturing Richard with a Taser gun or cattle brand. "You told me to keep the contract short."

"You're the lawyer, here. Just do your job. Or I'll find someone who can."

Technically, Simon was a lawyer. He'd graduated from Pitt Law and passed the bar exam on his second attempt. He'd spent two years at Rooney & Paine, a respected downtown firm. But these days, he rarely felt like a lawyer. His official job title at Commonwealth was Legal Compliance Specialist. Since they had no legal department, Simon reported to Richard. And when the shit storms hit, Richard called the attorneys at Mitchell & Burns. They had Ivy League degrees and worked in downtown Pittsburgh offices with views of the riverfront and the baseball stadium. Litigated multimillion-dollar cases, wrote elegant briefs, filed complex pretrial motions. Worked seventy hours a week, billed fifty. Drank single malts and smoked Cubans at the Duquesne Club. They had thick wavy hair, gleaming white teeth, square jawlines. They wore tailored suits and polished wingtips. Meanwhile, Simon drafted contracts, filled out forms, and tried to look busy until five o'clock. He had skinny legs, a round jawline, and a slight paunch. He wore wrinkled khakis and running shoes. He was Simon Yoder: Half-Man, Half-Lawyer.

When people asked why he'd settled for doing paralegal work for a coal company, he'd mention the bad economy and the tough job market. He knew he should be somewhere else, but had no idea where. He came from an over-achieving family. His father, a steel company executive. His older brother, a Wall Street banker married to a tax attorney. They belonged to a yacht club and lived in Greenwich. They had a nanny. On paper, overachievement seemed appealing, but to succeed on their terms, Simon would need to harness such large amounts of energy and ambition, there'd be no time left for the quiet enjoyment of life. The American Dream was fool's gold.

"Anything else?" he asked Richard.

"George is here next week. We need to put this fire out now, before he finds out."

George was President and CEO of Commonwealth Energy, which operated coal mines and natural gas wells in the region. He made the big decisions but was frequently out of the office, meeting with investors or visiting a company site.

Before lunch, Simon found the bathroom. Staring down at the pink urinal cake, he thought about Richard, or more precisely, Richard's family. He pictured his two kids skiing at Jackson Hole, carving giant slalom turns, and summering in Vermont, hitting topspin forehands on their private tennis court. Perfect models of Hitler Youth. But soon they'd head off to college and rebel against their parents for programming their lives and ignoring them. Richard's daughter would migrate to a southern liberal arts college, where she'd party five nights a week — molly, her drug of choice — and sleep with half the lacrosse team, but soon, tired of the academic tyranny and the vapid superficiality of her sorority friends, she would drop out and follow a neo-hippie jam band around the country with her poet boyfriend, ending up in Idaho, where she'd use her trust fund to start an organic potato farm. Meanwhile, Richard's smart but antisocial son would spend two years at MIT, using his coding skills to hack into global corporations and government agencies. He'd start his own tech company and sell it to Apple or Google for a hundred million, then spend the next twenty years indulging his weird sexual fetishes, splitting time between Thailand and Miami Beach.

Simon left the office and drove through Millburg, his hometown. Past the empty Woolworth's building, Phat Matt's Tattoos, the Elks Lodge, and Thompson's Funeral Home. The WELCOME JOE NAMATH banner above Main Street had been up since December. Although Namath hailed from Beaver County, he'd been the Grand Marshal of Millburg's Christmas parade: Simon watched him limp to the podium with a cane and thank the crowd. Much like Broadway Joe, Millburg had aged poorly. Once a vibrant town of immigrants, mostly from southern and eastern Europe, today it was a strange mix of churches and bars. Another notch along the rust belt. Some meth houses had sprung up on the edge of town. There were a few Amish communities in the western part of the county, but they weren't hardcore Amish: you'd see them at Wal-Mart, or eating Blizzards outside Dairy Queen.

In the eighties, thousands of laid-off steelworkers had left the region. The Armco steel mill had survived until '89, when a Japanese company took over and laid off half the workers. While Pittsburgh had embraced the new information economy, Millburg had not changed. Yet somehow, the town endured, dying but not dead. One reason was coal: the mines east of town had been running full tilt for the past decade. War in the Mideast and the spike in oil prices had triggered a national coal boom. So, rather than joining the twenty-first century, Millburg survived by returning to the Stone Age.

One day, Simon would invent an infomercial product that could instantly erase these dingy row houses and empty stores and factories. He'd call it THE EXPUNGER: If you want to eradicate the lingering disease and decay, even zap those stubborn feelings of shame and regret, just spray on The Expunger and watch them disappear! He could sell it to every Rust Belt town from here to Detroit and become a billionaire!

He decided to eat lunch at the only Indian restaurant in town, Curry Favor. Nearly empty, like most days. The same Bollywood movie played on the television in the back. He seated himself and used his phone to check his email.

"John Yoder, is that you?"

Simon glanced up at a black-haired woman with a familiar face.

"Anita?" He stood up. Awkwardly, they hugged. He hadn't seen Anita Sekran since high school. "How are you? I didn't know you were a waitress here."

"I'm not," she said, laughing.

"Sorry," he stammered. "You want to join me?" She sat down across from him.

He'd been in French Club with Anita. Quiet and smart, she hung out with the cool kids. She played varsity tennis and dated a football player who probably treated her like shit.

"So, you thought I worked here because I'm Indian?" Anita was biracial: Indian father, white mother. Exotic for Millburg. And beautiful.

"No, um, I saw you holding that notepad, and –"

"I'm kidding. My uncle owns this place. I worked here my college summers."

He could not believe his luck, the serendipity of this encounter.

When the waiter came over, Anita ordered something in Hindi.

"Tikka masala," he said. "Spicy."

"So you've been here before?"

"I love Indian food. And it's quiet here, so I can read."

She smiled. "My uncle's a great cook, but a lousy businessman."

Simon's neck twitched. His nervous tics were induced by stress. His left eye would blink and his hands would flap without warning. Over the years he'd learned to control them, but he could not eradicate them. As a kid he'd been hyperactive, ADD before people knew the term. His parents and doctors called it a phase, but as he aged, his anxiety grew. Sometimes, when his mind raced, his thoughts would pile up like cars hitting black ice on Interstate-80. He saw a shrink after his breakup with Lindsey, but the pills deadened his senses and emotions, as if he was covered head-to-toe in Bubble Wrap. He flushed the pills because he'd rather feel raw emotion than nothing at all.

"It's been a long time," Simon said. "What are you up to these days?"

"I live in Pittsburgh and write for the Press. I'm here for a story, hence the notepad."

"What's your beat?" Simon wondered if journalists still used that word.

"Mainly local stuff," Anita said. "Crime, obituaries, politics.

At Penn State he'd written a sports column for the student paper but was granted no journalistic freedom. Our readers want football, his editor kept repeating.

"What about you?" she asked.

"A lawyer for Commonwealth Energy. It's a coal and gas company."

"So, what kind of legal work is that?"

"Corporate stuff. I draft contracts with phrases like nondisclosure of confidential information and material breach of performance. I write memos to the VPs. When I get bored, I revise the employee policy handbook."

She laughed.

Simon pushed up his glasses. "In law school, I pictured myself as a hot-shot litigator, cross-examining evil men until they confessed everything."

"Reality is never what we expect."

They exchanged information about high school friends.

"Mike Ellis is an architect in Chicago," he said. "Chris Paserba is a commercial pilot, based in Charlotte. Drew Stadler got laid off during the recession and moved back in with his parents, along with his wife and two kids."

"Brutal," she said. "Julie Bandura moved back home, too."

"I thought she was living out west."

"Yeah, Portland, until she overdosed on heroin."

"What about Megan Chang?"

"Med school."

"She was my lab partner in Physics. Thank God."

"Hey, whatever happened to Joe Singleton?"

"Suicide." Simon paused. "I remember his funeral. Not a dry eye in the house."

"Oh my God," she said. "I had no idea."

Simon didn't see a ring, but he wanted confirmation. "So, you're not married?"

"Hell no." She rolled her eyes. My dad keeps trying to set me up with Indian men, like family friends or younger doctors he works with."

"You don't seem very enthusiastic."

"It's hard enough to find the right person, so why limit yourself to one race?"

Simon mentioned his busted engagement. Feeling self-conscious, he ate his chicken too fast and burned his tongue. Then he gulped his water, and half of it rolled down his face.

She smiled. "Here, let me clean you up." She wiped his chin with her napkin. "I'm a train wreck sometimes."

"You're not that bad," she said, but maybe she was just being polite.

"Remember that French Club trip to Montreal?" Simon asked.

"It's a blur. I was drunk the whole weekend."

"Same here," he said, but he clearly remembered their first night in the hotel when, walking down the hall to get some ice, he rounded a corner and bumped into her.

She wore a half t-shirt, exposing her pierced bellybutton, and black tights. She smelled like lavender. But before he could force a word out of his mouth, she'd vanished.

As the waiter took their plates, Simon offered to pay for lunch.

"Not necessary," she said. "Family members, and their guests, eat free."

He left a generous tip. Outside, he tried to read her body language and nonverbal cues, but he was nonverbally illiterate. *Just don't be too fucking weird. Don't scare her away.*

"It was good seeing you, John. We should get a drink in the city sometime. Here's my cell number." She wrote it down on the back of her business card.

"I'd love to," he said. "By the way, I don't go by John anymore."

"What should I call you, then?"

"Simon."

"It suits you," she said.

That evening, he grilled a pork chop and started watching the Penguins game, but he felt the urge to go out. He picked a bar in Lawrenceville called the Brillo Box, named after the Warhol painting. Cultured Pittsburghers claimed Warhol as their native son, even though he'd defected to New York after college and slandered Pittsburgh most his life. It was an eclectic venue that occasionally hosted events, like open mics and poetry readings, but tonight it was rather dead. Simon posted up at the bar, ordered a bourbon, neat, and looked around. Two lawyers or bankers sat beside him, in pressed slacks and polo shirts, discussing their golf games and the stock market. Some college kids – guys in skinny jeans and white sneakers and mesh caps, girls with bangs and thrift store sweaters – filled out a large table. Art or theater majors at Carnegie Mellon or Pitt. Still living on their parents' dime, free to sleep late and follow their creative muse. He remembered a line from a comedian on HBO: In your twenties, you think you know everything. In your thirties, you realize you don't know shit. He wondered what happened in your forties. Maybe it didn't matter by then.

He could not identify with anyone here. Not that he cared, but at least they had their own people. Simon didn't have his own people. He lived on an island, but not some lush Caribbean island with umbrella drinks and turquoise waters. More like a remote, barren island in the North Atlantic that repelled warm ocean currents and was surrounded by ledges that sank boats. He called it the ISLE OF SIMON, and for a long while he felt at home there. But now, perhaps, it was time for him to build a raft and paddle back to the world.

After applying his Breathe-Right nose strip and inserting his mouth guard (he looked like a linebacker when he slept), Simon climbed into bed, thinking about Anita. She was his best romantic prospect in years.

He wanted to ask her out, and considered his options. He could text her something ironic, like: If you want to go out with me, please reply "Yes." Or: If you don't go out with me, the terrorists will win. He could also make her a mix tape. In high school, he'd mastered the art of the mixtape. He could throw in some Black Sabbath and Led Zeppelin. On second thought, the mixtape idea might backfire.

He couldn't sleep. Since he was fresh out of weed, he flipped around the television for an infomercial. The creepy doctor was back again, selling his Frontal Lobe Lube. The testimonials were incredible. One woman climbed from secretary to CEO of a Fortune 500 company, after her IQ jumped fifty points. Simon imagined the new-and-improved version of himself: Simon, 2.0. Smarter and polished, minus the social awkwardness and nervous tics. What did the future hold? Would he become a badass lawyer? Would Anita fall head over heels? The possibilities were endless.

When he finally drifted away, he dreamed about her. In the dream, he was a Viking warrior who had just conquered a walled medieval city, and she was the exotic daughter of a blacksmith. After rescuing her from certain death, she rode away with him on the back of his horse, a gray steed named Thor.

Denise McCurdy scanned Lake Erie for Luke's boat. Sunny and seventy, warm for late March. This morning, she and Luke had driven up to her brother's lakeside cabin, her favorite place on earth. She was reclining on a deck chair in shorts and a t-shirt, reading a novel. Luke was out fishing, but he should've been home by now.

A boat, much bigger than Luke's little skiff, approached the dock and slowed down. The captain waved as if he knew Denise. She walked to the end of the dock for a closer look. He had blonde hair and plaid shorts. She pictured him in a sweater vest, holding a croquet mallet.

"Is Brian around?" he yelled.

"Next weekend," she said. "I'm his sister."

"You should come out to The Anchor Pub tonight, it's karaoke night!"

"Can I bring my husband?"

"Sure," he replied, but with less energy.

As the yacht pulled away, Denise tried to remember her life before Luke, when she was Denise Sadowski and boys competed for her attention. She'd been an awkward and insecure girl, but in eighth grade, when she returned to school with breasts and long legs, the boys took notice. At sleepovers, she and her girlfriends compared notes about other girls, boys they liked, and how far they'd gone with their own boyfriends. She started dating Luke at seventeen. Hard to believe they'd been together ten years, married the last two. Their first date, at the Seneca County Farm Show, they shared a funnel cake and watched the smash-up derby. That night, in a cornfield behind the fairgrounds, she let him go up her shirt but stopped him when he tried for third base. After high school, he started mining and she enrolled in Slippery Rock's nursing program. Some nights he drove up and stayed at her apartment, above Molinari's Pizzeria. She remembered the mornings they made love, when he'd stand naked by the window, like a Greek statue. They got married at St. Michael's, both Catholic, and honeymooned at the Jersey shore. Her dream had been to live in a farmhouse – and fill it with kids and dogs – but they couldn't afford a down payment, and she wondered how much longer her marriage would last. She'd fallen in love with Luke the Boy, the one who did backflips off the rope swing and left notes in her locker, but she needed to see more of Luke the Man. The low point came after her miscarriage. One evening while driving past the Pour House Tavern, she saw him leave with Brandi, his ex. "Nothing happened," he claimed. "She needed a ride home, all her friends had left." Denise moved out for a month. During their brief separation she'd had a few dates, but she also used the time alone to understand how her needs and desires had changed. She ignored his calls at first, but he persisted. Right or wrong, she gave it another shot. And things had improved. He'd been less angry, more affectionate.

She heard the whine of a small outboard engine and glanced up. Luke's boat emerged from around Wolf's Neck. Near the dock, he cut the motor and coasted in. He tied off the boat and hopped out. He wore a Cabela's t-shirt, camo shorts, and flip flops. "Make a new friend today?" He pointed to the yacht in the distance.

"Relax. He's just a friend of Brian's."

He pulled two fish from the cooler and threw them on the grill. Even after all these years, she still felt lust. The bulk of his forearms, the heft of his calves. His crooked smile. They ate outside, enjoying the quiet. After dinner they walked to the end of the dock, sat on a beach towel, and watched the stars. She heard minnows jumping. He pulled her closer.

"Let's go inside," she said. "There's people around."

She took his hand and led him to the bedroom, where she slipped off her bikini and unzipped his shorts. On the bed, he took her from behind. It felt good, until it got rough and he started pulling her hair, hard. Was he doing it to piss her off, she wondered, or had he forgotten who he was fucking?

Denise woke first and started breakfast. When Luke came in, he tried to kiss her.

"Brush your teeth," she said, handing him a plate of pancakes and bacon. "Donny won his fight the other night. Larry came along, too."

He'd mentioned Larry before: a quiet older guy who just started at the mine.

"Is there any coffee?" he asked. She pointed to the top right cupboard.

She was almost thirty with no kids. She pictured her life as a crazy blue-haired woman with ten cats. She wanted a family. Time for Luke to choose. Shit or get off the pot, as her dad used to say when she hogged the bathroom. Last week, she'd interviewed for a nursing job at Presbyterian, Pittsburgh's largest hospital. They made an offer, but she hadn't told Luke yet. Waiting for the right time. Either way, she was sick and tired of changing diapers – making nine dollars an hour – at the senior home.

"Where'd you guys go after the fight? You seemed hungover yesterday."

"Tree's place. Just had a few drinks. I got home around midnight." Since she'd worked until seven this morning, she had no way to verify this.

"Why do you stay friends with losers and meth addicts?"

"Don't start with Tree. The war messed him up. He's getting his shit together."

Denise shook her head. "You protect him too much."

"He's my best friend, Denise. He's family. His mom basically raised me."

Luke's parents had divorced when he was young. His mom spent her nights going to bars and bringing home different men.

"By the way, I interviewed for a job at a Pittsburgh hospital last week." She paused. "They called Friday and offered me the job. I'd start a week from Monday."

"Come again?" He squinted at her. "Why is this the first time I'm hearing this?"

"I could never find the right time. It's in the Orthopedic Surgery wing. Twenty-five bucks an hour. That's like sixty thousand a year." She started washing plates.

"I don't want you to take it," he said, raising his voice.

"You'd love Pittsburgh. Great bars and restaurants. Steelers games. And it's not like we'd be moving across the country. Just forty miles away."

"Denise, we're not city people. Change your hair and your clothes all you want. You're still not fooling anyone."

She folded her arms. "What does that even mean?"

"I'm a miner. I got coal in my veins."

She threw a plate against the wall, shattering it. "Enough with that romantic miner bullshit! Maybe you got coal in your lungs, too, like my dad. I won't go through that again."

"I thought you were happy. You wanted to look for a house."

"Things change." She peered out at the calm, flat lake. "People change."

CHUTES AND LADDERS

Despite it being a Wednesday night, the Pour House was packed with miners, bikers, businessmen, cougars, college kids. Even a few wannabe cowboys, in bucket hats and boots. Larry found Tree, Luke, and PJ at the bar, drinking from a pitcher.

"There's some talent in here," said PJ, pouring a fresh glass.

"Case in point, it's Brandi." Tree pointed to a table of women across the room. "I still remember that Motley Crue concert, when she flashed her tits on the big screen."

"That wasn't her," said Luke. "It just looked like her."

"Let's find out." Tree got Brandi's attention and waved her over.

She wore a tight skirt and black boots and a low-cut red top. "Hey Luke," she said, her hand touching his forearm. "I like the beard." She lit a Camel Crush. The Pour House was one of the last bars in town where you could smoke. They'd been grandfathered in.

"Hey Brandi, were you at that Motley Crue concert in Pittsburgh? About five years ago?"

"Hell yes. They put me on the big screen!" Great show, too."

Tree was giggling like a teenage girl. "You, or those big titties?"

Brandi squeezed her breasts.

The house lights blinked and the bartender announced last call. Tree invited Brandi and her friends over. "Make sure he comes." She pointed at Luke.

They watched her strut away, like kids at the zoo watching a dangerous animal.

Larry glanced around. Community college girls dancing with each other. Bikers playing pool. He turned to Luke. "Is Denise working tonight?"

Luke grimaced. "Thanks man, for that buzzkill."

Larry was just making small talk, but he should've kept his mouth shut.

"I haven't seen her all week. I think she's taking a new job in Pittsburgh."

"Let her go," Tree said. "You don't need that bullshit."

"Damn it Tree," Luke said, raising his voice. "You have no idea what I need."

Luke stumbled as he walked to his truck. Larry noticed it and offered him a ride. "No sense taking two cars."

"Damn, that Brandi." Larry said as they pulled onto Valley Road. "She's fine."

Luke rolled his eyes. "She's like one of those windy back roads. Fun to drive at first, hugging those curves. But then it narrows and turns to dirt, and you know it'll dead-end soon, so you keep looking for a place to turn around." They passed the Buffalo Creek Trailer Park entrance. "That's where I live."

"You want me to drop you off?"

"No. Keep going."

Larry closed his window as a light drizzle fell. In the western sky, lightning flashed like a defective lamp. Millburg at midnight was dead quiet: only the high-pitched whir of a crotch rocket pierced the silence. He followed the river downstream, past the sand and gravel dredgers, past a rickety old houseboat. On the far bank, webs of fog shrouded the glass factory. The corroded mouth of a drain pipe poked through the weeds, spitting brown gobs into the river.

They pulled into Tree's driveway, behind Brandi's Grand Am. She and her friends were smoking on the porch. PJ and Tree sat on lawn chairs, warming their hands over a fire pit. Tree squirted lighter fluid and watched the flames rise.

"Right on time," Brandi said, following everyone inside.

"Fuckin cold out," Tree said, reaching into the fridge. He grabbed two Iron City cans and handed one to Larry, then walked into the living room. Larry followed him to the couch. There was an NBA game on television but the sound was muted. The camera zoomed in on two men in suits, sitting in some luxury box.

Larry had spent much of his life hating wealthy men, for whom happiness seemed effortless. He'd grown up in a poor mining family, with no discussion of college. He barely missed Vietnam, too young for the draft, so after high school he had two choices: miner or mechanic. He chose the family business. As a young miner, Larry was making decent money and had a nice car, a Pontiac GTO he'd restored. Still, he couldn't let go of his jealousy and anger, using them as crutches to engage in destructive behavior. By some miracle, his son Josh had inherited his best qualities and none of his bad ones. Smart and hard-working, but quiet and unselfish, with no addictive personality. He'd been a decent father. He read books to Josh, and took him to museums and ball games. For Josh's graduation, he fixed up the old Jeep CJ-7 and gave him the keys. But watching him go off to war and not return: Larry never quite recovered from that. Nothing could prepare you for the death of a child. Most people remained ignorant of their true nature, not knowing if they possessed a lion heart or a wretched soul. But whatever lay hidden within your core, the death of your child exposed it.

Tree took a plastic baggie from his pocket and spilled the white powder onto the glass coffee table. After snorting a line, he twitched like a river rat.

"Larry, you look like your dog got run over," he said. "Go ahead, take a spin."

As a kid, Larry's favorite board game was Chutes and Ladders, a game that could summarize his life: climb two levels, slide down three. He remembered the year after his divorce. Weekend-long benders. Strippers. Piles of cocaine. His dealer and bookie on speed dial. He'd stitched his life back together, but now he felt himself sliding down another long, steep chute, and he couldn't slow his momentum.

Larry pulled out his library card and leaned over the table. He cut a fat line and vacuumed it up. The stadium lights in his brain surged on.

He wandered into the dark hallway, searching for the bathroom. Luke and Brandi were against the far wall, her hand running up and down the front of his jeans. Brandi curled her finger at him and led him into a bedroom.

Before closing the door, Luke turned to Larry and smiled. He pointed his finger and thumb at his head, like a gun. Then, he pulled the trigger.

DISASTER PORN

Mired in a chemical fog from the previous night, Larry drove across the Allegheny River. He passed rickety old houses with broken windows and rotting porch steps crammed together on the bluff. The low, gray clouds concealed the ridge tops, and patches of snow covered the hillsides. The trees were like naked old men: skinny and bent.

Tina had moved out early this morning while he slept. April Fools' Day, the irony not lost on him. She took everything, even his flat screen, but at least had the decency to leave his album collection and box full of Josh's things. Glancing down at the water, he thought of his dad and their fishing excursions upriver at Brady's Bend. When Larry was six, his dad picked him up by the ankles and dunked him in the river. "Now you'll be invincible," he said. For a long time, he'd believed those words.

His truck climbed the access road, past the coal tipple and the two boney piles that resembled black pyramids. He parked and walked to the change room. Sam, the onsite manager, stood outside the office trailer. Sam's head was so far up the ass of George Blount, he needed a goddamn flashlight.

"Larry!" he yelled. "C'mon up. We need to talk."

Inside the trailer, Larry sat beside a younger guy he didn't recognize.

"Here's the deal," Sam said. "We need six cuts of coal per shift. That rule comes straight from Mr. Blount, who signs our checks. This is Jamie. We brought him in to—"

"Take my job?" Larry interrupted.

"No. You guys will split time running the continuous miner. You make one cut, he makes the next. When you're off, stay busy by loading coal on the conveyor. Jamie's got some experience, and a little competition is healthy for everyone."

Larry shook his head and grinned. Then he scanned the new kid: spiky hair, shifty eyes. "Got a note from your mother?" he asked.

"Don't get too excited and shit your pants, old man."

"What's your last name?"

"Lubinski." Larry knew a Lubinski in high school. He was a dickhead, too.

Outside, Larry started coughing: bent over, spitting up phlegm.

"Take it easy," Tree said, "We ain't even started work."

"They brought in a ringer to take my job." Larry pointed out the new kid.

"Who, that dude? Looks like he can't even find a G-spot."

This little circus reminded Larry of '86, when scabs broke the picket lines, but that was back when unions had leverage.

Outside, the sky opened up, catching him in a downpour. Thunder boomeranged around the ridge, and lightning flashed like a strobe.

Larry was first up on the big machine. Today it ran smooth, and he finished the first cut in forty-five minutes. Solid time.

When the new kid took over, he was going even faster. Clearly, he'd done this before.

"Watch and learn, old timer!" the kid yelled. Larry gave him the finger.

Over the years, he'd heard stories of guys who'd killed themselves underground. One caused a roof to collapse on him, killing three other miners in the process. Larry wondered if he could pull it off. The machine was so wide, the operator couldn't see behind it when he backed up, and a two-ton machine running over his chest would surely do the trick. Even better, they'd call it an accident. He'd been dying for years now. Why not finish the job?

Things hadn't always been this bad. He remembered the best moments, like that trip he and Kelly took to the Outer Banks. Late October, some twenty years ago, they rented a house on stilts. Wrapped in a blanket on the empty beach, they made love as the waves crashed behind them. He remembered his son's first hunting trip when Josh killed an eight-point buck. The Millburg Eagle published his photo.

Larry stood behind the machine and picked out the best spot to lie down. But when the moment arrived, he froze. He couldn't go through with it. With his luck, he'd wind up deformed or paralyzed. Disgusted, he walked down to Section Two, where Tree and Luke were bolting the roof. He watched Tree struggle to drill a steel rod into a hole in the shale above his head.

Suddenly, they heard a loud noise, like a boom or blast. A thunderstorm churned outside, but the noise had been too loud for thunder. Then came a low rumble, shaking the floor.

Be careful what you wish for, Larry said to himself.

"We need to haul ass!" Luke yelled.

"How far to the entrance?

"Half mile, maybe."

Pale light spilled from Larry's helmet lamp as they staggered through the cold dark and heavy smoke. They only made it a hundred yards. A roof collapse had dumped a large heap of rock, shale and dirt, covering the width of the tunnel and blocking their path.

"Can we get past it?" someone asked.

Coughing, Larry turned away from the smoke and covered his face with a bandana.

"Too dangerous," said Hank. "The rest of it could collapse on us."

"We need to turn around and find the end of the tunnel," said Luke. "Build a curtain. Wait for the rescue team."

Hank and Ron, the oldest miners on their crew, agreed it was the right call.

"Fuck that," said Jamie, the red hat. "I'm leaving the same way I came in."

"You'll never dig through by yourself, dumbass."

"Watch me."

Larry considered staying with the new kid and trying to get out. The idea of building a barricade defied his core survival instinct. It seemed like digging your own grave. But the other guys had more experience – Hank had even survived a mine fire – so he kept his mouth shut and followed, even if his gut said otherwise. They came to the end of the tunnel and stopped.

"Make the curtain airtight to keep the bad air out," Luke said. The ground was littered with rock and debris. "Start with big boulders, then fill in the holes with smaller rocks."

"What about the new kid?" Larry asked. "Should we go back and get him?"

"Leave him." Luke shook his head. "If he makes it, they'll know where to find us."

From the bay window, Denise watched two ambulances race down Fulton Street, heading east. Her mother was in the kitchen, wearing a velour jumpsuit, sipping coffee from a yellow mug.

"Come talk to me," she said. "Before you move to the big city and never return."

Denise had just accepted the nurse job in Pittsburgh – at Presbyterian Hospital's Orthopedic Surgery Center – and would be starting in a few days. "It's not California. I'm only two hours away. And I'll come back weekends, to see Luke."

"He's not moving down there with you?"

Denise shook her head. "I'm staying with Kathy, until I find my own place."

"You and Luke will patch things up. You always do."

She pulled a Gatorade from the fridge. "Feels different this time."

"Marriage isn't a sprint, it's a marathon. Remember that."

"You want to get lunch? I was thinking that new Panera, by the mall."

When her mom asked if she needed a coat, Denise turned on the radio, hoping to catch the local forecast. Instead, she heard: "Breaking News: We're getting multiple reports of a coal mining accident in Seneca County."

Her mom frowned. "Can you turn it up?"

Denise cranked the volume: "We're still trying to confirm the location, but we believe it's the Sarver Mine, near Millburg. Reports of several miners trapped inside. No more details right now, but we'll keep tracking this story all morning."

"Is that Luke's mine?"

"Shit." Denise hardly ever swore in front of her mom. "I gotta go."

"Call me, soon as you can."

She staggered to the guest bedroom and grabbed her hoodie. A dim ringing noise, like a dinner bell, vibrated through her head.

In the car, she cracked her window and lit a cigarette. She'd been trying to quit, but not today. Outside Morgan's Diner, a group of older men talked with their hands. Kids poured out of the elementary school, cancelled for the day. She parked in the Methodist Church parking lot, near the access road. Half the town was already here, wandering along the road like a lost ant colony. She spotted her Uncle Bob, a retired miner, and ran over.

"What are they saying?" she asked.

"Last I heard, ten or twelve are still down there."

"Luke?"

Bob looked down, adjusting his Penn State cap.

"Oh my God." Denise rubbed her temples.

A nearby journalist interviewed a young woman.

"Damn reporters." Bob shook his head. "Been stirring up shit all morning."

Denise glanced at the sky, darkening with anvil clouds.

Bob pointed to the Methodist Church. "They opened the church up to family members. You should go in. Find out the latest."

A frantic woman ran past them. "Where's my son?" she repeated.

Denise sat in the back pew and glanced around. She recognized a few faces from the company cookout last summer, but had forgotten their names. The only woman she knew was her high school friend, Gina, also a miner's wife. Gina was always on Facebook posting photos of her kids in matching outfits like denim overalls.

Denise felt like a heretic. She hadn't seen Luke since their weekend at the lake. She wanted to start fresh and make a new life in the city. The word divorce had been floating around her head. Still, in the back of her mind she'd expected this. Mining had killed her dad. Black lung. A slower method, but the same result. In the end, we can't shed our fate.

A large, dark-haired man entered the church. Blue button-down shirt, dark jeans, cowboy boots. Everyone got quiet as he marched down the center aisle and climbed the steps. His face was notched and grooved, like the surface of some cold, distant planet devoid of light and heat. He looked familiar, somehow.

"Good afternoon, folks. I'm George Blount, president of Commonwealth Energy. We're still gathering information. It looks like an explosion. Lightning could've struck a power cable that ran into the mine, and triggered a blast. But the high-methane sections are sealed off with concrete walls, so the miners should be fine. Trust me, we're doing all we can."

When he said the word explosion, something inside Denise cracked. Groans and whispers issued from the other pews.

An older man in front stood up. "How many are down there?"

"Ten, we believe." Blount replied. "We don't have names yet. But don't worry, all the miners have access to oxygen, first aid, and food."

"How can you know that for sure?"

"No need to panic." Blount raised his hands like stop signs. "The rescue teams are going in soon. We'll provide updates. The church will remain open. Meals will be provided."

Blount escaped out the side door, escorted by two state troopers.

The woman beside Denise with a mullet and camo jacket shook her head. "I don't know. Smells like horse shit to me."

Denise covered her face, fighting back tears.

"Don't worry." The woman touched her shoulder. "The Lord will look after them."

Denise glanced up at a stained-glass window depicting the image of Christ: resurrected and risen from the grave.

≪०⋘

At first, the miners treated it like a work break. Their makeshift wall seemed airtight, keeping out the carbon monoxide. Larry played Texas Hold 'Em with a few other guys. As Hank dealt the cards, guys compared local hunting spots and fishing holes.

"The best buck are in Tioga County," Ron said. "A couple years ago, I snagged a twelve-point up there."

Larry had never been trapped in a mine, but he understood the need to maintain positive energy and goodwill. "What's the first thing you guys'll do when you get out?" he asked.

"Buy a fishing boat," Hank said.

Larry glanced at Ron. "And you, Papa Smurf?" Ron's nickname had two sources: he was short, about five-four, and he loved talking about his kids.

"I'm taking the family to Myrtle Beach."

"Will you guys keep mining after this?" Luke asked.

"Not me," Larry said with conviction. "I'm done."

"Nothing else around here," Tree said. "Flip burgers. Work at Wal-Mart."

Larry chuckled. "Might move to Mexico. Fish every day."

As he ate his granola bar, Larry pictured turquoise water and white sand. Still, he couldn't block out the fear. Everyone wanted a happy ending, another heroic story of survival. But what about the stories that never got told, about miners who never made it out? Did they spend their final hours holding hands and confessing their worst sins, or fighting over the last drop of water?

"I remember those Shanksville miners," Hank said. "They survived three days and nights underground. Drilled down and brought them up, one-by-one, in cylinder cages. They all came out dazed, like babies being born."

"What ever happened to them?"

"They sued, but got nothing. A few are still fucked up. Post-traumatic stress."

"Guess you need to die," Larry added, "before you can win in court."

Tree snorted. "Sounds about right."

"Those copper miners in Chile spent a month underground," Luke added.

"But there wasn't any explosion or fire."

"I remember that dude whose wife and mistress were both waiting on him." Tree's wide smile glowed in the dark. "Someone had a ménage-a-trois that night!"

Like a puzzled dog, Ron tilted his head.

Tree laughed. "It's French, Ron. You should try it sometime."

By mid-afternoon — as smoke began to filter through the wall — the mood had changed: their laughter was replaced by a tense, awkward silence.

Tree pulled out his oxygen canister and took a few hits.

"Remember, those self-rescue devices are a last resort," Hank said.

Larry sat against the wall beside Luke, who looked pensive. "What're you thinking so hard about?"

"Stupid stuff," Luke said. "My best football game, when I scored two touchdowns against Aliquippa. Hunting trips with my dad. Quiet Sundays with Denise." He paused. "Hey, if I don't make it out, promise me one thing. Find Denise and tell her I'm sorry. For everything."

Larry studied his face. "You can tell her yourself, man."

Deep down, however, Larry was starting to panic. The goddamn rescue team should've been here by now. He felt dizzy. His oxygen can was half-empty. Since a few cans were defective, they'd all been sharing, but guys were becoming more possessive.

"Hey Ron," said Tree. "You been hoarding that for an hour. Pass it back here."

"I got bad lungs. I need it more than you."

"Bullshit."

Ron glared. "I got a wife and three kids up there."

"I get it. Your life is more valuable. Let the black guy with no family die first. "

"All I know is I'm getting out of here alive. My wife won't be a widow and my kids won't grow up without a father."

Tree smiled. "Don't worry, Papa Smurf. She'll find a good man to replace you."

"That's it, asshole," Ron said. "Get up."

Both men circled each other. Though Ron was a foot shorter, he charged Tree and tackled him, then climbed on top and started punching him.

Larry studied the other miners' faces. They looked like kids watching a back alley fight, yet their expressions revealed something darker. Nobody tried to break it up, not until Ron pulled out a knife. Luke got behind Ron and locked his arms. Ron dropped the knife.

"That's enough!" Luke yelled. "Nobody's dying down here. Not like that, anyhow."

"Dying ain't the worst thing." Tree had a bloody lip and swollen eye. "Remember that."

⁌⁍

As word of the accident spread around Commonwealth's corporate office, Simon found his friend Julie, always his best source of information, and asked her what she knew.

"A fire or explosion," she said. "Several miners trapped."

Even if he had no connection to the accident, Simon's natural curiosity would have led him to the disaster site. He'd inherited the ambulance-chasing gene from his dad, who used to follow sirens all over town. But as luck would have it, Simon's job position provided him with a front-row seat.

Around two o'clock, Richard gave Simon his instructions. "Find George and stick by him all day, especially when he talks to the media or gives a press conference. He might need your advice to answer any legal questions."

"Will I have to address the media directly?"

"Probably not." Richard scrunched his face. "Look, make sure George doesn't say anything completely stupid or false. Got it?"

Simon nodded. "Yes sir."

He drove east, following the heavy traffic on State Route 422, and parked in a field and walked a quarter mile to the mine entrance. At first, he stayed on the perimeter of the crowd, noticing the tension and fear on the surrounding faces. They looked like members of some addict support group. He watched a young woman, perhaps a miner's wife, smoke a cigarette. She was tall, with dark hair and sharp features. She reminded him of Lindsey, his ex.

The first time Simon had laid eyes on Lindsey, he went blind. As she reclined on a deck chair beside the shared pool of their same apartment complex, the sunlight reflecting off her tan legs – lacquered with lotion – was so bright that, momentarily, he lost his vision. Within a year, they were living together and planning a wedding. Too fast, but it felt right. She was a middle school math teacher. Smart and sarcastic. Her beauty had a sharp edge, the kind that could slice you open. And it did. One day in February when he stayed home with the flu, he noticed her cell phone on the coffee table. Scrolling through her texts, he read a message from Kevin, her social studies teacher friend: *Can't wait until you ride my joystick again!* Simon broke off the engagement and moved out. She gave the ring back, but he pawned it for half-price because the jeweler had a no-returns policy. That was eighteen months ago.

Glancing around, Simon felt charged with a perverse energy. Lonely people like him appreciated the gravity of these moments. While the media wanted blood and carnage and disaster porn, he came to witness humanity in its raw, crude state: people struggling with emotions they could not name or articulate.

Near the church he spotted George, flanked by two state troopers. Despite the weather – thirty-five, cloudy, and chance of rain or snow later – George wasn't wearing a jacket, only a blue oxford with the sleeves rolled up, along with jeans and boots.

Simon waved and approached him.

"So, what brings you out here?" George asked. "Got the day off?"

"Richard sent me. To offer legal advice, if needed."

"Of course." George chuckled. "My brother hates when I go off script. But he doesn't get it. During a crisis, you need to speak from the heart. If we give the media boilerplate answers, the public will turn against us."

"So I don't need to speak?"

"No. But if a reporter asks you a question, don't be rude. Say you're unable to comment at this time. And one more thing. Take your coat off."

"Why?"

"It shows weakness. We need to show that the cold doesn't affect us."

It seemed ridiculous, and paranoid, but Simon complied.

For the next few hours he followed George, watching him play the role of a politician, benevolent and patriarchal. Calmly answering questions from aggressive journalists. Comforting anxious mothers and wives.

As the sun went down, Simon watched a candlelight vigil form, started by family and friends of the miners, most of whom had been here all day. Soon, Simon got wind of a circulating rumor: something about the voices of the miners heard by the rescue team. When George heard this, he and the state governor issued a quick press conference. Simon didn't like the idea, telling his boss to wait until they all came out alive, but George disagreed.

"The families need some good news, and so does the public."

As George spoke to the world – declaring that the miners were alive and would be coming out soon – Simon rubbed his forehead.

George thanked him for "working overtime" and said he could leave, since the miners wouldn't be out for a couple hours.

Around nine o'clock, Simon returned home to the Ketchup Factory. He ordered take-out lasagna from Mama Rosa's, the Italian place down the street. After dinner, he smoked a joint and watched the news. CNN was reporting that all the miners were alive. He'd hoped to stay up long enough to see them emerge, but was too exhausted and fell asleep.

Two tables of home-cooked meals – meatloaf, chicken noodle casserole – were set up inside the church. After Denise finished a plate of casserole, she went out for a cigarette. A rheumy mist blanketed the valley. Colder now. The rain had changed to sleet: roads and sidewalks freezing over, ice coating tree branches. Pellets of ice stuck to Denise's hair.

Across the road, as a silver-haired journalist in a white button-down delivered a live report, Denise crept closer and listened:

> Good evening from the coal region of western Pennsylvania, where a methane gas explosion left several miners trapped inside the Sarver Mine. A rescue team has been deployed, but they must get through smoke and carbon monoxide. In a press release, Commonwealth Energy indicated that the miners are trained to survive these in conditions. But fines and safety violations have been issued against the Sarver Mine by the federal Mine Safety and Health Agency.

Feeling a tap on her shoulder, she turned around.

Her friend Gina greeted her with a wide smile. "Denise McCurdy, right? I thought that was you in church." She'd put on weight and cut her hair short, but she still had the same girlish face. "So, is your husband down there?"

"Think so."

"Mine too." Gina wiped her eyes.

Denise forced a smile. "They'll be okay."

"I wonder how long can they survive."

"A long time. Maybe a few days."

Denise's uncle approached, running up the hill.

"You girls hear the news?" he said, out of breath. "They're alive. The rescue team radioed a message. Said they heard voices."

Word spread like a gasoline fire. Friends and strangers hugged. Cameramen ran back to their vans and retrieved equipment. George and the governor gave a press conference. They stood before the cameras and microphones, chests puffed out. "Believe in miracles!" George proclaimed. Church bells rang. The silver-haired reporter issued another report:

> Here is what we know. This is unconfirmed,
> but we've been told that all the miners are alive.
> Stay tuned for more updates.

Because she was told the miners would not emerge for another hour or so, Denise drove down the road to Sheetz for a coffee. She returned before midnight, as a light snow began to fall. Another candlelight vigil had formed, and the cameras kept rolling. Hollywood, she thought, had come to Millburg. Off to the side, a small circle of men – George Blount, two cops, and two men in polo shirts and khakis – spoke in hushed tones. When they broke their huddle, they rounded up the family members and told them to report back to church for an announcement. Denise followed the herd back inside.

Blount took the podium, once again, now with bloodshot eyes and a pale face. Behind him was a sculpture of Jesus nailed to the cross. "Folks, I'm afraid there's been a mistake. We had some bad information. The truth is we found all ten miners, but only two are alive."

Somewhere, a baby started to wail. Denise recalled that Bible story about King Solomon and the child. Two women knelt before the king, both claiming the same baby as their own. Then Solomon gave his answer: he'd resolve the dispute by cutting the child in half.

A miner's wife in the front row stood up and approached Blount. She cried "No!" Then, she lunged at him, but her punch missed. She collapsed near his feet. Two state troopers picked her up and took her outside, her screams fading into the night air.

Denise wanted to rage, too, yet something in her body told her Luke had survived. Thus, when a state trooper took her aside and confirmed her intuition, she remained calm. She didn't know what to feel. Joy? Relief? Guilt? The cop told her Luke was being flown to Pittsburgh Presbyterian Hospital. Her hospital, where she'd start work Monday. What were the odds?

Driving south toward Pittsburgh, she thought about her people – poor country people – and how they were always paying for the mistakes of the privileged: CEOs, journalists, and politicians who didn't have to live with the consequences, who could wash the blood off their hands and return to their normal lives.

In her head, she replayed the image of the woman in church throwing a punch. She hoped someone with a video camera or iPhone had recorded it. So the world could truly understand what happened here. So they could see the damage done.

❦

At some point, Larry had drifted off. When he woke, his chest felt tight. He sat upright, propped against the wall. He glanced around. No one else, except Luke, was awake. No one else, he soon recognized, was moving at all.

Luke jostled him. "You awake? I hear something."

Sure enough, he heard voices in the distance.

By the time the rescue crew sledge-hammered through the wall, Larry's breathing sounded like a boat engine. They loaded him and Luke on stretchers and rushed them out. They were less urgent with the others, using body bags instead of stretchers.

As their helicopter rose off the ground, Larry figured they were headed for some large Pittsburgh hospital better equipped to treat them. Beside him, Luke mumbled something incoherent. Both men were trapped in the same bizarre dream.

PART TWO

PART TWO

THE PARIS OF APPALACHIA

Stumbling out of the shower, Simon grabbed a towel and opened the medicine cabinet. He pulled out the jar of Frontal Lobe Lube, removed the cap, and whiffed: it smelled like sour milk and menthol. He rubbed a dollop of the white cream into his forehead. Cool and tingly. He paused before the mirror and squeezed an inch of flab around his waist. He'd been skinny as a kid, so in college he started lifting weights. He never got ripped, yet adding muscle to his frame made him more visible to women. But that was college. He hadn't worked out in six months, not since the Lindsay breakup, and now he looked four months pregnant. At least he still possessed his two best features: a thick head of light brown hair and his bluish green eyes.

While shaving, he tried to retrace the last two decades of his life, wondering how he'd arrived here. He'd completed his degree at Penn State– History major, with a pedestrian 3.1 GPA– but remained in State College for another year, bartending at a side-alley pub called Dark Horse. Then he returned to Pittsburgh, and after several interviews, took the first job offered, as a Customer Service Rep for a large health insurance company. They gave him a cubicle on the fifth floor of their downtown Pittsburgh office. When people asked if their MRI was covered, he said "No." When they asked why, he said: "Preexisting condition," or "Nonessential procedure." But those were the company's words, not his own, so he changed the script. He said: "You're not only covered for that MRI, we'll throw in a colonoscopy, free!" Simon's boss Maura, with rust-colored hair and a chronic scowl, despised the new script and fired him. He decided to apply to law schools, since lawyers seemed to have the ultimate backstage pass. They dined at five-star restaurants, had expense accounts, billed five hundred bucks an hour. But, he soon discovered, those were the lucky few. The rest scavenged for leftovers, like crows.

Simon had come to terms with being a lawyer, yet he resisted becoming another corporate douche. Generally, his politics leaned left. He recycled, shopped at farmers' markets, patronized indie record and bookstores. Believed in equal marriage and equal pay. Listened to NPR. He could never give up red meat but respected the choices of others. He worried about climate change and, despite his job, supported renewable energy over fossil fuels. Yet politics didn't shape his identity. He'd flirted with Marxism in college, but law school had crushed his idealism. Ideas and opinions, he'd learned, carried little weight in the real world.

In the car, he scanned the radio, searching for news on the miners. Last night he'd gone to bed happy, but now KDKA was reporting that two miners were found alive. At the office, the hollow, blank faces of his coworkers – huddled around the conference room table – confirmed the grim news. All the executive managers, except George, were present.

Richard scowled at him. "About fucking time, Simon."

Nobody smiled or said hello. Not even Hippie Jim, the company geologist.

Simon asked his friend Julie, the office manager, what exactly happened.

"Eight miners died. Two survived, both in serious condition."

"Do we know what caused the explosion?" someone asked.

"No," Richard said, with dark lines under his bloodshot eyes. He hadn't slept. "But there was a heavy storm at the time. A lightning strike could have hit a cable or wire running inside the mine. It's happened before."

"Why couldn't they escape on foot?" asked Julie.

"The main tunnel was obstructed by a roof collapse."

Bob, the computer guy, asked if they had enough oxygen, because he'd heard the miners were trapped for hours. Pat, a new temp, replied that her cousin was a former miner at Sarver, and he'd once mentioned that the oxygen cans were "old and hard to use."

Richard glared at them. "That's total bullshit." He paced the room like an angry coach at halftime. "Listen, we're getting off track. We need to get on the same page."

"Why'd it take so long for the rescuers to find them?" Hippie Jim asked.

"Exactly. That's the right question to be asking. We kept telling them to get in there sooner. Their lack of urgency, in my opinion, was a major factor in the outcome."

The real tragedy, in Simon's mind, was that the entire nation had gone to bed believing miners were alive. Thus, the cable news networks – eager to break the story without confirming sources – shouldered some of the blame.

"This is ugly," Richard continued. "If one or two died, we could brush it off. MSHA would believe whatever we told them. But not eight or ten. They will investigate this. Somehow, we need to reduce our exposure and control the media narrative."

"Does anyone know the survivors' names?"

"Luke McCurdy and Larry Jenkins."

After Richard adjourned the meeting, he called Simon into his office.

The door was wide open. He stepped in.

"Simon, we need to talk legal strategy. At some point, you need to meet with the Mitchell Burns lawyers. If we get sued, they will litigate. But I want you to take an active role. Drafting pretrial motions, taking depositions, and so forth. This is your chance to shine, okay?"

"Thanks for the opportunity," Simon said, faking enthusiasm.

Richard frowned. "George is holed up at his hunting lodge in Westmoreland County. I can't reach him by phone or email. If he's not back by tomorrow, I'm sending you up there."

Simon loved assignments that took him out of the office. "Yes, sir."

"Also, type up a press release for the media. Keep it short and to the point, but with a sympathetic tone. And let Julie review it."

Simon went back to his office, shut the door, and drafted the press release. He included a description of the accident, a list of the confirmed dead, and a short bio of the two survivors:

> Luke McCurdy, 29, and Larry Jenkins, 55, were evacuated and flown to Presbyterian Hospital in Pittsburgh last night, where both are in serious condition. Both McCurdy and Jenkins are Millburg natives with years of mining experience.

After completing the first draft, he checked his phone and noticed a missed call. He put the phone up to his ear and played the new voicemail: *Hello Simon. This is Ken Schultz, the former compliance manager at Blount. I've been following the mine explosion, and you need to know some things. Maybe you've heard my name around the office. People say I'm crazy, right? Well, they're dead wrong.*

He paused the message and closed his office door. Was this a joke, or some weird prank? He tried to think. *Ken Schultz, Ken Schultz...* The guy he'd replaced. Richard had mentioned that mental health issues forced Ken to resign. And Deb said he went batshit. Simon wondered how he'd gotten his cell number. He continued to play the voicemail: *Leaving this message may be crazy, but I had to tell someone. Some evil shit has been going on at the Sarver Mine, for years. Safety fines and violations. Defective equipment. Bad things. For your sake and mine, erase this message. The Blount Brothers will do anything to cover their asses. But if you want to discuss this in person, call me back soon.*

Simon's eye twitched like a bird's. Electric currents surged through his veins. He stared at the phone, his mouth half open. He thought about deleting the message, but for now he'd keep it.

Denise's first shift at the hospital came on Saturday morning, two days after the accident. She was told to shadow Dr. Turner, a semi-retired orthopedic surgeon with crumbs in his white beard and a Band-Aid on his forehead.

"In my day, surgery was like metal shop." Dr. Turner wiped his eyeglasses with a soiled handkerchief. "They used electric saws to cut off limbs, and with no anesthesia you'd hear their screams ten floors below. Of course, that was back in the Dark Ages."

Denise felt queasy. "What about the nurses back then?"

"They didn't know as much as you gals today. Their main job was to lift spirits and boost morale. You know, show a little thigh or cleavage."

She wasn't getting paid to abide the misogynistic opinions of Dr. Old Balls. She wanted to slap him, but she just stopped listening instead.

Around noon, she met Kathy for lunch in the cafeteria. Kathy started six months earlier. They went to nursing school together, and Denise was crashing with her until she found her own place.

"Relax. You're doing great," Kathy said, grabbing a tray.

"I'm still trying to process it all."

They found a corner booth. "How was Dr. Turner?"

"Creepy."

"He loves to scare new nurses."

He does a great job, Denise thought. She devoured her slice of pizza and yogurt, but was still hungry. Must've been the nervous energy burning her calories faster.

"I can't believe you're working today," Kathy said.

Denise agreed. This wasn't the ideal way to start a job — with her husband fighting for his life a few floors below — but what could she do about it?

"Have you seen him yet?"

"Last night," she said. "Vitals were fine, but still unresponsive."

"You need me to do anything?" Kathy asked.

"I just don't want to forget something or make some huge mistake."

"Don't worry. My first week, I kept giving the wrong pills to the wrong patients."

"Seriously? What happened?"

"Nobody died," Kathy said. They both started cracking up.

Kathy pointed to a broad-shouldered man picking up a tray. He had dark hair and dimpled cheeks. "Look who just walked in. The new orthopedic resident. Dr. Dreamy. Ooh, I'd like to check under that hood!"

Not too shabby, thought Denise, but too clean cut for her.

"So, what other doctors have you met?"

"Campbell. Burke. Vavro."

"Stay away from Vavro. Arrogant bastard. Always leering at me, too."

"Yeah, I got that vibe," Denise said. "What about the other nurses?"

"Barb can be nebby, always asking about your personal life. But she's a good resource. Hilary sucks at the job, she can't keep up. She just wants to marry a doctor."

Denise looked at her watch. "I need to check on Luke again."

Kathy cleared her tray. "I'm sorry you have to deal with all this right now. You want me to go down there with you?"

"No thanks, I'm good."

"I'll cover for you."

In the elevator, Denise thought of the two chief reasons she became a nurse. Her father. His lung cancer. His slow, painful decline. His body whittled down to nothing. And her schizophrenic Aunt Eileen. On Sunday dinners at Granny and Pap's house. Eileen would stare at her food and make screeching sounds. She'd spent much of her adult life at Western Psych. They shocked her with electric current, fed her psychotropic drugs, lobotomized her. She died young, at forty-three. Physically, Denise always resembled Eileen. During her first semester, lonely and homesick, Denise was consumed by the fear she'd inherit her aunt's disease, and she pictured it like a big wad of Play-Dough festering in the back of her brain. But she overcame her fear with knowledge, studying biology and psychology. She decided to specialize in Sports Medicine because, unlike mental illness, the success rate for treating a torn ACL or rotator cuff was high, and Denise liked seeing the fruits of her labor.

"No changes from yesterday," said Rhonda, the senior ICU nurse.

She stood over Luke and studied his face.

His eyes were shut, and his cheeks were pale and swollen.

Rhonda shrugged. "You never know with coma patients. Medicine has come a long way, but there's still an element of mystery with comas. Some people come out after a week, some after a month, and some never do."

"What are his chances of a full recovery?" Denise asked.

"Once the swelling on the brain decreases, we'll know more. But he's young, so I'd give him a pretty good chance."

Denise nodded and checked her watch. Break was over, back to work.

"Don't worry," Rhonda said. "He's in very good hands."

She wanted to tell Rhonda the truth: that she'd come to Presby to leave her old life behind and hit the RESET button. But now, she couldn't escape her old life.

She hated when people said, "God has a reason," like her mom did on the phone last night. "Or maybe," Denise had replied, "The only reason is that Presby is the biggest hospital in the city! Why did there have to be a preordained explanation for everything?"

Still, Luke had no other family nearby. His mother was dead, his father was never in the picture, and his brother worked on oil rigs in the gulf coast. Denise had to be the responsible one, but now that she was working ten-hour days, she had no time.

Quit feeling sorry for yourself, she thought, *put your big-girl pants on and deal.*

❧

Pittsburgh: The Steel City. The City of Bridges. The Paris of Appalachia. During the French & Indian War, it was a tiny frontier outpost called Fort Duquesne. When British troops invaded, the French decided to burn their own fort, rather than surrender it to their enemy. Simon admired the purity and passion of their hatred.

But Pittsburgh today looked far different. Since the turn of the century, the city had greened itself — cleaning rivers, erasing industrial blight — and transitioned from a blue-collar steel town to a center of finance and technology, even as the surrounding rust belt continued to corrode.

Approaching downtown, Simon surveyed the skyline: the US Steel Building, convention center, PPG Towers, the new stadiums. He missed Three Rivers Stadium and its ugly bowl shape, going to Steelers and Pirates games as a kid, watching old heroes like Franco Harris and Andy van Slyke. He crossed the Fort Pitt Bridge, spanning the confluence: the marriage of the Allegheny and Monongahela Rivers, their union spawning the Ohio. Perched on the cliff above sat Mount Washington, which owned the city's best views. But the road leading up there was so gnarly that, once or twice a year, some demented old man would drive his car off the cliff. Speaking of demented old men, Simon's current mission, as instructed by Richard, was to find George and persuade him to return to the office.

Yesterday, the day after the explosion, George escaped to his hunting lodge in Ligonier, saying he needed a couple days of solitude to clear his mind. But, local and national media were all over the story and not going way, and Richard simply couldn't handle the fallout by himself: he needed his older brother to help steer the ship.

From the South Side, Simon followed East Carson Street to the Homestead Waterfront — a cluster of trendy shops, bars, and restaurants stood on the same patch of land where a Carnegie-owned steel mill once blocked out the sun. Since the Civil War, western Pennsylvania steel built the nation, but nearly all of the region's steel mills were now gone. Modern capitalism no longer had loyalty, no sense of history. Corporations would not hesitate to leave a region for greener pastures.

Leaving Pittsburgh, Simon followed winding roads into the Laurel Mountains, passing dairy barns and cattle grazing on hilly pastures. He crossed an old, wooden bridge that creaked and groaned under his tires. When his GPS signal faded, he used his handwritten directions. On Donegal Road, he checked the mailboxes for house numbers. Then, he followed the whir of a chainsaw until he laid eyes on George Blount, attempting to cut down a large oak tree.

Simon parked in front of George's chalet — a large structure of wood and glass — and walked around to the backyard. For a minute he stood unnoticed, as George hacked away at the tree trunk. George was built like a bear: barrel-chest, jet black hair, thick mustache, and dark eyes. Wearing a flannel jacket, jeans, and work boots, he could've played the role of lumberjack, but he didn't know shit about cutting trees.

Eventually, George turned off the chainsaw and lifted his goggles.

"Hello Simon. What a nice surprise."

"Richard sent me."

"I figured he would. Once I finish up here, we'll talk inside."

"You're cutting it wrong," Simon blurted.

"Excuse me?"

"You're cutting in the wrong direction. It could fall on your house."

George handed over his gloves and goggles. "Okay Paul Bunyan. Show me."

Here was Simon's chance to impress. He'd spent a college summer in Maine working for a paper mill, felling white pines in the North Woods. The hardest job he'd ever worked.

He grabbed the chainsaw, a newer-model Stihl, and found a firm grip. "You need to start at the back. The side where you want the tree to fall. Then, cut an open-faced, V-shaped notch." He revved the machine and made the under-cut, a twenty-degree angle from low to high, and stopped at the tipping point, halfway across the trunk's diameter. Then he made his top cut, finishing at the same point. "The open face gives the trunk more room, so it falls the right way," he yelled over the engine. "If you just made one straight cut, there's no telling where it lands."

"What now?" George asked.

"One more cut." Simon walked to the other side of the trunk and made a straight horizontal cut, meeting at the V-point he'd just made. He turned off the saw and stepped back. "Wait for it." The tree started tipping, gaining force until it crashed and shook the ground.

"You missed your calling," George said. "Where'd you learn all that?"

"Summer job. In college."

"But you didn't come up here to cut trees. C'mon inside."

The chalet's great room had a wood-burning fireplace and high-raftered ceiling. Through the large glass window, the mountains seemed to sprout up from the backyard. Above the fireplace, the head of a ten-point buck was mounted, along with various photos of George standing beside dead animals and large fish. The opposite wall held pictures, plaques, and trophies from his college football days: George played for Penn State in the seventies.

"You like Rachmaninoff?"

"Sure." Simon was surprised by the selection.

George pulled a compact disc from the shelf. "Piano Concerto Number Three. Do you know this one?" He loaded it into the stereo and pressed play.

"Sounds dramatic."

"The Pittsburgh Symphony performed a stellar version of this last season," said George, returning from the bar with two full tumblers, handing Simon a glass.

"Thanks." Simon examined the brownish liquid. "Whiskey?"

"The finest bourbon, made here in Fayette County. My friend Wayne's distillery. Family-owned for two hundred years. Among the first Scots-Irish clans to settle here. When the new government tried to tax their revenue, they triggered the Whiskey Rebellion."

Simon tried it. He winced. Strong as fuck. Tasted like paint thinner.

"Wayne is a true craftsman. Handmade, no mass production." George held up his glass and examined it like a critic. "He's a dying breed."

Simon stopped beside a framed picture of George in his football uniform, posing with Joe Paterno, his former coach, who wore his customary khakis and dark-rimmed glasses.

"When was that taken?"

"1976."

The year of Simon's birth. He was a bicentennial baby.

"Paterno was a great coach and great leader of men. A great shame to see his legacy tarnished by the sins of another."

Simon assumed he was referring to Jerry Sandusky, Paterno's longtime assistant coach who'd been convicted on several counts of child sexual abuse. For years, he molested young boys that attended his summer football camp. Simon had been a Penn State fan his whole life, but after the scandal, he lost his enthusiasm.

"Sandusky was a monster," George said. "He lived a double life. He fooled Joe and betrayed his trust. And he's not the only one. We live in sad times."

Simon turned around and pointed to a glass-encased football. "What's that?"

"My game-winning touchdown in the Cotton Bowl. Best game of my career. The following season, I ruptured my Achilles tendon, an injury that ended my career."

Simon swilled his bourbon, feeling the slow burn, and studied George: his face appeared to be cut like a piece of granite.

George stood by the window. "I've been thinking a lot about the mine explosion. We're getting slammed by the media."

"Richard thinks you should do an interview or press conference. Did you read yesterday's New York Times story? It's pretty scathing."

"I built this company from scratch. With these." He held up his oven-mitt hands. "I don't listen to critics or spectators. A lot of people resent success. It's easier to tear down than to build something. Tell me, Simon, would you rather be liked or respected?"

"Respected, I suppose."

George's pupils darted around like pinballs. "Like is fleeting. Respect is durable."

Simon wondered how far down this rabbit hole his boss would go.

"Carnegie and Frick were lions. They built bridges and cities. Today, what do we make?

"Plastic things?" Simon said, playing along.

"Exactly. Poorly made shit that lasts a few months. Ironically, Carnegie got all the attention, because steel is sexier than coal, but Frick was the better businessman. Carnegie would've failed without Frick."

"How'd you get into the coal business?" Simon felt like a pitcher in a slow-pitch softball league, lobbing up balls for his boss to crush over the fence.

"I'm from West Virginia. Appalachian, but not Southern. No mint juleps or seersucker suits. More like moonshine and overalls. My daddy played a mean fiddle. But I was the athlete of the family, and Penn State gave me a full ride. Studied Engineering. Then, Armco Steel offered me a job, overseeing their production."

Simon's father mentioned they worked together at the mill.

"By 1980, the steel industry was imploding, so I returned to my roots and took a job with Blackburn Coal. Dan Blackburn is one crazy bastard, but a great businessman. He once told me, 'If you stay in the mining business, get a nice black suit and plan to attend some funerals.' Anyway, when the time was right, I struck out on my own."

Dan Blackburn was the Darth Vader of Coal. He was best known for intimidating journalists and environmentalists, and sacrificing the safety of miners for profit.

"Is this the first mine explosion you've had to deal with?" Simon asked.

"First one at my company. But when I was at Blackburn, there was a fire that killed seven men. The point is, mining accidents happen all the time. It's a dangerous job. We need to ride the storm out. Don't talk to the media. They've betrayed us too many times. Richard disagrees, but my brother is a coward."

Simon considered telling him about Anita – that, maybe, she could be persuaded to write a story casting the company in a positive light – but he held his tongue. "What do you think caused the accident? I heard some office rumors about those dense foam blocks–"

"Rumors and gossip are the language of the weak. Even if we'd sealed off that high-methane section with cast iron, it would've made no difference. A major explosion destroys everything in its path. Legally speaking, it was an act of God."

Simon stared at his empty glass of bourbon.

"The coal boom will soon be over. The future is natural gas. All the new power plants use gas. That's why I bought all that land in the Marcellus Shale."

"Smart move."

"We'll survive this." George stood up. "I need to piss like a racehorse. Stay here."

Simon walked around the room, taking it all in. On the shelf beside the flat screen television, he browsed the collection of DVDs and compact discs. He removed one, titled EXECUTIONS, which he assumed was some thriller or horror movie.

"I guess you're the curious type," George said, directly behind him.

Startled, Simon dropped the case and the disc popped out.

George picked it up. "It's not legal to own this." Instead of placing the disc back in the case, he inserted it into the DVD player. "A friend of mine, a four-star Army general, gave it to me."

"Is it, like, one of those snuff films?" Simon asked.

"No, just classified. You want to see?"

Simon nodded. They sat back down and George turned it on.

The video began inside a small soccer stadium, filmed by someone in the stands. The field was empty, but the stadium was full and the crowd was buzzing.

"It's a Taliban village in Afghanistan," George said. "This video is several years old, before the war, even before Nine-Eleven."

The camera followed a group of bearded men in robes and turbans as they walked onto the field. Two men were escorting a blindfolded prisoner, a young woman. They walked to the midfield circle, where she knelt down. Then a tall man, holding a machete, stepped forward.

"They're going to kill her," Simon said. "What's her crime?"

"Infidelity," George said. "Unfaithful to her husband."

The man raised his machete. In one clean sweep, he severed her neck. Her head rolled off to the side, about ten yards. The crown erupted.

"Turn it off," Simon yelled. He clutched his own throat.

George stopped the film. "Public executions are a Taliban custom. Before the war, it was an effective way to show power and deter criminal acts." He paused. "But now, public beheadings are so common. All those splinter terrorist groups, videotaping executions of informants and western journalists and aid workers. The shock value is gone."

Simon looked at his watch. Eight o'clock. He started thinking of excuses to leave.

"The world is a cruel place, Simon. We don't appreciate how good we have it here."

"Yes sir, I understand. You know, it's getting late, and I'm meeting friends for dinner back in the city."

"You're not staying?" George looked surprised. "I have two guest bedrooms."

"No thanks." There was no way in hell he'd be spending the night in Dracula's castle. "But you'll be back to the office Monday, right? Richard wanted me to get confirmation."

"Tell Richard not to worry. I'll come back and clean up his mess, just like always."

Simon thanked him and walked out the front door. Outside, it was pitch dark. Free from city lights or pollution, the stars were urgent and reckless, an electric layer of dust.

Part of Simon felt sorry for George, who was divorced and estranged from his kids. Simon's father had described him as a shrewd businessman, but his ego and ambition clouded his judgment. Yet he also feared George, even more so after seeing that video.

As for the explosion, Simon didn't buy George's theory. Mine explosions could often be prevented or mitigated with safety measures. He knew the Sarver Mine had problems, but he lacked information. He needed to dig deeper and get some answers.

Closer to Pittsburgh, his phone vibrated. The office number.

"I assume you talked to George," Richard said.

"He'll be back Monday."

"Good. On Monday morning, before you get to work, I want you to go to Presbyterian Hospital in Oakland and visit with the two surviving miners. I emailed two documents."

"What kind?" Simon asked.

"Boilerplate settlement agreements. I need you to revise the language."

"What's the money amount?"

"Two hundred thousand each," Richard said. "That's three years of salary, and we'll pay all medical bills. In return, they agree not to sue the company."

"What if they don't sign?"

"Be persuasive."

Simon drove through Oakland, passing Pitt's Cathedral of Learning, that Gothic tower. (His Environmental Law class had met there one semester, in a basement room that resembled a medieval dungeon.)

Farther down Fifth Avenue, he glanced over at Presbyterian. Luke and Larry, the two survivors, were somewhere inside. He'd visit them in a couple days.

He cruised down Bigelow Boulevard, past the hockey arena, across Veterans Bridge.

Just as he reached the Ketchup Factory, he received a new text message: *Dinner? Tomorrow tonight? – Anita.* She'd read his mind.

HOSPITAL FOOD

Larry's dream unfurled like a carnival of memories. A little league baseball game at Pullman Park. Camping under the stars in Eugene, Oregon, after a Grateful Dead show. A Mississippi juke joint, jamming to the hill country blues. Early spring in Nebraska's Platte River, watching the Sandhill Cranes, awe-struck. The oldest birds on earth, their long wings draping the sky like ptero-dactyls, their distant cousins. Diving, like streams of ribbon, to a sandbar in the middle of the river. He'd lived a full life, and was ready for whatever came next, but when he opened his eyes and saw that he was connected to machines and tubes holding bags of fluid, it all came back to him.

A tall, thin Vietnamese man walked in, wearing a white lab coat over his scrubs.

"Good afternoon, Mr. Jenkins." He had a flat, Midwestern accent. "I'm Dr. Vo, your attending physician." Larry returned his smile. "How are you feeling?"

"Kinda sore all over," Larry said. "Could be a lot worse, I'm sure."

"So, you know why you're here?"

"Almost died in a coal mine. Right?"

"You inhaled a lot of carbon monoxide." The doctor sat down.

"What day is it?"

"Saturday morning."

"They brought you in late Thursday night, and you slept all day yesterday. You've experienced severe trauma, but you seem poised to make a full recov-ery."

"Good thing I quit smoking!" Larry winked.

"You chart indicates scarring of lung tissue from coal dust exposure." The doctor looked up from his clipboard. "Considering your medical history, we need to keep you here for a while and monitor things."

"How long?"

"Hard to say. Perhaps a week or two. Depends on how your body responds."

"C'mon doc." Larry chuckled. "There's no way I'm staying that long."

"You've been through a lot, Larry. When you first arrived, we had to stick a tube down your throat to remove fluid from your lungs."

His throat did feel sore, come to think of it.

The doctor asked if he had chest pains or shortness of breath.

"Not lately. Once in a while, my heart speeds up, like a panic attack. But when I do those deep-breathing techniques, it goes away."

"You quit smoking, but what about alcohol?"

"Just a couple beers now and then."

The doctor made a note on his chart. "What do you recall about the accident?"

Larry described the loud blast, the ground shaking, the smoke, the collapsed roof. The new kid, who tried to get out by himself. How the rest of them retreated, then used boulders and cement blocks to build a wall meant to keep out the smoke.

The doctor put his hand on Larry's shoulder. "You're a brave man."

"What about the other miners?" he asked. "Are they here, too?"

"I'm sorry to be the one giving you this news." The doctor shook his head. "But you and Luke were the only survivors. He's now in the ICU. His condition is more critical."

Larry dug into his ear canal. Maybe the wax blocked his hearing. "You serious?"

"I'm afraid so. Luke is in a medically-induced coma. We're doing all we can."

"Jesus Christ." Larry scratched his head in disbelief.

The doctor walked to the door and turned around. "A nurse will be in shortly, and I'll be back later on. For now, just try to get some rest."

On his first attempt to climb out of bed, Larry's weak legs gave out, and he fell. He picked himself up and sat in the bedside chair. He stared at the tray of food. Cup of mixed fruit, bowl of pale green soup. He craved a burger.

He smiled at the nurse when she came in. Tall, brown hair, deep brown eyes, full breasts. *Goddamn,* he thought, *maybe I'm dreaming this after all.*

"Hi Larry," she said. "I'm Denise. I work upstairs, in orthopedic surgery."

"You're not my nurse?"

"I'm Luke's wife."

He remembered everything Luke had said while they were trapped and waiting for the rescue team. "Oh, that's right. Luke told me."

"I came down to see if you need anything."

"Hospital food." He pointed to the tray. "Can you smuggle in a ribeye steak?"

Denise laughed. "The doctor says you're doing well."

"Someday, they'll study me in medical school textbooks!"

"Can I ask you something?" She hesitated. "Do you remember anything about Luke? I mean, like what happened to him down there in the mine?"

His chest felt tight, as if his emotions were sparring with each other: the guilt of being so attracted to his friend's wife, pitted against his anger with Luke for cheating on her. "We were all together. And I can tell you one thing. Luke saved me. That's the God's honest truth. You know, I still can't believe me and him are the only ones that made it."

Larry touched his arm, picking at the spot where the IV tube was attached. He thought about guys like Ron and Hank and their families.

Denise pointed to his forearm tattoo. "What's that?"

"An old mining symbol. Two pick axes."

"My dad was a miner," she said. "Died about five years ago."

"I made it twenty years with no accidents. But I guess it was my time."

"Luke mentioned you a few times. He said you'd just returned to the job."

"Long story." Larry glanced out the window as a medical helicopter passed.

"I'd like to hear it sometime." She checked her watch "But I need to get back."

"How long you been working here?"

She laughed. "This is my first week, believe it or not. It's chaotic, but I like it. Some lineman for the Steelers had knee surgery this morning."

She started for the door, then turned around. "By the way, have you talked to any reporters yet?"

Larry shook his head.

"They're crawling around here. Let me know if they bother you."

Larry smiled. "I think it'd be fun. I got some good stories."

"Suit yourself," she said. "But I'm not letting them go near Luke."

Larry hesitated, not sure how to ask the next question. "How's he doing?"

"We don't know much yet."

"It's crazy, they took Luke to the same hospital you work at."

"I know." She paused. "Not sure why I'm telling you this, but Luke and I had a big fight just before the accident." Her voice cracked. "I was too hard on him."

Larry wondered if she knew about Brandi. "It's not your fault, Denise."

"Did Luke ever talk about me?"

"Of course. Matter of fact, he made me promise I'd find you and tell you how much he loved you. Luckily, you weren't too hard to find."

She laughed through her tears. "Everyone's telling me there's a reason God put Luke and me in the same hospital. Like they got nothing better to say."

"Well, maybe they're right."

Larry searched her face. It felt like they'd known each other a long time.

She touched his shoulder. "I'll come back tomorrow."

He winked. "I hope so."

WEREWOLF

On Sunday night, Simon coasted down Murray Avenue, searching for the perfect parking spot. Luckily, Anita agreed to meet him directly at the Squirrel Cage. Picking up a woman in a soccer-mom sedan, he'd learned from experience, made the wrong first impression. Maybe it was time to reinvent the Simon Brand with a sporty Audi or BMW. When he noticed a car pulling out of a parallel spot, he uncorked a U-turn in the middle of Murray Avenue, ignoring the honks, and slipped into the opening. City driving brought out the worst in everyone. He checked his face and hair in the mirror. With his three-day beard stubble, he'd hoped to show Anita a different side. His dark, brooding side. He arrived ten minutes late: just right, since he didn't want to seem eager.

Sitting at the bar, Anita wore a shiny, emerald-colored dress, and her shorter haircut made her look girlish. He walked over. She smiled and kissed him on the cheek.

"Good cocktails here." She glanced at the hipster bartender – suspenders, a bowtie, handlebar mustache – making a round of martinis.

"The burgers here are the bomb, too." *Oh my God,* he thought. *Did you use the word bomb earnestly, without irony? You fucking jackass.*

After getting seated at a window booth, Simon ordered the fried-egg burger and a beer. "How long were you waiting?" he asked.

"It's fine. I'm early for everything. My high school tennis coach used to say *If you're on time, you're late.* Maybe I took him too seriously."

Self-deprecating humor. Good sign. "You still play tennis?"

"I burned out. My dad played in college. He started coaching me once I could hold a racket. At age twelve, I was winning USTA tournaments. I had a big kick serve and a solid backhand, but my forehand was inconsistent. Anyway, by eighteen, tennis had become a job, not a sport. In college, I wanted to try new things. Reinvent myself."

He considered that idea. "I quit basketball after ninth grade. Not from burnout, more like Darwinism. Natural selection. I rode the bench that whole season. By the end, I'd stopped wearing my shorts under my warmups. The final game, we're getting blown out by Aliquippa, and the coach calls my name."

Anita's eyes widened. "What happened?"

"I wasn't about to walk around the court in plaid boxers, so I kept sitting there with my pants on. The coach walked over. 'Yoder, get in the game,' he told me."

"And?"

"I told him I was sick. 'Bad diarrhea,' I said."

Anita covered her mouth, stifling a laugh.

"The coach shook his head at me in disgust. He pointed to the locker room, telling me to spend the rest of the game there. My NBA dreams died that day."

Simon still remembered that moment of recognition, when it dawned on him that he wasn't good enough to pursue his dream, no matter how hard he worked, because he did not possess a crucial trait. His junior high coach said he lacked killer instinct, and that he thought too much on the court. He had skill and athleticism, but during the game – when the lights came on and the seats filled up – something changed. Normally a good shooter, he'd miss wide open shots, and if he drove to the hoop, he'd miss the layup or dribble the ball off his leg. For the great athletes, the game slows down, but for Simon, the game sped up.

"Anyway," he said. "You went to college in New England, right?"

She nodded. "Amherst. One summer, I interned at the Boston Herald. They offered me a job after college. Spent five years there. Then came the recession. They cut half their staff."

Simon glanced at the pendant of her necklace. Some kind of Hindu symbol or character. It resembled a swastika. He knew so little about her, yet he was willing to learn.

"You were so quiet in high school."

"If you were a new girl from the Midwest, and half-Indian, you'd be quiet, too."

Her family, she reminded him, had moved from Wisconsin.

At the table beside them was an attractive, platinum-hair woman dining with a younger man. Mother and son, Simon thought, until the older woman started caressing his forearm.

"Remember Allison Moore?" he asked.

"Ditzy, but beautiful."

"In sixth grade, I tried to ask her out."

"Oh, I need to hear this." Anita inched closer to the table.

"I'd sit by the rotary phone and practice my lines, but each time I started to dial her number, I'd hang up before finishing. My mom would say, How hard can it be? But she never understood boys. She grew up with three sisters."

"What'd your dad say?"

"Nothing. He stayed out of conversations that might involve him giving life lessons. He believed in learning from your own experiences."

Simon felt like he'd slipped into a wormhole, or time machine, and had somehow landed in the Millburg High cafeteria in 1993. "Does this feel strange to you?" he asked. "I mean, do I feel like a stranger?"

"You resemble the cute guy who tutored me in Physics. But his name was John."

He flashed a crooked smile. "The name change is the only difference."

"I feel like there's a story behind that."

"A girl I dated in college said I was too boring and generic. Some people change their hair or clothes. Some get a tattoo. I changed my name."

"Girls are so mean. But why Simon?"

"I thought it sounded smart. And it's my middle name." He paused. "So, what about Anita? Any hidden meaning there?"

"Well, it means graceful in Hindu. But, most days, I'm the opposite of graceful. What would that be, anyway? Graceless?" She looked around. "Where are the bathrooms?"

"Behind the bar."

"Excuse me a minute, I want to wash up. Be right back."

Although Simon would never be called a sex panther, he was by no means a virgin. He'd known a dozen or so women – in the biblical sense – but he'd never known love, that camouflaged creature always evaded him.

He admired Anita's sense of humor, and she had plenty of grace, two qualities lacking in the few women he dated seriously. Hannah, his girlfriend at Penn State was a sweet girl from Ohio, but morally rigid. In law school there was Maggie, an ambitious redhead who swam the butterfly in college and had a matching butterfly tattoo. A serious, hard-charging girl, she didn't have the patience for him. Then came Lindsey, with her raw beauty, sarcastic wit, and need for control. She chose the restaurants, the movies, the vacations. She wanted a husband she could conquer and possess. Simon decided her cheating was a blessing, even though he'd woken up in physical pain almost every morning for a year. In a weird way, he missed that pain. He was the kind of man, after all, better taking orders than giving them.

Anita excused herself to find the bathroom. "Be right back."

Since the Lindsey breakup, his dating life had been a joke, a poorly-timed joke with no punchline. The blind dates felt arranged, and the internet dates were train wrecks. Some women looked nothing like their photo. Others couldn't remember his name. Like cheap champagne, internet dating left a chemical aftertaste and went flat overnight. He wanted somebody who was honest. Smart and funny would be a nice bonus.

Anita returned from the bathroom and sat down.

Simon asked her how Pittsburgh compared to Boston.

"It's easier to live here. Less intense. But I get strange looks. Could be my ethnicity. People have guessed Greek, Arabic, Spanish, Mexican, Brazilian. In Boston, nobody asked."

And the Pittsburgh news cycle, she pointed out, was slower than Boston's, so finding good stories could be more challenging here. She just wrote another story about the city budget, and the anger of residents over another bus fare increase.

Simon leaned closer to the table. "I've read your articles on fracking in Pennsylvania. You really know the issues around natural gas drilling. The politics and the science. But it sounds like you believe all fracking companies are evil."

"Well, it's disturbing how many water sources have been poisoned."

He held out a finger. "Natural gas is still cleaner and cheaper than coal or oil."

She looked surprised. "Not when you factor in long-term environmental costs."

Simon resisted his impulse to debate. He was starting to sound like a lobbyist. Then again, she sounded like an eco-snob. He glanced at a picture on the wall, a black-and-white shot of Pittsburgh in the 1940s. Steel mills lining the rivers. Smoke and soot filling the air.

After the waiter came with their burgers and a bottle of wine, she took the opportunity to pivot the conversation. "So, you live in the city? What part?"

"The old Heinz plant on the north shore. It's a loft."

He peered out the window. Across the street, a man with a camera stood under the Manor Theater marquee. It seemed like was he taking photos of people inside the restaurant, but it was dark and Simon couldn't see very well.

"And what's your escape?" she said. "I mean, what do you do for fun?"

"I have too many escapes. I've spent my life escaping."

He glanced outside again, but the photographer was gone.

"I did some research and found your college band. MAD DOG, right? I listened to a few songs online. Sounds like grunge, or heavy metal."

Her curiosity impressed him. "Our lead singer was a crazy German metal head with a high falsetto."

Anita's face was a kaleidoscope, each expression a new mystery.

"What did you wear on stage?"

"Flannels, baggy jeans, Timberland boots."

She ran her fingers through her shiny black hair. "You have any old video?"

He smiled. "We burned all the tapes. You know, speaking of Boston, we played The Middle East, in Cambridge. And the Paradise, near BU."

"Sometimes I miss it," she confessed. "It was easier to be anonymous there."

After dinner they walked down the block, passing the Manor Theater and Silky's Tavern. Two kids on skateboards weaved between them. They went inside the 61 Café, a bookish coffeehouse favored by grad students. They ordered espressos and found a corner table.

"So tell me about this explosion," Anita said.

"It was tragic, but every big mining company has an accident. Last year, thirty people died in a Blackburn coal mine in West Virginia. Yet we're getting hammered by the media."

"Death and destruction sells papers and boost ratings." She adjusted her glasses. "But I do have a serious question. You need to put your lawyer pants on for this one."

He considered a joke about wearing lawyer jeans, but resisted. "I'm listening."

"Is your company responsible? Did they somehow cause the explosion?"

"Honestly, I don't know all the facts. Negligence means the breach of an ordinary standard of care. We've been cited and fined a couple times for safety violations. But they were minor citations. There needs to be willful or reckless disregard of the law."

She raised an eyebrow.

"You asked a legal question. You got a legal answer."

"Sorry," she said. "We can talk about it later."

They left as the barista started closing up. He walked Anita to her car.

"You want a tour of the ketchup factory?" he asked.

"Nice try. But I'd like to see you again."

She waited for him to make a move, but he felt the tics coming. He was like some tourettic werewolf: he could get through dinner, but late at night, under a full moon, his body would jolt, jerk, and flail. He looked down at his feet, to distract his mind, but his legs began to do a weird dance, hopping back and forth, defying Simon's brain signals that commanded them to stop moving.

"Simon, why are you hopping from one leg to the other?"

"Oh, it just happens when I'm nervous."

"Are you nervous now?"

He nodded. She leaned forward and kissed him. More than a polite kiss.

As she drove off, his mouth hung open, like a dog that smelled bacon.

He wanted to package this feeling and sell it as an infomercial product.

SHOOT THE MESSENGER

By Monday morning – four days since the accident — Larry felt no pain in his lungs, and his breathing was free and clear. For the first time, he felt ready to leave the room and explore the hospital, but his plans were interrupted by another visitor. He'd never been this popular before the accident. This time, a short gray-haired woman in wire-rimmed glasses and a black robe with a preacher's collar had entered the room.

"I'm Reverend Southwick, the hospital's spiritual advisor." She smiled from the foot of the bed, her hands clasped together. "I heard your amazing story. My grandfather mined coal in Greene County."

He'd heard this before. When he told people what he did, some folks would mention a steelworker relative or coal-miner ancestor. It didn't offend him. Quite the opposite, Larry appreciated those who took pride in their working class roots.

"We're blessed that you survived such a traumatic ordeal," she continued. "I'd like to invite you to join our weekly prayer and support group. Your presence would help our patients, especially those facing serious illness or chronic disease."

"Thanks ma'am, I appreciate it. But I've tried church, and it doesn't work for me. I believe in God, I just talk to him in my own way. Does that make sense?"

Larry remembered the fundamentalist church he once attended. Born-again hypocrites. He saw prominent church members verbally abusing their kids in the parking lot. Church leaders in bars Friday nights, hitting on college girls. But on Sunday mornings, they always looked righteous.

"Of course." She smiled. "If you change your mind, we meet Tuesday nights, and all faiths are welcome."

After she left, Larry ventured out of his room. He passed the empty nurse station and took the elevator from the fifth floor to ground level. Searching the information directory on the wall, he located the ICU: third floor. When he turned around, a young Latina woman holding a microphone, next to a TV cameraman, was smiling at him. "Are you Larry Jenkins?"

"Who's asking?"

"I'm Wendy Gomez, Channel 4 News. Can I ask some questions?"

He squinted as the camera's bright light turned on. She'd ambushed him, caught him totally by surprise. "I guess so," he said.

"So how does it feel to be a hero?"

He kept blinking. "I'm not a hero."

"Do you feel any survivor's guilt?"

Her heavy perfume smelled of lavender and tobacco, which made his head spin. "I don't know. Am I supposed to?"

"Your story is everywhere. There's even a Larry Jenkins fan page on Facebook!"

Larry shrugged. "I don't own a computer."

"Well, now is your chance to send a message to all your new fans!"

"Thanks for the support, I guess."

"And what about your friend Luke? Is it true that he's near death?"

That's one of hell of a question to ask, he thought. "Luke is in serious condition, but he's a tough kid. He'll get through it."

She turned to the camera. "Reporting live, Wendy Gomez, Channel 4 News."

Off the air, she gave Larry her card. "I'd like to do a longer interview, when you're ready. By the way, this interview will air tonight, on the late news."

He watched her and the cameraman shuffle toward their van, parked by the curb. Then he walked to a trash can and ripped her card into little pieces. He glanced around the lobby. A Starbucks and a wireless internet lounge. Flower shop. Pharmacy. It looked more like a four-star hotel than a hospital.

On Monday morning, before making his hospital visit, Simon stopped by The Parlor, a high-end furniture store in the North Hills. Framed by large white columns, the store's exterior had a Southern antebellum aesthetic. Adam, his best high school friend, owned The Parlor. His family's business, Adam was third generation. He'd graduated from West Point and fought in Bosnia, but after completing his military service he came home to help run the business.

While the receptionist paged Adam, Simon browsed the showroom floor. He admired the library, with its grandfather clock and mahogany bookcase with classics like Jane Eyre.

Adam emerged from around the corner, wearing a gray, double-breasted suit. He'd put on weight, maybe twenty pounds. "Another vacation day, Simon?"

"What's with all the books? You never finished one in high school."

"An old customer donated them."

"I like the double-breasted suit. Very European."

"And hides the beer gut."

They'd met in seventh grade, while campaigning against each other for student council president. Adam, who wore ties and carried a briefcase in middle school, won the election, but Simon was content to settle for VP and let his friend make the hard decisions. In high school, they took the same honors classes and played varsity tennis. They could have been twins, except that Simon was almost a foot taller, and Adam was Jewish. In Millburg, a small Catholic town littered with bigots and racists, Adam couldn't hide his heritage. In the high school cafeteria or football stadium bleachers, Simon heard whispers of jewboy and kike, but somehow, Adam concealed his rage in public.

"How's business?"

Adam shrugged. "The recession hit us hard. But thank God for wealthy customers. The wife of the Steelers' head coach came in the other day. She bought something new for every room in their new mansion, which has like thirty rooms!"

Simon laughed.

"I heard about the mine accident," Adam nodded. "I saw your boss on television. He looked like a politician."

"George? Yeah, he's smooth. When he needs to be."

"You don't want George Blount on your bad side, from what I've heard."

"He's a scary fucker." Simon paused. "And this accident doesn't feel right."

"Eight people died. It shouldn't feel right."

"They're keeping me in the dark about something."

"Accidents happen. Don't go looking for answers. It's not worth it."

Simon nodded. "You may be right, but they treat me like a paralegal. Meanwhile, they make millions and pollute the environment. My company pride is pretty damn low."

"Don't be a hero," Adam said. "You know what happens to whistleblowers? They end up in witness protection, living in some random place like Sioux Falls. Or they're found dead. Either way, not a good career move."

Simon folded his arms. He disliked Adam's paternalistic, condescending side: dishing out his opinions and advice like it was charity work. "Can we talk about something else?"

"What about a new couch for your loft? Like this one?"

Simon collapsed into the brown leather sofa. "How much is this bad boy?"

"Let's make a deal," Adam said, sitting in a love seat.

Simon eyeballed the price tag, then recoiled. "Four grand. Is that a typo?"

"This is high-quality, finely crafted furniture, not that Discount-Outlet shit. Besides, I've seen your loft, and you need furniture."

They walked to the Entertainment Section, which included a pool table, pinball machine, various wet bars and barstools. "You also need some real toys. Not those damn infomercial products."

"By the way," Simon bragged. "I had a date last night."

"With your hand?"

"Remember Anita Sekran?"

Adam's face perked up. "Nerdy, but cute. Wait, she lives in Millburg?"

"Pittsburgh. She writes for the Press. I bumped into her a few weeks ago."

"So, how'd it go? You close the deal?"

"Did I close the deal?" Simon stifled a laugh. "I still have no idea how you ever talked Jenna into marrying you."

Adam answered his cell phone. He whispered hold on, then walked off.

A few minutes later, he returned. "So, where were we? Oh, your date."

"No more details. You can't keep your mouth shut. Remember eighth grade, when I told you about going up Rana Miller's shirt behind the Clearview Mall? Two days later, half the junior high knew about it."

"C'mon. Tell me a story. Married guys need stories. Did you scratch?"

Adam's phone rang again. "I need to take this, but let's grab lunch soon. And buy some furniture next time."

In the car, Simon weighed Adam's advice. He was right. Why get involved with the explosion? He didn't need to be some whistleblower, like those guys in Scorsese films who get whacked. Yet something in him burned to find out what really caused the explosion.

He parked in the garage beside Presbyterian Hospital and crossed the street. He followed signs for the information desk, then waited for the receptionist to get off the phone.

"Can I help you?" she asked, without looking up.

"I'm looking for two patients. Larry Jenkins and Luke McCurdy."

She raised her head. "No reporters or lawyers are allowed."

"No. I work with them. I wanted to come down and show my support."

She scanned him up and down. "You sure don't look like a miner."

Simon laughed. "Yeah, I get that a lot."

"Mr. Jenkins is in Room 705. You can see him, but not Mr. McCurdy."

Simon thanked her, then rode the elevator to the seventh floor, beside an old woman with a walker. She gazed at him like a child staring at the moon. Her gaunt, hollowed-out face reminded Simon of his grandmother before she died: the cancer had eaten through her organs like a depraved parasite.

He watched nurses shuffle in and out of rooms. He peeked into one room. Deflated balloons were tied to the bed, while a blond-haired toddler, surrounded by adults, batted the balloons with his hands. He found a bathroom and straightened his hair in the mirror. In his blue Oxford and khakis, he looked casual but professional.

Finally, he reached Room 705, knocked on the open door, and stepped in.

Larry sat in a chair beside his bed, reading a book. A long, opaque tube connected an IV bag to a vein in his forearm. He had a gray ponytail and high forehead. He looked wiry but strong. He had a forearm tattoo.

"Hello Larry. My name is Simon, and I'm here on behalf of–"

"Judging by your clothes, I'm guessing you're a lawyer. Or journalist."

"Well, yes. I'm the Legal Compliance Manager for Blount Coal."

Larry's eyes were tracking Simon like a panther. "Hold on." He ripped the IV tube from his arm. "I hate these goddamn tubes."

Simon felt weak and powerless, like he did in the junior high locker room after basketball practice, when Jason Rockenstein gave him wedgies and headlocks.

"I'll keep this short. First, I feel terrible about the accident. I respect what you guys do, putting your lives on the line every day."

"What else?"

Simon pulled out the contract and placed it on the bedside table. "In light of the hardship you've suffered, Commonwealth Energy is offering you a settlement agreement for one hundred-fifty thousand dollars plus all medical costs."

Larry scratched his beard. "Funny how you said agreement, not contract. Good lawyer trick. Now, what do y'all get in return?"

"Confirmation, I suppose, that the accident was not the fault of the company."

"In other words, I waive my right to sue for liability regarding the accident."

Simon nodded. His cheeks felt hot.

Larry glanced down at the contract. Finally, he said, "You got a pen?"

Surprised, Simon pulled one from his bag. "That means you'll sign?"

"Sure. I know the game is rigged against people like me."

"What game?"

"Contracts. Courtrooms. The law. You know what my dad called lawyers?"

Simon ventured a guess. "Assholes?"

"Carnies in suits and ties."

"Never heard that one."

"And besides, George Blount owns all of Seneca County. No use fighting him." Larry pointed at the Dixie cup of water on his tray. "Little help?"

Simon passed it along and watched him swallow a few pills, all at once.

"Cheers," Larry raised his Dixie cup. "By the way, I knew who you were the moment you walked in. The lawyer for the miners' families came in yesterday. Tried to sign me up."

"What'd you tell him?"

"Same thing. You can't beat George Blount in court." Gripping the pen, Larry signed.

Simon reviewed the contract, to make sure he'd signed in the right places. As he discovered, Larry not only signed it, he'd also crossed out the money amount– $150,000– and wrote in a new number: $300,000.

"What's this?"

"You made a lowball offer," Larry said. "I'm not a hick. I know how this works. You need me to sign this form. You don't want me joining the miners' case."

"Yes, but– "

"I had to fight for my goddamn life down there."

"But I don't have the power to negotiate. George and Richard make the decisions."

Larry smiled. "You got more power than you think. Take it back, see what happens."

His reasoning made sense, and Simon admired his boldness. He glanced up at the television, a replay of the Super Bowl two years ago, when the Steelers lost to the Packers.

"You a Steelers fan?" Larry asked.

"Of course."

"Did you read that obituary of the Cleveland Browns fan?"

"No." He'd already seen it online, but wanted to hear Larry to tell the story.

"Apparently, the man had requested six Cleveland Browns players for pall-bearers. So they could let him down one last time!"

Simon found himself laughing alongside this cagy old miner, who looked like he'd been raised by wolves. He'd feared him just a minute ago, and now he wanted to stick around and hear more stories. But visiting hours were over. Time to scoot back to work.

ৡৡ

Stationed in the Long Term Care ward, Denise felt light years removed from yesterday, her worst day on the job. All new nurses rotated their first two weeks, and yesterday she'd been assigned to the Urgent Care Wing. The ER smelled like a slaughterhouse: a mixture of bodily fluids, organs, and shit. One patient, a schizophrenic homeless woman, lost control of her bowels and shit herself. Then came the man with a neck tattoo, bitten in the ass by a stray dog. His rabies shot had to be injected at the source of the injury. And a young single mother with no healthcare, who'd waited three hours to get treatment for her kid's sinus infection. The overworked ER doctors and nurses were jaded and burned-out. Even without a life-threatening case— no gunshot wounds or overdoses— yesterday showed her the ugly side of nursing.

Today, in Long Term Care, things were much quieter. A welcome change. She carried a tray with packaged meals and pill cups labeled with room numbers. The secret to being a nurse in a large hospital, the veterans told her, was being orga-nized. Give the right meals, pills and shots to the right patients, and give the right tests and procedures. Each patient had a different chart, and their charts often changed. Denise kept detailed notes and didn't let her tasks pile up.

She walked into Room 27 and set down the tray. She glanced at the bed-rid-den man with wispy hair and a pained expression. "Mr. Wilson, how are we?"

He was watching a Weather Channel show about freak tornadoes. "Same shit, new day!" he said with a rapid fire, high-pitched laugh. He had a bulbous nose and ruddy cheeks.

She lifted his robe and examined his hip. The skin around the bandage was purple. His chart listed hip surgery, over a month ago. She assumed his age and alcoholism caused the poor circulation, resulting in a slow-healing wound.

"How is your hip? Do you feel a lot of pain?"

"Everything hurts, honey. Just give me your best drugs."

"Only what Dr. Rivers prescribes," she said, handing him a Dixie cup of pills.

"Doc Rivers is a fuckin' moron." The old man swallowed his pills and chased them with a glass of apple juice. Then, with his pinkie finger, he drilled into his ear canal, picking out a lump of ear wax and wiping it on his robe. "When you're old and mean, most nurses ignore you."

Normally, she'd keep him talking – most patients wanted to unload their problems – but today she wasn't in the mood. This is what the older nurses warned her about. A thankless job. Taking shit from both sides, doctors and patients. Find happiness outside work.

"I need to check your wound." She peeled off the tawny, crusty rectangle of gauze in the area of his left hip. Raw and puss-filled, it gave off a sour smell. It hadn't been cleaned in days. She doused a cotton ball with rubbing alcohol and scrubbed it.

"Goddamn!" he shouted. "That stings!"

Denise ignored his words and focused on treating the infection. She applied antibiotic ointment and fastened a new bandage over the wound.

"Okay. Done."

"At least I can still feel something," he said.

"When was the last time you walked around?"

"I walked to the bathroom this morning."

"That doesn't count," she said. "C'mon, let's do a lap around the floor."

He chuckled. "Good luck with that."

Before he could protest, she yanked him out of bed and led him into the hallway. "Hold onto the side rail if you need to."

"I had surgery 'cause it hurt to walk," he said, wincing. "Now it hurts more."

They walked toward Larry's room. He'd been the most pleasant surprise of her first week. She appreciated his easy smile and dry sarcasm. Visiting his room helped make the days go faster and forget her problems. Unlike her husband, Larry was a good listener, quiet and unassuming, although she could tell by the occasional wry grin, or gleam in his eye, that he'd been no saint as a younger man.

She noticed a man– tall, light brown hair– leaving Larry's room. As he passed, she stopped him. "Did you just come from Larry Jenkins' room?"

He said yes, flashing a goofy, crooked smile.

"Stay right here." She held up her index finger.

She turned to Mr. Wilson. "Let's head back."

"You said do a lap."

"Baby steps."

When she returned, the man was still waiting in the hallway. At least he could listen better than most members of his species. He wore glasses, a navy polo, and gray slacks. Round face, soft features.

"I'm Simon," he said, extending his hand.

"How do you know Larry?" she said firmly, hands on her hips.

"We work for the same company," he stammered.

"You're not a miner. I can tell."

"I'm a lawyer for Commonwealth Energy. Legal Compliance Manager, to be technical about it."

She took his arm. "Let's go down to the lounge. We can't talk here."

"What's this about?" he asked.

"That's what I'm going to find out."

They sat in cushioned chairs next to a coffee table. She spoke first. "So what are you doing here? What do you want with Larry?"

"Are you nurse or a cop?"

She folded her arms and glared at him.

"I'm just doing my job. My boss asked me to visit the miners."

"About what?"

"I don't think it concerns you."

"Do you know who I am?" She waited. "Luke is my husband."

He tilted his head sideways. "Wow, small world!"

His tone sounded sarcastic. "Hey smartass, you'd better tell me why you're here right now, or I'm calling security."

"I asked Larry to consider a proposal from the company."

"You mean a settlement offer, so he won't sue, right? I'm not stupid."

"Take it easy. Don't shoot the messenger."

"What if the messenger deserves to be shot?" Her mouth was a tight line.

"I'm not the enemy."

"You're not my friend. And I hate lawyers." She thought about the attorney who fought her dad's disability and worker's compensation benefits, even as he was dying.

"Honestly, I hate them too," he said. "It was not my choice to come here."

"Were you dragged here against your will?"

"Not literally."

"Whether you see it or not, the blood of those dead miners is on your hands."

"How do you figure that?" he asked.

She pulled her chair closer and leaned forward. "Because your actions are guided by your employer, and your company is driven by greed."

"Larry was offered a fair settlement offer, and he chose to sign it."

"He signed it?" It felt like she'd been slapped in the face. "You're lying."

He pointed to his bag. "I have the proof right here."

A few nurses walked past. She waited for them to get out of earshot. "Show me."

He handed her the folder.

She opened it and read the document. "You guys only offered one hundred-and-fifty thousand?"

"Plus all medical expenses."

Her blood was boiling now. Impulsively, she crumpled up the contract into a ball and threw it at his feet.

"Jesus." He picked it up and tried to flatten it out. "Are you insane?"

"It's not valid. He signed it under duress. You coerced him."

He flattened the document and placed it back in his bag. "Ask him yourself."

"Your company put my husband in a coma. Do you get that?"

"Denise, I feel terrible. But it was a freak accident."

"Why do people like you never apologize?" She stood up and started pacing, shaking her head. They were speaking different languages.

"I was born and raised in Millburg," he said. "My dad worked for Armco Steel. I care about what happens to Larry and Luke. It's personal."

She figured his dad was some corporate VP who belonged to the country club. He'd gone to a fancy private college, then law school. And now he drove a BMW or Mercedes, using his money and status to pick up the kind of women who'd ignored him in high school.

"Just think about what side you're on. You can't jump around. You have to pick a side."

Before he could respond, she got up and stormed down the hall, not turning around. Maybe she'd been too hard on him, but she wanted to send a clear message: she was prepared to fight.

THIS NEVER HAPPENED

On Sunday morning, Simon drove north to Slate Lick, a sleepy river town east of Millburg. He'd arranged a breakfast meeting with Ken Schultz, still wondering why he'd changed his mind and called him. Maybe the verbal lashing he'd taken from Denise at the hospital, accusing him of guilt by association, like a good German who remained silent during the Nazi regime. Whatever the reason, he returned Ken's call.

Simon knew the town of Slate Lick well. When his grandparents lived here, Simon's family drove over for church, followed by brunch at the Hot Dog Shop. He remembered how his Papa, always dapper in a suit, would hang up his fedora and cane, and then order his usual: butter-thin hotcakes, bacon, and black coffee.

Just off the exit ramp, he pulled into the Sheetz gas station— their meeting point— and waited. He kept alert for anyone suspicious. He'd heard a rumor that George kept two security personnel on the payroll, guys who did his grunt work but rarely showed their faces in public.

Sifting through his console for a piece of gum, Simon heard a loud tap on his window. Standing beside his car was a man in a camouflage jacket and sunglasses. He had an acne-scarred face and short brown hair with a widow's peak.

He lowered his window. "Ken?"

They shook hands.

"Sorry I'm late. I was out hunting this morning. You hungry?"

The man's yinzer accent was heavy, his vowels stretched and flattened.

Simon nodded, assuming they'd get breakfast or lunch somewhere.

"Good, but I want to show you something first. Leave your car, come with me."

Despite his better judgment, he climbed into Ken's truck.

They drove west on 422, toward Millburg. He noticed a shotgun in the backseat.

"Where are we going?" Simon asked.

Ken removed his sunglasses. Simon noticed a black eye patch over his right eye.
"I'm taking you to the crime scene. The Sarver Mine. Just a few miles away."

"What's with the eye patch?" Simon asked.

"Hunting accident."

"From this morning?"

Ken let out a quick burst of laughter. "You're funny, for a lawyer."

"Well, that's a pretty low standard."

"As a kid, I caught a stray arrow. From a crossbow."

"You grew up around here?"

Ken nodded. "East Brady."

They bounced along a potholed road, deep into the hills. The road curled around a pig farm, then it narrowed and turned to gravel. They passed a massive bony pile standing beside a coal tipple. Ken drove by the COMMONWEALTH ENERGY sign and the empty security booth.

They got out and walked past a doublewide trailer, the former onsite office. Ken stopped beside the string of yellow Caution tape. Simon studied the mine entrance, surprised by two things. First, how small the mine entrance looked. Somehow, he'd assumed underground mines were larger, with wide tunnels and openings, but this mine had small narrow tunnels, where most guys couldn't stand upright. Second, the ridges that flanked both sides of the mine were incredibly steep, like two walls that could not be scaled.

"I'd love to show you the damage up close, but they've got it sealed up." Ken pointed to the metal wall blocking the entrance. "Still a crime scene."

"This feels wrong. What if we're being watched?"

"Look around," Ken said. "It's dead quiet. It's been over two weeks since the accident. Everybody went home. The story's over, no one cares anymore."

"What about security?"

"It's Sunday morning. I don't see any security guards, do you?"

"No, but what about video cameras?"

"George is too cheap for that. This barbed wire fence is the only security he's ever used for his mines."

"If we could get in there, what do you think we'd find?"

"They've cleared it out. But I do have photos of how it looked right after the accident. I snuck in one night, before they sealed it off. I found several of those defective oxygen cans. And hundreds of tiny, shredded pieces of dense foam, scattered all over the tunnel floor."

Simon nodded. "I heard about those foam blocks before. What's the relevance?"

"Some mines have pockets or sections with naturally high methane gas levels, and sometimes the standard procedure won't reduce those levels."

"Like spraying the walls with crushed limestone?"

Ken nodded. "Federal law requires that you seal those sections with a hard material, like concrete blocks. A few years ago, George started using dense foam blocks in his mines. He claimed studies showed dense foam material could withstand as much force as concrete. But I've never seen proof. Nobody has."

"Then why did he make the switch?"

"Money, probably. The foam blocks are cheaper. George is also an investor and part owner of the company that makes them."

"Holy shit," Simon whispered, as if talking to himself.

"Before leaving Blount, I copied hundreds of confidential documents. Safety violations and citations. Important email threads. They're in a nearby storage unit."

"Can you show me?"

"Not now, it's too dangerous. George employs two full-time personal security guards. I doubt you've ever seen them, they keep a low profile. But they know I have evidence against the company. They've broken into my house and hacked into my cell phone. That's why I only use disposable cell phones."

"Did you go to the cops?"

"You're kidding, right?" Ken laughed. "George Blount owns this county. He essentially pays the salaries of the local police. And I can't risk them finding my storage unit. But you could get in there, undetected."

He took out a business card, wrote something on the back, and handed it to Simon. He flipped the card and read the back: BOB'S SELF STORAGE. Unit 13. Lock Combo: 31-07-23.

"So, you want me to find this?" Simon asked.

Ken nodded. "If something happens to me, I want you to get those documents. It's that storage facility on Route 356, near the high school."

"Thanks, I guess."

Simon heard tires crunching gravel. He turned around and watched a gray Crown Vic, unmarked, crawl up the hill.

"Speak of the devil," Ken said. "Cop."

A tall, muscular man stepped out of the car. He wore jeans, but his black coat and baseball hat had a gold shield, similar to what Pennsylvania state troopers wore on their uniforms. He had on Ray-Bans, and blonde hair, almost shoulder-length, under his cap.

He stopped about ten yards from Simon and Ken. "State police," he said, flashing a badge, then tucking it back inside coat. Simon noticed a handgun clipped to his belt. "I heard report of some activity up here."

"It's job related," Ken said. "We both work for Blount."

"On a Sunday?" The man had an accent, maybe German or Swedish.

"Tough boss," Simon said.

"This area is a live crime scene. It's off limits to everyone, even personnel."

Ken pointed to Simon. "My coworker has never been here. He just started, in the corporate office. I'm showing him where the accident happened. The outside, anyway."

The cop took out his citation book and started writing something.

"There's no need for that," Simon said. "We were just leaving."

He put his book away. "I don't want to see you here again," he warned.

They thanked him, and quickly shuffled back to Ken's truck.

"That was fucking weird," Simon said.

"You still hungry?" Ken asked. "Want to grab lunch at the Hot Dog Shop?"

"Sure. One of my old favorites."

Walking down Water Street, Simon surveyed the old Victorians. He used to admire their grandeur, but most of them had withered. A frail man with a tangled nest of gray hair and a torn coat walked past him. He carried a large plastic bag, full of smaller bags, and was talking to himself. "Time to make the donuts," he repeated, looking down at the pavement.

They walked three more blocks to the diner. He followed Ken to a booth in back, passing the same grungy kitchen, smelling the bacon grease. And the same old menu, in large print, was painted on the wall.

"That dude didn't seem like a cop," Ken said. "You see that hair?"

"Maybe he's one of those office cops. Like an investigator."

"Yeah, but what about the accent?"

"Who else could it be?"

"One of George's goons, but it's impossible to be certain."

Simon made a mental note. "So, tell me more about what's in your storage unit."

"You don't need to know that information right now."

"Why did you contact me, in the first place?" Simon asked.

"I had to tell someone." Ken glanced anxiously around the dining room.

"What's wrong. Are we being followed?"

"I'm just on alert. I told the hostess to let me know if anyone strange comes in."

Simon felt queasy. "Look man, I'm not Robin Hood. I won't risk my life."

"You're not in danger. Not yet, anyway."

The waitress came back for their order.

"Burger and fries," Ken said.

Simon ordered hotcakes and bacon. "Best pancakes north of Pittsburgh. My grandparents lived around here. We'd come here for Sunday brunch, after church."

"I live in East Brady. Just up the road."

"Home of Jim Kelly. The old Buffalo Bills quarterback."

"Right," Ken said. "He still owns a place on the river. I think he has cancer."

They traded complaints about working for Blount.

Ken smiled. "Legal Compliance Manager is the perfect title, since you must comply with George and Richard every time. I could never give my opinion. It was like Stalinist Russia."

While he didn't look like a typical lawyer, Ken had a firm grasp of the law— environmental, land use, contracts— and he knew everything about the company.

"So, what keeps you busy these days?"

"Preparing for the end of the world."

Simon spilled his coffee. "Pardon me?"

Ken smiled. "The apocalypse. The end of days. My bunker is stocked. Canned food, water, frozen deer meat. Clothing and batteries. Guns and ammo."

Simon poured another creamer into his coffee.

"Look around. All these freak storms. Sea levels rising. Food and water shortages and power blackouts are coming. Better build your ark now."

"Why did you leave Blount?" Simon asked. "I mean, was it your choice?"

Ken flashed a crooked smile. "You know, I didn't think you'd have the balls to call me back. You haven't told anyone about this meeting, right?"

"Of course not."

The waitress refilled their coffee. She looked scared. "There's a guy up front, waiting to be seated. I've never seen him before. And he looks, um, different."

Ken poked his head around the booth. "We need to get out of here."

Turning his head, Simon eyeballed a short guy, built like a brick outhouse, wearing a brown leather jacket and wraparound sunglasses.

"There's a back exit through the storage room." The waitress pointed.

Simon and Ken ran along the back wall and through the storage room, a giant pantry filled with bulk sized cans of ketchup and gravy, big boxes of flour and sugar. It was dark. Simon tripped over a box. The back door led into a back alley. The temperature had plummeted, and a low bank of anvil clouds marched across the sky.

They jumped in Ken's truck and raced back to the gas station.

Simon got out. "Thanks for the info. I'll be in touch."

"No." Ken wagged a finger. "This never happened, we never met. Trust me. Once you look inside that storage unit, you'll know what to do."

Simon went inside the convenience store and grabbed a Gatorade. He studied the other customers. A fat guy in a Steelers jacket. Two teens. An old couple. Nobody stuck out. No goons. He was safe again. At the counter, he asked for a can of Skoal.

"What kind?" asked the short, gray-haired woman.

"Sorry. Long cut, mint."

She grabbed the can from the shelf behind her, then rang him up.

"I don't dip that often," he added. "Just when I'm stressed."

"I ain't judging you, hon. Only God can do that."

In the car, he packed a wad of tobacco under his lip and reflected on his morning. He felt frazzled, yet invigorated. Sneaking around a coal mine— an ongoing crime scene— and being followed by violent men was more exciting than his average day: Revise a contract. Draft a memo. Reply to emails. Read the news online. Check social media. Go home, order takeout dinner. Watch a game. Read a book or watch an Infomercial until his brain powered down. Wake up and repeat. He hated the robotic repetition. The absence of wonder or discovery.

But things were changing. His life was gaining velocity.

POST-DRAMATIC STRESS DISORDER

Each day, Larry's room felt more like a prison cell. He'd been here eight days, and he couldn't endure it much longer. But this morning Dr. Vo had delivered some good news. Because his lungs scans were clear, barring any setbacks, he'd be released in a few days.

Larry walked to the window ledge and examined the cards attached to flower baskets and vases. The arrangement from Hank's family held thistle, rhododendron, and Mountain Laurel. It smelled fresh, unlike the generic fruit basket sent by the Commonwealth Energy Corporate Office. Their card read: "You're in our thoughts and prayers." Nobody had even signed the damn thing.

He grabbed the television remote and flipped to Channel Four. For some reason, they'd been replaying his interview on the morning news all week long. Sure as shit, there it was again, with his photo appearing in the top right corner of the screen, as the anchor summarized the key facts about the mine explosion.

"Reporter Wendy Gomez interviewed Larry Jenkins," the anchor said. "A true survivor."

They cut to him, at the hospital, answering her questions. The camera zoomed out. Even though he'd seen this video three or four times, he still hated how small and frail he looked, in his loose-fitting hospital robe.

Just then, Denise walked in. She stopped at the foot of the bed and faced him, her arms crossed, blocking the television.

"Did you see my interview?" Larry said. "I look like a sad bastard."

"Did you speak to a lawyer the other day? A lawyer for Commonwealth? "

"Yeah, Simon. Nice guy."

"Did you sign any documents?" She pulled the chair beside his bed and sat down. "And don't bullshit me, because I'm not in the mood."

Larry sat upright. "Look Denise, I'm too old to play the hero. Somehow, I survived this ordeal. But I need to move on with my life. I don't have the energy for a legal fight, and I can't wait two years for a big jury award that may never come. I just want my fair share." He paused. "So yes, I did sign a settlement agreement."

"Oh, I see. Once you walk out of this place, you'll forget about the rest of us. You'll turn your back on your friend, who's clinging to his life down the hall."

She sounded hysterical, he thought. "I'm not turning my back on anyone."

"I didn't ask for this either," she said. "But I can't ignore it."

"Denise, you need to do what's best for you and Luke. But I've seen this movie before. Everybody thinks they'll walk away with millions. It never happens like that."

"You think it's about the money?" She paused. "It's about making them do the right thing, and admitting responsible for eight dead miners. Maybe nine."

"Luke's a tough kid. He'll get through this."

She walked to the window and looked out. "What if he doesn't'?"

"Look, I can't tell you what to do."

"Why are you being like this? I thought we were in this together."

"We are."

She started to cry, her sobs growing louder. When he opened his arms, she let loose with the kind of emotion she couldn't show on the job. He thought about Josh, crying on his shoulder when he'd skin his elbow or get stung by a wasp. After a minute, she lifted her head and composed herself.

When she reached for the glass of water on the tray, she noticed the blood-spotted napkin. "What is this? Have you been coughing up blood?"

"It's nothing."

"How long have you noticed it?"

"That's the first time it happened since I've been here."

"We need to tell Dr. Vo."

"No," he pleaded. "I need to get out of here. Please, I can't stay in this room any longer. Do me this one favor."

She studied him for a minute. "Fine, but you owe me a favor in return."

"Name it."

She winked. "I'll save it for a rainy day."

Once Denise left, Larry embarked on his mission. Seeing Luke was the last thing he needed to do before leaving. He walked down the corridor – his robe sliding off, exposing plaid boxers – before pausing at the nurse station.

"Hello Mr. Jenkins, can I help you?" asked Stacy, one of the nicer ones.

"Where's the ICU at?"

"Two floors down, but you're not supposed to leave this floor."

"I need to see Luke." He tried to sound convincing. "Denise approved it."

She looked around. "Okay, but please come right back."

He smiled. "I promise."

At the main doors of the ICU, he waited for a diversion. When two nurses carted a post-surgery patient inside, Larry fell in behind them, keeping his head down. He glanced into the opening of each curtain, searching for Luke's face. When he reached the private rooms, he peered through each glass windows. Near the end of the row, he found Luke's room.

His friend was hooked up to every kind of machine. A breathing tube poked out of his mouth. Another line connected an IV bag – hanging from a metal pole behind him – to a vein in his right arm. Chapped lips, pale skin, atrophied muscles. They'd shaved his head and his goatee. He looked like a frail ghost. This had to be a joke. How, in God's name, could this healthy young dude could be clinging to life? It made no sense. Luke's condition reminded him of the wounded soldiers at Walter Reed, where he'd gone to identify Josh's remains.

He heard a knock at the door. It was Dr. Vo, but without his trademark smile. "Stacy told me you were here."

"I had to see my friend, before I leave here."

"I understand. But there's nothing you can do for him."

"How is he?" Larry asked "Any changes?"

"The nurse on duty last night said he opened his eyes, but I don't want to give false hope. Sometimes coma patients appear to be awake and alert, when they're really not. But we'll keep a close eye on him, you can be sure."

"Take good care of him."

"Of course." The doctor's smile returned. "Let's go back upstairs now."

Reluctantly, Larry obeyed the doctor's instruction.

From his room window, he peered down. Umbrellas filled in the sidewalks. He'd give anything to feel rain on his face, and sleep in his own bed. He was ready to unload these feelings on anybody, but when Tina knocked on his door, he changed his mind.

"What a pleasure," he said, not hiding the sarcasm.

She set her umbrella in the corner. "Look at me, I'm drenched." She was dolled up, with a fresh spray-on tan.

"What are you doing here?" he said, clenching his jaw.

"Oh my God baby." She bent over to hug him. "Look at you."

Selling the drama, like always. Her perfume smelled like a stripper's. No big surprise, considering they'd met at Teaser's in Ford City, where she used to dance.

"I was so worried about you!" she said.

Larry narrowed his eyes. "Why are you even here?"

"I needed time to get my head right." She grabbed his hand. "When I saw them take you out on a stretcher and put you in that helicopter, I was so scared."

Larry tilted his face up toward ceiling, fixing his eyes on the tiny video camera.

"I've missed you so much. Did you miss me?"

"Tina, let's not dance around this any longer. We had a good run, but it's over. Your moving out was the best thing for both of us. I can't give you what you need."

"You're not thinking straight," she said, hands on her hips. "Darren said this might happen. He said you might have that post-dramatic stress."

"It's called post-traumatic stress. And who the fuck is Darren?"

"A lawyer I know. I told him about that miners' lawsuit. He said with your injuries and trauma, we'd get millions! He kept saying something about punitive damages."

"First of all," Larry said. "There is no we. And second, I'm not suing anyone. The company gave me a fair settlement deal, and I took it."

"How much?" she asked.

"It doesn't concern you."

"Even if you signed a contract, Darren said it's void. Since you were drugged."

"I wasn't drugged!" He tilted his head. "Wait, are you fucking this guy?"

"You're crazy," she muttered. "You don't know what's good for you."

"Well, I know what's bad for me. I'm looking right at it."

She pointed finger at him. "Keep it up, asshole."

"You know what, Tina? Since I've been laid up in here, with nothing to do and nowhere to go, I've tried to understand why it didn't work between us."

"And what'd you come up with, Einstein?"

"You're completely self-absorbed. There's no room for anyone else."

"It's a two-way street. You need to quit living in the past. Your son is dead."

She still knew his weak spots. She knew where it hurt the most.

His smiled vanished. "Get the fuck out of my room. Now."

Calmly, she turned, grabbed her umbrella, and left.

Larry knelt down beside the bed, clasped his hands, and whispered a quick prayer: *Lord, please take me out of here, before she comes back.*

GUILLOTINE

From his desk, Simon heard Deb's scratchy voice, coming through the PA system. She was announcing a company "ice cream social" in the conference room. It surprised him, since there were no birthdays or special events marked on the calendar.

He watched a line of his coworkers shuffle into the kitchen. When he joined them a few minutes later, most of the chocolate layer cake and half the tub of vanilla ice cream had already vanished. Simon served himself, then sat down beside Julie.

"What's the occasion?"

"Beats me," she said. "No birthdays this week."

Computer Bob devoured two large slices of cake using his hands, no utensils. Hippie Jim walked in, smiling and rubbing his belly. He wore a Hawaiian shirt and jeans. His hairy toes poked out of his Birkenstocks. He once dropped acid with Bob Weir.

"Why is Jim allowed to wear jeans and t-shirts, but not us?" Simon asked.

"Because he can find natural gas underground," Julie said. "Can you?"

"Good point."

Richard seemed upbeat, even happy, as he sat down.

"What's the occasion?" Scott asked him.

Richard smiled. "As you know, we had record profits last year. And our first quarter numbers are even better. So, thanks for your hard work. Give yourselves a pat on the back."

Bob, Scott, and Deb followed along. Yes, they patted themselves– earnestly, with no hint of irony– on their fucking backs.

Simon chuckled. Oh, what a jolly bunch of ass-clowns he worked with.

"Also," Richard continued, "I'd like to do an office field trip this summer. I considered Kennywood, yet not everyone likes roller coasters. But most people like games and good food, right? So, how about Dave & Busters?"

Scott and Bob high-fived each other. "We love that place!"

"And games are free," Richard said. "The company will pay for it."

"Is the beer free, too?" asked Hippie Jim.

Simon howled. Jim's snarky jabs always made the day go faster.

Richard ignored it. "Well, back to work for me. Enjoy the cake."

Simon whispered to Julie. "I bet the field trip is our Christmas bonus."

She rolled her eyes. "You mean, instead of Walmart gift cards?"

"No shit, right? My brother works on Wall Street. His bonus was like eighty grand."

"But did he get a field trip to Dave & Busters?"

"Good point," Simon said. "I'll try not to rub it in the next time I see him."

At five o'clock, Simon locked his office and prepared to slither away, but before he reached the front exit, Deb stopped him.

"George and Richard want to see you. She stared at him with empty eyes, chomping on her gum like a Holstein eating grass.

"Where?"

"George's office."

Simon's eye twitched. "I thought George was out today." His mouth felt dry.

Deb's eyes were empty black holes. "Guess not."

Walking back, he pictured a guillotine. He'd heard rumors that "heads would roll" after the accident, and he was a perfect candidate. The door was half-open.

"Grab a seat, Simon" said George, from the leather chair behind his desk.

Simon eased into the captain's chair, beside Richard. He studied their faces. As usual, Richard looked agitated.

He surveyed the bookshelf behind George's chair. Along with the customary books on business and leadership, there were nonfiction books on military history – World War 2 and the Civil War – and biographies of industrial captains and financial tycoons like Carnegie, Frick, Ford, Rockefeller, Vanderbilt, and Morgan. He also noticed *The Art of War* by Sun Tzu.

Beside the bookshelf was a gray metal filing cabinet. The other day, Julie had told him George kept copies of sensitive and confidential document locked in that cabinet. Because he distrusted computers, he printed out emails and files he deemed important.

"Haven't seen you since you came up to the lodge" George said. He appeared calm, but alert. "Richard and I have been busy all week, managing the chaos."

"Of course."

"Richard tells me you visited one of the surviving miners in the hospital?"

"Larry Jenkins." Simon cleared his throat. "Quiet man, but pleasant. He seemed healthy. I was told he'd make a full recovery, but the other one– "

"Did he sign the settlement offer?" George asked, cutting him off.

"Yes." Simon pulled the contract from his satchel. "I meant to give it to Richard sooner, but his office door was always closed, and —"

"Let me see it," George said.

He handed him the crumpled document.

"I hope there's a good reason why it looks like this." George flattened it out and ran his finger down it. "Wait a second. He wants more money?"

Simon nodded. "He crossed out our number and doubled it."

"He's got balls, I'll give him that." George paused. "But why is it crumpled?"

"On my way out, a nurse confronted me. Turns out, she's married to Luke, that miner still in the coma." George and Richard exchanged a nervous look. "She asked what I was doing there. When I showed her Larry's signature on the agreement, she crumpled it up."

"What else did she say?" Richard asked.

"Not much. But she hates the company, and lawyers."

"It's no problem," George said. "We'll handle this."

"Thank you, sir."

"And next week, I want you to meet with the Mitchell Burns lawyers. We need to map out a legal strategy. Call Mark Wentworth to set it up."

"Sure." Simon stood up to leave. "Is that all?"

"One more thing," George said. "Do you know Ken Schultz?"

The air smelled like burning leaves. His eye wanted to twitch, and his elbow wanted to jerk. But he kept his poise. "That guy who worked here before me?"

"Has he ever tried to call or email you?" Richard asked.

"Now that you mention it. I did get a strange voicemail last week, after the accident."

Richard looked pissed. "What, exactly, did it say?"

"He sounded manic. He was talking super-fast about how it was the company's fault. I'd heard he was crazy, and the voicemail confirmed it. So, I ignored it."

"Did he go into any details?" George asked.

"He called you guys capitalist pigs. He sounded like a conspiracy theorist."

George addressed his brother. "I knew he'd try to call him."

"You still have the voicemail?" Richard asked.

"I erased it," Simon said. "It didn't seem like a big deal."

Richard scowled. "Are you kidding?"

"Calm down," George said, chiding his younger brother. "Simon, we were afraid of something like this. Ken has a mental disorder. We tried to be patient, but he got worse, until he could no longer handle the work. He had other issues. Messy divorce. Drug addiction."

"I had no idea."

"Sometimes, people crack." George paused. "Simon, do you play golf?"

"Yes, but not very well."

"I'm hosting a charity scramble next month. You should join us."

"Sure."

"Great, you can be my partner!" George smiled. "That's it for now. You're a free man."

Simon left the room, but instead of returning to his office, he lingered outside the door. He put his ear against the wall, as George and Richard continued their conversation.

"What are we going to do about him?" Richard said.

"You need to relax."

"George, you know he's lying."

"We don't know anything yet. It's too early. But we do need to keep an eye on the situation at the hospital."

"Luke's wife?"

"Both her and Luke. I'm not worried about the older guy anymore. But if Luke wakes up and suddenly remembers things about the accident, we're fucked."

"And if he dies, the media will crucify us. We're fucked either way."

"Not necessarily," George said. There was a long pause. "What if, somehow, he stays in a coma, at least until the legal shit-storm has passed?"

"We can't control that."

"We could encourage his doctors to keep him connected to those machines."

"How?" Richard asked.

George cackled. "Money, you retard. Are we really brothers?"

"What about Simon?" Richard said. "He can't be trusted. He's a cancer."

"We can't make rash decisions. We'll talk about this later."

Simon raced down the hall, blowing past his office, to the men's room.

He entered the last stall, knelt before the porcelain god, and vomited up his cake.

LAW-BOTS

Riding up the U.S. Steel Building elevator, Simon thought about last week's conversation with George and Richard. He was confident they'd believed his story about Ken, but the encounter had left him totally fucking paranoid. How much did they know, and what did they know about Anita? He hadn't seen her since their dinner date. Resisting his physical desire, Simon knew it was best not to involve her, to keep her off George's radar.

On the fifty-seventh floor, he found the Mitchell & Burns office and checked in. The receptionist, in a sandpapery voice, told him to wait. He walked to the window. Spectacular view. He could see the infield of the Pirates' ballpark– they must have been playing an afternoon game, since the lights were on and the seats were filled– but all the lawyers and paralegals on this floor seemed too preoccupied to admire the view.

A woman with nice legs and big mall hair approached. "Mark is waiting."

In the conference room, dozens of lawyers and paralegals sat behind laptops, iPads, and large stacks of paper. Mark, the head litigator, greeted him. "Welcome to the war room."

Mark was the perfect lawyer to greet clients. Polite and polished, but not abrupt. His colleagues looked and acted like drones. No smiles or "hellos," no acknowledgment another life form entered the room. They looked to be junior associates or paralegals– not partners– prepping for a big trial. Simon pictured them as Law-Bots: robots created by the mad scientists at Carnegie Mellon.

"This is how it looks when we get serious. Big trial next week. We're defending a big pharmaceutical firm in a class action suit. Defective drug claim."

"Sounds exciting."

"I need to step out for a minute, but my colleagues, Lauren and Seth, will handle things."

A woman in her late twenties with short brown hair, glasses, and a light gray suit introduced herself: Lauren, a junior associate. She smiled and brushed her hair out of her eyes. She reminded Simon of the young female attorneys at Rooney. Smart and confident. But guarded, never revealing too much.

"Let's take a seat, and then I'll ask you some introductory questions."

"No problem," he said.

She turned on a voice recorder. She questioned Simon about the compliance part of his job, safety protocols, and communication with company managers. She was pleasant, although it felt more like a deposition than a strategy meeting.

"Great," she said, wrapping up. "Now, Seth will ask a few more questions."

A short, beady-eyed man entered the room and took Lauren's seat. He made no eye contact as he opened his laptop.

The Inspector General, Simon thought.

"Why did Commonwealth Energy fail to comply with the MSHA safety citation, from two years ago, requiring new oxygen masks and canisters?" Seth asked, with no introduction.

"Well, I wasn't working there at the time. But I assume they were working properly."

Seth raised his head. "How would you know that?"

"They were probably tested by someone."

"By whom?"

"By people who do that kind of testing." Dumb questions get dumb answers.

Seth looked annoyed. "How long have you been with the company?"

"Six months."

"And what did you do before that?"

"I worked at Rooney for two years."

Simon glanced at the portraits on the wall: four old white men in dark suits, none of them smiling. The firm's founding partners, long dead.

"And you were fired from Rooney?"

"Excuse me?"

"Were you fired?"

"I resigned. How is that even relevant?"

"It's my job to ask questions the other side might ask. Since you spent less than two years at that firm, it's a valid question. Your background impacts your credibility as a witness."

"I know the rules of court procedure, thank you very much. The bottom line is, Commonwealth was a better opportunity for me."

"What are your chief responsibilities in your current position?"

"I make sure our coal mines and gas wells are fully compliant. I draft contracts with landowners, customers, and other companies we deal with. I also help to draft the legal sections of the annual and quarterly shareholder reports." Simon fidgeted, as Seth jotted something on his legal pad. "Oh, and I update employee policies and regulations. Finally, I help our office manager, Julie, with paperwork."

Seth flashed a quick smile. "So, part of the job is paralegal work."

Simon hated him. Seth was like those douche bags in law school who argued everything. At Shadyside bars, they'd debate the reasoning of Supreme Court opinions and drink overpriced Heinekens. Simon preferred cheap pitchers, usually at dive bars like Silky's or Panther's Hollow.

Seth continued his interrogation. "Regarding compliance of coal mines, are you familiar with the mine's safety practices and procedures? Did you write the miners' safety manual?"

"Yes. And I rewrote major portions of the safety manual."

"Since 2010, Pennsylvania mines are now required to seal off high methane areas with concrete block. Yet, Commonwealth still uses the dense foam blocks. Why?"

Simon adjusted his glasses. He felt like a hostile witness being cross-examined.

"Richard handles that issue."

"Is it done for financial reasons, in other words, to save money?"

"I have no fucking idea," Simon replied.

"Please find out and get back to me."

When Mark returned, Seth got up to leave. They were like a tag-team wrestling team. Simon gave them nicknames: Mark the Magnificent tags in for Seth the Scorpion!

"Okay, Simon. As you can see, we're trying to gather the best information about the accident, in case of a lawsuit, and perhaps a trial."

"Do you think we'll get sued?"

"Do you I think any criminal charges will be filed? No."

"What about a civil lawsuit?"

Mark nodded. "It's possible that the families of the dead miners will seek a monetary award. They might argue that the company's negligence caused the explosion and, by extension, the deaths of the miners. But they haven't yet filed a complaint. Also, a trial would not take place for several months, at the earliest."

"Okay. Good to know."

"If there is a trial, you'd be expected to testify." Mark paused. "As the in-house legal expert, you'd be the linchpin of our case." Mark leaned back and crossed his legs. "By the way, I apologize for Seth. He's passionate about his job."

Simon shrugged it off. "No worries."

"Remind me of your legal education and experience. You went to Pitt Law, right?"

"Yes. I clerked for a judge in Scranton for a year. Then, two years at Rooney."

Mark jotted down notes on a yellow legal pad. Mark had played basketball at Vanderbilt. He was 6'5" and spoke with a south Virginia drawl.

"And while at Rooney," he continued. "Did you work on any Environmental Law cases?"

"A few, but I worked more on the industry side."

"Good. Your background is solid. But the plaintiff lawyer will test you with some tough questions."

"Such as?"

"They might ask about the citations and fines Commonwealth has received in the past year, like for defective oxygen devices. How do you typically handle such violations?"

He told Mark how they would pay the fine, then make the required changes within six months or so. They recently ordered new oxygen cans for their Freeport Mine, but Richard said the ones at Seneca were good for another year, at least.

"What about training for miners?" Mark asked.

"They undergo three days of safety training sessions before they start."

"Good. Did the Sarver Mine have any alternate exits or evacuation routes?"

"The engineers would know that," Simon said.

"No problem. If you don't know an answer, that's fine. Just don't volunteer information." Mark paused. "One more thing. About you leaving Rooney –"

"I already told Seth. I left by choice."

"But there were six months in between your leaving and starting at Commonwealth."

"I needed time to sort things out." Simon chewed on his fingernail.

"Your Rooney file says you failed to meet your billable hours. More than once."

"I wasn't the only one. It's hard to meet that quota some weeks."

"Trust me, I know. But some jurors might take that to mean you were fired."

"And some people believe in Creationism! Look, I hit a rough patch. My fiancée cheated on me. My dad died a few months later. I was a mess."

"Fair enough. I think we're done." Mark put his pen away. "Let me walk you out." He patted him on the back, like a coach rebuilding a player after tearing him down. "You're a straight-shooter. I admire that. No matter what happens with this case, I'm sure you'll land on your feet."

Simon wondered what he meant.

"Any trial would be a long way off," Mark said. "Late fall, at the earliest. But you and I should meet again in a few weeks. If the company does get served with a complaint, we'll draft a response and go from there."

Simon questioned the real point of this meeting. Was it trial preparation, or a fishing expedition?

They shook hands.

"Can I ask you a question?" Simon asked. "Do you like being a lawyer?"

Mark paused. "I've made peace with it." Then, he winked. "The paycheck helps."

Simon walked down Grant Street. Lunchtime. Primanti Brothers was just a few blocks away, in the Strip District. He craved a cheesesteak sandwich, Pittsburgh style: mayo, shaved sirloin, melted provolone, tomato, and oil and vinegar, with steak fries and slaw piled between two slices of French bread.

BEST. SANDWICH. EVER.

He followed Smallman Street past the loading docks where produce trucks unloaded. The Strip District had several ethnic food markets, along with a dozen tourist/souvenir shops, where you'd find Steeler swag in great abundance. Primanti's was hopping: families, college kids, office workers. Two women in suits, eating beside a construction worker. The hostess led Simon to a two-seat table beside a window. My waitress, an older woman, had dark, Italian features and a strong Pittsburgh accent.

"Are yinz ready to order?" He loved that she used the plural yinz– Pittsburgh's version of y'all– even though he was alone.

"The steak and cheese. And a Coke."

"You got it, hon. You want the fries and slaw on top, right?"

"Of course," Simon said, surprised at the question. "Doesn't everyone?"

"Just makin' sure," she said. "Some tourists don't even know why we're famous. Then they see the fries and slaw inside. And they got the nerve to complain about it!"

While he waited, he watched the foot traffic outside. Guys in suits. Women in pink Steelers jerseys. Kids skipping school. He noticed a short, thick guy in sunglasses, across the street, but he vanished around the corner. He resembled the guy from the Hot Dog Shoppe, one of George's goons, but Simon knew his paranoia might be distorting his judgment. After all, there were hundreds of short, stocky, Italian guys in Pittsburgh.

The waitress brought out his sandwich, but he could only eat a few bites. Embarrassed, he tipped thirty percent.

Driving back to work he kept checking the rear view mirror, as bad thoughts swam around his head like baby sharks.

SOMETHING AIN'T RIGHT

Denise threw off the comforter and jumped in the shower. Even in the summer, she slept under the covers and turned up the fan or air-conditioner, because she liked feeling protected.

She checked the calendar: April 15, tax day. She hadn't had time to even think about filing her return. She just moved out of Kathy's guest room and found her own pad: the third floor of a Victorian, above two quiet grad students. She wondered where she'd be now, had she gone to college at Pitt instead of Slippery Rock. Her parents rejected the idea, claiming a young girl living in the city was too dangerous. After getting her nursing degree, she'd spent four years at an assisted living facility in the North Hills, making nine bucks an hour with no benefits, not even health insurance. In other words, she paid her dues.

Denise preferred the city in the morning, while the undergrads slept. Instead of taking the bus, she walked down Fifth Avenue, admiring the geraniums blooming outside the art museum. At Kiva Han Café, she stopped for a coffee and waited behind a young professional woman wearing a low-cut dress, Prada heels, and a designer handbag. Denise looked at her scrubs. God, how she'd love to rock a pair of killer heels to work once in a while.

She shuffled down Craig Street and wandered into a used bookstore, where she browsed the fiction shelves for a good summer read. In the EROTICA section, she grabbed a paperback called Maiden Voyage and turned to a random page:

> Dirk untied Heather's robe, unveiling her luscious breasts and bearded clam. She reached into his briefs and unsheathed his sword. "Is Sinbad ready to sail the high seas?" she whispered with horny breath. "The jib has been raised." She guided his vessel into port. Dirk navigated the tight channel like Captain Ahab. Ready to explode, he dropped anchor.

Despite the pathetic prose, she purchased the book because her sex life was in a coma, and she needed some escapist pleasure.

She continued down Forbes past the dorms, walking behind a girl in gold shorts with PITT across the butt. They could've said: LOOK-AT-MY-ASS. Wasn't that the point?

She thought about Larry. He was scheduled to go home tomorrow. She tried to come up with ideas for a surprise gift, but nothing clicked.

Approaching the hospital's main doors, she noticed a cluster of reporters.

Once the first one turned and yelled "Denise!" the rest swarmed around, invading her space with microphones and voice recorders.

"Any comment on Luke's condition?" asked someone.

Flustered, she tried to ignore them. "Excuse me. Let me through."

Luke had been in a coma for two weeks. The uncertainty of his recovery, combined with a lack of new information, had dimmed Denise's hopes. And while something must have changed overnight, she wouldn't let herself guess.

Denise passed some nurses, all seeming to avoid her. She elbowed her way through the crowded ICU wing until she reached Luke's room, then she approached Rhonda, beside the bed.

"Denise, glad you're here. Last night, the nurse on duty said he opened his eyes. He seems to be awake, but he hasn't spoken yet."

"Is he responsive?" Denise asked, studying Luke's face.

"He seems to respond to noise, but not verbal communication."

"The tubes are still hooked up."

"We're being cautious," said Rhonda. "He seems to be in that middle stage. The next couple days are important, whether he regains full consciousness and brain cognition."

Luke was propped up by pillows. His face looked gaunt, his cheeks hollowed-out. She'd always admired the girth of his forearms. Now, they were like skinny branches.

She rolled him over: his bed sores had gotten worse.

"Luke, it's me, Denise!" She repeated her name, but still got no response, verbal or otherwise. "Can you understand me?"

What's going on, she wondered, moving closer to his face. His eyes were wide open, and his face expressed wonder, but not recognition. Like a baby responding to pictures in a book. *Something ain't right,* she thought. She could feel it. She feared the hospital was keeping him alive to avoid liability and bad publicity.

She looked at Rhonda. "He still doesn't recognize me."

"It's hard to tell right now. Things are changing so fast."

"Bullshit. If anything, he's getting worse."

Rhonda shrugged. "My hands are tied. There are politics involved."

Denise raised her voice. "What politics? I'm his wife! And if he can't survive without being hooked up to machines, then what's the point?" She paused.

"Luke and I talked about this possibility, and we both agreed."

"But as you know, without a living will, those decisions must include the doctor."

Denise knew she was right, and that she couldn't argue around this point.

Rhonda hesitated. "Look, if you're worried about money, you don't need to be concerned. George Blount promised to pay all Luke's medical expenses."

"Excuse me?" Denise narrowed her eyes. "What did you just say?"

"I meant to tell you, first thing." Rhonda flashed a big grin. "Mr. Blount came in yesterday and spoke to Dr. Vo. He said, do whatever we need to do to keep Luke alive. He also made a big donation to the hospital. Isn't that wonderful?"

"So, the CEO of a coal company has more influence than me over my husband's healthcare? That is totally fucked up, and you know it!"

Frustrated and fed up, Denise walked back to the elevator. As the doors opened, her eyes narrowed. Standing in front of her was Brandi. Luke's ex-girl-friend. She wore a tight black dress, looking like the skank she was. Their eyes met. Brandi looked down, pretending she got a text.

"You've got some nerve coming here," Denise said, holding her glare.

Brandi looked up. "Excuse me?"

"You heard me."

"I have every right to see him."

Denise stepped into the elevator, but as the doors closed she jumped back out. She chased Brandi down the hall, then she jumped in front of her, blocking her path.

"Get out of my way."

"Don't go in there," Denise said. "Haven't you done enough?"

"He doesn't love you anymore!" Brandi yelled. "He was going to leave you!"

"For you?" Denise let out a high-pitched shriek. "He'd never marry trash."

Brandi grabbed her arm.

"Don't touch me." Denise slapped her hand away.

Another nurse had to separate them. "What's going on here?"

"Ask Barbie. I'm done here."

Denise ran down the hall and descended five flights of stairs to the ground level. She walked out the back entrance and smoked a cigarette, glancing over at Western Psych, where her Aunt Eileen had been treated, or tortured. Maybe Luke would end up there, too. She crushed the cigarette butt with her heel and walked back in. She rode the elevator to the Orthopedic Unit where, for the next ten hours she'd examine X-rays of broken clavicles and MRI scans of torn knee ligaments, while trying to act normal. Another day in paradise, asking patients how far they could bend their knee or how much pain they felt. But nobody would ask how much pain she felt. Nobody cared.

UNDERTOW

After he signed all the release forms, Larry busted through the main doors. The sun kissed his face. No need for a jacket, he wore jeans and a white t-shirt. He spent fifteen days in the hospital, but outside things looked totally different. The morning of the accident, April Fools' Day, snow had covered the ground, while today felt like late summer, muggy and hot.

It also felt like the last day of school, or the day he got out of prison. He still remembered doing a month in the Gulfport, Mississippi county jail, his sentence for growing and selling weed. (His lawyer, a miracle worker, had reduced the sentence to thirty days and a year of probation.) He glanced back at the hospital. He'd miss Denise, but that was about it. She'd promised to come visit him, but he had no idea when, or if she was even serious.

The Friday afternoon traffic hummed, horns blaring on Fifth and Forbes. He wandered the parking garage for ten minutes looking for his truck. Then, he remembered the helicopter ride. His truck must still be at the Sarver Mine lot, unless they towed it.

He walked to the intersection and hailed a Yellow Taxi. It stopped at the curb. The driver lowered his window.

"Where you headed?" asked the young white dude with thick dreads.

"Millburg."

"That's forty miles away, man. You're looking at sixty bucks."

Larry checked his wallet. Two twenties and five ones. "Make it the bus station."

He wandered through Pittsburgh's Greyhound terminal, dark and cavernous. He checked the monitor beside the ticket booth. The next bus to Millburg left in forty-five minutes.

He bought his ticket, then sat on a bench, and did some people-watching. Most eyed him cautiously. Did he look scary? Did he look homeless? *But I'm not asking for change*, he thought, *and I don't smell like piss or booze.*

His ride – heading to Youngstown, with stops at Millburg and New Castle– was packed with a weird mix of people. Commuters in business casual attire. Mothers with babies and diaper bags. A skinny white guy, wearing a wife-beater tank top and black Pirates cap. He looked paranoid, his eyes darting around. Larry remembered his own younger days, when he popped speed pills like breath mints. He wanted to tell the guy to relax, that life gets better, but you could never tell how a stranger might react. Best to say nothing.

He sat behind two teenage Goth girls with pale skin, jet black hair, and piercings. Beside him was a white-haired man, seventy or eighty, wearing a Scottish cap and nipping from a flask. He craved a cold beer and a juicy burger. He wondered if alcohol withdrawal had caused his headaches and hand tremors. At least he'd stopped coughing up blood.

He gazed out the window as the bus chugged up Route 8, past a glass factory and The North Park Lounge, once a great watering hole before it turned into another cheesedick sports bar. They passed Hilliard's Truck Sales and the Chevy dealership, owned by the McConnell Brothers: two high school football legends who'd played at Notre Dame. Almost home, he thought, as the bus raced down Armco Hill and crossed Hansen Avenue Bridge. It stopped at the Pullman Shopping Plaza, where Larry and a few others unloaded.

He would need to call someone to retrieve his truck, but his immediate concern was finding a cold beer. So, he walked down the road, half a mile, to the Chester Hotel. There was a faded GENESSEE CREAM ALE sign on the door.

Inside, he posted up at a bar stool under a ceiling fan. The place was nearly empty. He wiped the sweat off his face and neck with his red bandanna.

"You can cut that humidity with a fuckin' knife."

"Got that right," said the younger bartender. He had a thick beard and wore a tie-dyed shirt. He smiled. "Hey, aren't you Larry Jenkins?"

Larry, still adjusting to celebrity, figured he was another cult follower.

"It's me, PJ. We went to that fight together in West Virginia, with Tree and Luke."

Now he remembered. The fight, the casino, the drugs. "Good to see a friendly face," Larry said. "But I thought you worked at the Pour House."

"I quit. Better money here. What're you drinking? It's on the house."

"A shot of tequila and a beer."

"What kind of beer?"

"Don't matter," Larry said. "Coldest one you got."

PJ came back with a full shot glass and a frosty mug of Yuengling.

Larry buried the shot. He winced, then started laughing.

They gazed at each other: two lost men, searching for words.

"You look good," PJ said.

"Just got out of the hospital today."

"How's Luke? He doing any better?"

Larry said nothing, just shook his head.

৯৵৶

Right after Simon's breakup with Lindsey, his father died of a brain aneurysm. These events triggered what skiers would call a yard sale: when you don't just fall, you lose your skis and poles, cartwheel through the air, smack your head on the ice, and slide down the pitch like a ragdoll. There was nothing graceful about Simon's yard sale. He lost his job and his pride. He watched old movies on cable. When they shut off his cable, he read comic books and crime novels. A steady diet of cereal, refried beans, and cheese sticks. He tried to pick up the pieces. He returned to the same bars he once patronized, but they'd become cesspools of meathead frat guys who wore sunglasses indoors and texted photos of their junk to young girls. So, he stopped going out.

But not tonight. Spring had arrived, and he wanted to numb his senses with music and liquor and drugs. He wanted to make some bad decisions. Tonight, he and Adam were meeting up in Millburg. The Clarks, a local alt-country band, were playing at The Chester Hotel.

Music had always been Simon's form of escape. His first real concert: The Who in '89 at Three Rivers, jammed in the back of a Volkswagen Bus packed with his older brother's friends. He went through a heavy metal phase in middle school, highlighted by a Metallica concert in pouring rain: eighty thousand heads banging in unison, like some Gnostic birth ritual. In high school, it was hip-hop – wearing black Adidas and baggy jeans, the Beastie Boys and Tribe Called Quest pumping through his headphones – followed by a jamband phase. (He'd lost his virginity inside a tent, the night of his first Grateful Dead show, the summer before Jerry died.) Finally, in college he cloaked himself in grunge and alt rock. After taking bass guitar lessons, he answered an ad from a grunge/metal band called Mad Dog. Their founder and lead singer, Uwe, was a German exchange student known for his high falsetto and red leather pants. Simon's bass guitar skills were pedestrian – he played the same three chords in different combinations – but he'd never felt more alive than during those two years: playing at bars and house parties in college towns like Amherst, Ithaca, Syracuse, and Morgantown.

Simon parked beside the Chester Hotel, whose name evoked the old liquor laws. Back when only lodging establishments could serve alcohol, some Millburg taverns kept a few beds upstairs. (Simon's uncle claimed he'd slept in all of them.) After the Chester burned down five years ago— they ruled it arson— the new owner rebuilt the place, adding a big stage. Simon wore his old band uniform: plain black t-shirt, jeans, Timberland boots.

Outside, a pregnant woman smoked a cigarette. There was a snake tattoo on her neck. Inside, it smelled like stale beer and buffalo sauce. On the fake wood-paneled wall hung yellow "support the troops" ribbons and framed photos of old Steelers players: Bradshaw, Swann, Franco, Lambert, Mean Joe Greene.

Simon ordered a Yuengling. The bartender pointed to a glass jug, half-filled with dollar bills. "You want to make a donation to the families of those dead miners?"

Simon threw in a twenty. "Glad to help."

Across the bar sat a bald man wearing a gray ARMY t-shirt and sunglasses. The left side of his head was concave. Roadside bomb, maybe.

Beside the vet was a short, wiry man with a gray ponytail. Simon studied his face, until it registered: Larry Jenkins. Simon walked over, wearing a big dumb grin.

"Hey, it's the mining company lawyer," Larry said. "Following me again?"

"You look good."

"They let me out of the looney bin."

"Glad to hear it," Simon said.

"So, you workin' hard, or hardly workin'?"

"Too hard. At a job I hate, for a boss I hate."

"Can't you leave and go work for some other firm or company?"

"Not now," Simon said. "George wouldn't let me."

"They got you by the balls, huh? Join the club."

"George doesn't play fair. He's got his own rules."

Larry shook his head. "From the day I started at that mine, I had a bad vibe."

Simon picked at the label on his bottle. "Can I ask you something?"

"I'm sure you will, anyway."

"Those miners that died. What were they like?"

"Most of 'em I didn't know. I started there a couple weeks before." Larry paused. "I knew Hank, an old fishing buddy. There was a younger black guy, Tree. Crazy as hell, but funny. And Luke, of course. Everyone loved him."

"I heard he's still in a coma," Simon said.

Larry's smile disappeared. In the dim light, his face looked like a jagged piece of granite. "Hold up, chief. Why you asking all these questions? You fishing around for dirt, so you can use it against them in court? You can go straight to hell."

Simon proclaimed his innocence. "I promise, I'm not here on behalf of the fucking company. I just came to listen to some good music and get high."

"Why do you even care about the accident?"

"I guess I feel responsible, somehow."

"Shit happens, kid. That don't mean it's your fault."

"For once, I want to do the right thing," Simon said. "Be on the good side."

"Don't glorify coal miners. We're assholes, too. Shit, Tree was a drug addict. Luke cheated on his wife. We're not heroes, man."

"You still have rights," Simon said. "The law should be on your side."

"What's the company's crime?"

"Negligence. Misconduct. They took shortcuts."

"Good luck proving it." Larry got up. "Hey, I need to piss like a racehorse."

"Can we talk about this later?"

Larry shook his head. "Let it go, man."

Simon turned to watch the band's roadies set up. When the lights dimmed, a horde of college kids moved to the front of the stage.

A minute later, Adam and Jeff, another high school friend, walked in.

"Yoder!" Jeff said, giving him a bro-hug. For some reason, his hometown friends still used his last name, as if they didn't want to acknowledge the name Simon.

They ordered three tequila shots. Adam buried his first and yelled, "Harsh!"

"Reminds me of college," Jeff said. "Thanksgiving weekends, we'd all meet here."

"I feel like a creeper." Simon glanced around.

"You're old," Adam said. "How's work? You look stressed out, big time."

"The mine explosion. It never ends."

"Keep your voice down." Jeff was now a deputy sheriff. Ironic, since he'd been a serious hell-raiser as a kid. "Yoder, we're friends and all, but people are pretty fired up."

"Trust me, I know." Simon watched Larry slide off his stool and leave. He wondered where he was going. He almost got up and asked if he could tag along.

Just then, the band's lead singer plugged in. "Millburg! Are you ready to rock?" The crowd roared back. Typical call and response. These guys had been playing for twenty years. They had gray hair, beer guts. Simon wondered about their lives: *Did they go to bed early and change diapers, or were they clinging to the rock dream, still partying with groupies?*

"Holy shit, look who just rolled in."

It was Jason Rockenstein. Or an older, bloated version of the former legendary athlete. Millburg's best running back, the best football player from Simon's generation.

"Dude could've played in the NFL," Adam said.

"Didn't he play at West Virginia?"

"Kicked off the team for gambling," Jeff said.

"Not the brightest bulb." Adam smiled.

"What's he doing now?" Simon asked.

"Sells luxury cars. Some dealership in the North Hills."

Simon had played junior high basketball with Rockenstein. Their best player, he roamed the locker room like a silver-backed gorilla. He had biceps, zits, and chest hair. Simon was short, scrawny, and prepubescent. Jason, ironically, called him Big Balls, and gave him wedgies and knuckle-punched him in the arm, leaving purple welts. One day at practice, Simon stole the ball from Jason.

Next time down the court, Jason sucker-punched him. Blood gushed from his nose like a hydrant. Nobody saw it, but coach stopped practice. "Who hit you?" he asked. Simon said he was prone to nosebleeds. The coach knew he was lying, they all did. After that day, Jason stopped bullying him, because Simon had followed the unwritten code of masculinity – keep your mouth shut. But the damage had been done. He'd wasted years of his life trying to reclaim the manhood stolen from him. Maybe that explained why he became a lawyer.

"Hey boys," said Rockenstein. He wore faded, designer jeans and a plaid, tight-fitting shirt. "I didn't know it was geek night!" His hand dug into Simon's shoulder. "What's up, Yoder? Little fucker, I haven't seen you in years!"

Simon nodded "Hey Rock."

"I heard you're a lawyer. Dude, I bet you're making bank."

"Doing alright. I heard you're selling cars."

"It's bullshit. I should be in the NFL right now."

"Didn't you play in Canada?" Jeff asked.

"Saskatchewan," Rock said, chuckling. "Those paint-sniffing rednecks only care about hockey." It felt like the junior high locker room again, listening to Rock's stories of conquest. "I also played in the World League. Amsterdam. Loose women and legal drugs!" Rockenstein tapped his jeans pocket. "Speaking of which, you guys want to step outside and do a bump?"

Jeff and Adam declined. "We're gonna check out the band," they said.

Simon stayed put. "I'm down."

Jason smiled, looking surprised. "Nice, Yoder! I like your fire, dude."

Simon followed him out to his car. He'd done cocaine twice, in law school, but snorting lines from the dashboard of an old Camry was a far different experience than partying in a Fox Chapel mansion.

"So what's it like, being a dick-swingin' lawyer?" Jason asked.

"Flaccid!" Simon said. "Mainly, I write and edit contracts."

"I heard George Blount is richer than God. But that accident sounds fucked up."

"You have no idea."

"I'm sweating balls," Jason said, checking his shirt. "So, you married?"

"Engaged a few years ago. Didn't work out."

"Smart. Don't take the bait. I'm divorced, waist-deep in child support." He laughed. "The sad part is, I sell luxury cars, and meanwhile, I drive a beat-up Toyota Camry to work!"

Simon hadn't expected this. Bonding and doing rails with his old bully. He felt pretty fucking high. "Life is a grand farce. A carnival of the absurd."

"Who said that?"

"Me, myself, and I."

"You're cracking me up tonight!" Jason punched his shoulder. "Hey, you remember those junior high basketball days?"

"Like yesterday."

"What was the name of that creepy assistant coach?"

"Troy Nelson," Simon said.

"Goddamn pervert. Always leering in the shower stalls."

He studied Jason's face: ruddy cheeks, dark lines under the eyes. They were about the same age, but Jason looked ten years older.

"Hey Rock, I got a question. Why'd you bully me in junior high?"

Jason cracked a smile. "I had to toughen you up!"

"Bullshit." Simon said, watching the Bud Light sign flash.

"Honestly? I was jealous, man. You were smart and from a good family. You know what my dad did when I played a bad game? He beat my ass."

"You still talk to him?"

"He died last year," Jason said. "My dad came from nothing. But it's almost like he cared too much. He thought a football scholarship was the Holy Grail."

If Rock's dad cared too much, Simon's dad cared too little. Never went to his games. Never told Simon he was proud of him. Never said he loved him.

"Hey dude, you got some on your nose," Jason said. "Let me rub it off."

Jason brought his face closer, then quickly pressed his lips to Simon's.

Simon recoiled, pulling his head back. "What the fuck, man?"

Jason paused. "I thought that's why we came out here. C'mon, you were flirting with me inside. Buying drinks, asking about football."

"I was being polite, dude!" Simon said. "I'm not gay, and I had no idea you were."

"Be careful with that word." Jason wagged his index finger.

"It's fine." Simon lowered his window halfway. "I'm not judging."

"You can't be gay in this town. At least, I can't." Jason slouched in his seat like a deflated raft. "People talk. Friends will drop you."

"You shouldn't have to hide it. I have friends in Pittsburgh. I could introduce you."

"Get the fuck out of my car," Jason said. He'd flipped some kind of switch.

"Thanks for the bump, anyway."

Walking away, Simon turned. Jason was punching his dashboard, over and over.

After a bizarre night, Simon wondered how to end it. Adam and Jeff had vanished back to their quiet, normal lives. He'd planned to crash on his mom's couch, but as he drove through Millburg, lost in his thoughts, he noticed the old radio tower and followed it like the North Star. He drove up South Main Street Hill, his tires bouncing over the red bricks.

He parked at Millburg Catholic, his old primary school, and pulled his Maglite from the glove compartment. He entered the woods, following the same old path to the radio tower. Empty beer cans and cigarette butts scattered in the grass. The new generation of kids, just like them: bored, disaffected, plotting their escape from this rusting shithole town. He sat beside the fire pit, where he smoked his first joint.

He walked to the edge of the plateau and looked across the valley. He found the spires of St. Peter's, his old church. In tenth grade, their youth group drove to South Carolina to rebuild houses for hurricane victims. On the last day, despite the riptide warning, they all hit the beach, eager to swim after a week of hammering nails and cutting wood. Six of them got pulled out by the undertow. Simon made it back to shore first. Exhausted, he alerted two lifeguards. They saved everyone. He could still picture the minister's wife lying in the sand: pale skin, long red hair, the lifeguard giving her CPR until she coughed up water.

His mind drifted back to Rockenstein. Maybe he'd been too harsh. Indeed, karma was a bitch. But they shared one thing: both were now pariahs in their hometown. Simon wondered how he'd ended up back here. Deep down, he knew: the undertow. But he refused to get trapped here for life, like so many of his friends. He was done with the Blount brothers. Done with the law. Done with Millburg, Pittsburgh, and every other shitty Pennsylvania town. He could move west or south – maybe even leave the country – and reinvent himself. Before embarking on a new life, however, he needed to find out what caused that explosion. Whether it required hacking into George's computer, or searching Ken's storage unit, he wouldn't quit until he discovered the secrets George and Richard were hiding.

PART THREE

ESCAPING THE CAGE

Leaving Pittsburgh on a Sunday morning in late April, Denise ashed her cigarette out the window. She cursed the slow line of traffic ahead. Lately, she'd been allowing the smallest things to deflate, and defeat, her. Must be living in the city, caged in with all the freaks and nuts. Or the job: exciting at first, but after witnessing several surgeries, she came to realize that orthopedic surgeons were glorified mechanics. For most of them, repairing a knee was like replacing brake pads or shocks on a minivan. But deep down, she knew the true source of her angst was Luke. She'd accepted the possibility of his death, but not his current state. A vegetable, barely breathing. How could she sit back and let him hang there, suspended in that void between life and death? But what choice did she have?

As the gridlock dissipated, she sped up and weaved through cars. She'd always been an aggressive driver, even as a kid, riding go-carts and ATV's with her older cousins. She cut through East Liberty. A century ago, home to steel barons. Now, Section Eight housing and vacant buildings. Recently, they'd built a Home Depot and Trader Joe's, part of the urban renewal project, and a row of colorful town homes. On Negley Avenue, church was letting out. Black families, dressed in colorful suits and dresses. She recalled Easter Sundays, watching the stylish church ladies in their colorful dresses, like Mrs. Kelly and Mrs. Snyder, hoping to be that beautiful and hating her mom for making her wear thrift-store clothes. Sometimes, she drew pictures with her dad during the sermon. After his lung cancer whittled him down to a toothpick, she quit going to church. What kind of God would let the most humble, decent man on earth suffer like that?

She crossed the Highland Park Bridge and climbed the hills into Fox Chapel. These were not homes, they were estates, flanked by mature trees and big yards. Some orthopedic surgeons lived back here. She wanted to peek inside their homes and see what happiness looked like. On Saxonburg Road, more modest ranch houses. Steeler flags on porches and Support the Troops ribbons on mailboxes. She passed that creepy old house on the bluff with the basement window light on. Home to a squatter, maybe, but she pictured something more depraved, like a mad surgeon cutting up young girls.

Passing into Seneca County, she whizzed by the mushroom farm, picking up the same foul odor that clung to her skin during the summer she worked there. She remembered the cold dark tunnels and helmet lamps, crouched over the mushrooms trays, slicing the stems with a paring knife. She crested a hill and glimpsed a fracking well above the tree line. These new ones were bigger. They wouldn't stop until they squeezed everything from the earth, until there was nothing left, all because people couldn't turn off their phones and iPads, because they were addicted. On the local news, there was a story each week about poisoned wells or streams. The road dipped and skirted past the cement plant. She drove another mile until the road came to a T, then turned up White's Hollow Road. She slowed down, reading address numbers on the mailboxes.

Larry waved from his front stoop and smiled as Denise pulled in the driveway. He was excited to have company.

"Nice car," she said, pointing to his black Pontiac GTO.

"Yeah, it's my baby. Restored it myself."

"My uncle has an old muscle car. A Bonneville. Maybe a Charger. Can't remember."

They walked into the living room.

"How about some coffee? Just made it."

"Sounds good."

He returned with a mug. They both sat on the couch. "So, how's Luke?"

"Not good. He can open his eyes but that's about it. And his bedsores are getting worse, like they stopped paying attention." She paused. "Can I be totally honest?"

"You don't need my permission."

"I think they're keeping him alive to avoid bad publicity. And I have no say, because we never made a will. It's up to the doctors."

"What're you going to do?" he asked.

"I can't see him like that." She paused. "It's not even him."

Larry scratched the back of his neck. "Don't know what to tell you."

"Yesterday the lawyer representing dead miners' families called me. He said I might have a claim for punitive damages, especially if Luke needs medical care for life."

"He called me too. Said I'd be a key witness at trial."

"I'm worried about you testifying."

"You can be my cheering section."

Denise walked to the fireplace. She studied a photo of a young Larry with Kelly and the kids on the mantle. "Your family?"

"Used to be," he said. "When Kelly and I divorced, she took Josh and moved to Johnstown. Around that same time, a doctor told me I had bad lungs and should stop mining. I sat around for six months collecting disability. Then I left. Bounced around the country. Had a blast, until I ran out of money and had to find work. I hit rock bottom in Nebraska."

"How so?" she asked.

"Worked in a meatpacking plant. The stench inside there– from the meat, blood and guts– was like nothing I ever smelled before, or since."

"What'd you have to do?"

He wagged his finger. "Trust me, you don't want to know."

"C'mon, I don't scare easy."

Larry explained the process. "After they cut off the heads and legs of the steers, the bodies rolled down the line on hooks. We had different knives for each section of animal. I'd come home with pain shooting through my hands and arms. Once or twice a month, there'd be an accident. Sliced fingers, hands caught in machines. Thank God, they transferred me outside. Where the cattle came off the trucks."

Denise covered her mouth. "So, you had to kill them?"

"We had this tool, like a stun gun. You stood on a plank right above them and held it to their heads, and a long steel tube penetrated the skull. Sometimes, the younger ones would sniff the gun." He paused. "I lasted four months. But it wasn't just the job, it was the place."

He remembered Nebraska's brutal winters, the flat brown land, the constant wind. With no hills or trees, he felt naked. And the people kept their distance from outsiders. He would see the same people every day, and they'd only discuss the weather or Husker football.

"Is that when you came back here?" Denise asked.

"Nope. I went south. I had a friend on the Mississippi coast, a carpenter who rebuilt homes damaged by Katrina. He had a growing business."

"Never been down there." Denise sipped her coffee.

"Great seafood. Fishing. The beach bars had decks looking out on the water. You could sit outside with a drink and watch the sunset. I loved it down there. And New Orleans was an hour away, whenever you needed to get crazy."

Denise laughed. "Let's take a road trip!"

"Anyhow, I had a scrape with the law. I lived a couple miles inland, a shack on stilts with a tin roof. Secluded. Lots of trees. And the humid climate was perfect for growing weed."

She raised an eyebrow. "I see where this is going."

"I just grew a small patch for me and my friends. But word got out. One day I'm working outside, when I looked up and see DEA helicopters flying real low. I ran into my back yard, cut down all the plants, and threw 'em in a ditch beyond my property line. When I finished, the cops were rolling up the driveway. But I cooperated. Hell, I even made coffee!" Larry chuckled. "They searched my property, but only found a couple plants."

"They busted you?"

"I got a month in jail and a year of probation. But it could've been a lot worse."

"There's an understatement," Denise said. "A friend of Luke's is doing five years over at the federal prison in Lewisburg. He sold pills and coke, too."

"After my probation, I left the state. It was time to come home."

"What about your son?" she asked. "I mean, you never talk about him."

He looked out the window and shook his head.

"I'm sorry," she said. "That's none of my business."

"No, I need to talk about it," he said. "Josh died in the war. Afghanistan. He enlisted. I told him the Army would chew him up and spit him out. On his second tour, he was killed by one of those roadside bombs. Didn't see his twenty-first birthday."

Denise wiped her eyes.

"Last year, I drove over to Shanksville, site of the Flight 93 crash. I met relatives of the passengers and heard their stories. I talked to the white-bearded old man who owned the land, the first one to find the plane. He told me the noise was so loud, it pierced his eardrum. He jumped in his ATV and rode into the clearing. He saw one of the wings on fire. In those few seconds, I thought I was listening to the voice of God."

There was a long silence. Denise searched his face. "Did you know that, before the accident, Luke and I were having problems? I was thinking about divorce." She stood up and walked to the window. "I knew he'd cheated on me. I was ready to start a new life in the city. But since the accident, of course, I've had to put everything on hold."

"I'm sorry. I had no idea."

"Not sure I would've gone through with it. I don't like to fail at things." She paused. "I ran into his Brandi, his ex-girlfriend, last week in the hospital. We had a confrontation."

Larry wanted to tell her what he knew – that he'd seen Luke and Brandi together the night before the accident – but he couldn't betray his friend like that, especially not now, not in Luke's current state.

"You know, Denise, I was never the greatest husband. When things got bad in my marriage, I'd escape. I'd go to casinos and strip clubs."

"But you're a good person." She walked over, touched his shoulder. "I can see it, and so can everyone else."

"Did I tell you about Tina? She came to the hospital, right before I left."

Denise giggled. "Sorry I missed her!"

He rolled his eyes. "She heard about the lawsuit. Once she gets a whiff of money, look out. She's like a bird dog flushing out geese!"

"Have you seen her since you got back?"

He smiled. "If she tries to come here, I changed the locks."

They both started cracking up.

JUST BECAUSE YOU'RE PARANOID

Since the corporate office was empty on weekends, Simon reckoned a Friday night would be his best chance of breaking into George's office. He spent all week scouring files on the shared drive, looking for documents showing the company's misconduct and exposing the Blount brothers. But he'd found no smoking gun, and hacking into George's computer was beyond his skill set.

Then, he remembered what Julie told him, about George's filing cabinet and his skepticism of computers. A long shot, but he had to try something, especially if his scapegoat theory was correct. After his meeting at Mitchell Burns, he suspected they might be building a case against him. If the miners' lawsuit made it to trial and things went bad for Blount, the litigators could change strategy and go after him, arguing that his job required him to monitor safety and compliance issues for all mines. And technically, they'd be correct.

He glanced at the clock. 6:45. While waiting for the last of his coworkers to leave, he tried to stay calm.

As George passed Simon's desk, he stopped, looking puzzled. "Still here?"

Simon looked up and smiled. "Just paperwork and filing, stuff like that."

"Very good. Carry on, soldier."

From the window, he watched George pull away in his Tahoe. The only remaining vehicle was an old Chevy Silverado, owned by Charlie the janitor. A tall, white-haired black man, Charlie been a basketball legend in the seventies, playing in the ABA. He had a smooth voice and always looked as if he'd just gotten laid, or was about to.

Simon bumped into Charlie outside the bathroom.

"Burning the midnight oil, counselor?"

"Something like that."

"Well, I'm ready to leave and get my groove on." Charlie gyrated his hips.

"Wish I could join you. It's been a long week."

Charlie winked. "Don't spend your life working. Life is a gift, young brother."

"Hey, I left a file in George's office. Could you unlock his door?"

Charlie detached the key ring dangling from his belt. As they walked down the hall, Simon asked about his pro basketball days.

"I played with Julius Erving one year."

Doctor J had been Simon's favorite player growing up, and the Philadelphia 76ers his favorite team. All his friends wore Celtics or Lakers or Bulls gear. But before Magic, Bird, Jordan, or LeBron, the Doc was king.

Charlie opened George's office door. "Lock it up when you're done."

"Thanks again. And nobody needs to know about this."

Charlie pressed a finger to his lip. "Time to get my drink on!"

Simon made a quick sweep of the office. He paused to examine a photo of George and the state's current governor, golfing together. He walked to the file cabinet and tried to open a drawer. Son of a bitch. Locked. He looked around. A small bowl on his desk held some keys. He grabbed all five keys and tried each. The last one unlocked it, thank God.

He opened the top drawer and checked the labels on each accordion folder. He pulled one out labeled 'Foam Blocks' and laid it on the side table. He did the same thing with a second folder: 'Safety Equipment – Sarver Mine.'

Simon checked the clock – 7:45. Nearly full dark out.

Suddenly, he heard a car engine and noticed headlights in the parking lot. No time to copy or scan the documents, so he returned them to the cabinet. He scanned George's office one last time, making sure nothing seemed out of place, before locking his office door.

He left out the back exit and punched in the security code. He heard the car, but it was out of sight. He sprinted towards the back dumpster, near the tree line, and crouched behind it.

Moments later, the car emerged from the far side of the building and made a wide turn. Its headlights settled on the dumpster as the car slowed to a crawl.

Simon froze. His hands trembled. His eye twitched. If the engine stopped, or a door opened, he planned on sprinting into the woods behind him. Instead, the gray Crown Vic with tinted windows rolled forward. He watched the tail lights fade as it pulled onto Technology Drive.

He ran back to his own car. Sitting behind the wheel, he paused a minute to catch his breath, and wondered the best way out of this fucking mess. *It could've been a simple a mistake,* he thought. Some guy who took the wrong exit off the parkway and was turning around. (One boring day at work, he'd counted six cars that made U-turns in the Blount parking lot.) Then again, it could also be one of George's goons making a sweep of the property. He had to assume the worst, and that the Crown Vic was sitting up the road, waiting for him to leave.

He kept his lights off as he pulled onto Technology Drive, but instead of going left toward the highway, he turned right, remembering there was a back way out of the business park, a seldom-used access road. He curled past other office buildings, pleading with his Nissan Altima to go faster. He checked the rearview and noticed headlights behind him, getting brighter.

On the straightway, he sped up, shifting into fifth gear. The road emptied onto a county road, but not for another half mile, and there were no other turnoffs. He was doing seventy, but the car behind him was gaining ground.

The access road paralleled the highway. No guardrail or divider, just a patch of grass. Acting on instinct, Simon braked hard and jerked the wheel left. He skidded across the grass and snaked into the far right lane of the interstate, narrowly missing a tractor-trailer.

Adam lived a few miles away from here. Hiding out there made more sense than driving twenty-five miles back to Pittsburgh. Simon called his friend's cell number, praying he'd pick up. No answer. Fuck. He called his house number.

Adam's wife picked up.

"Jenna, it's Simon. Sorry to call so late, but I'm in trouble."

A minute later, Adam came on the line. "What's up, man?"

"I can't explain now, but can I crash at your place tonight?"

"If you don't mind the couch."

"Thanks. I'll be in your driveway in about two minutes."

"The front door's unlocked," Adam said.

He took the next exit and followed Freeport Road. He kept looking in his mirror, but there was no sign of the Crown Vic, or any other cars.

Approaching Adam's mailbox, he turned and drove up the long, winding driveway leading back to his house. Luckily, the house was hidden from the road by a row of trees. He waited a minute, listening for any cars coming up the driveway. Dead quiet, crickets buzzing. Finally, he took a few deep breaths and walked to the front door.

Adam opened it before he could knock. "You look like shit."

Simon's face was pale and sweaty. His green Polo shirt was soiled from rubbing against the dumpster. "Thanks man. I worked late. Too tired to drive home."

They had known each other so long, Adam could tell when he was lying. Still, he fetched a pillow and fleece blanket from the closet. His children's toys— a Lego set, remote control car, and a few stuffed animals— were scattered on the living room floor.

"We've got leftover pasta in the fridge," Adam said. "Help yourself."

"I appreciate this."

"Simon, are you in trouble?"

"I don't know." Simon slumped on the couch, taking his shoes off. "Maybe."

Spirit Animal

Memorial Day Weekend, the return of summer. Simon couldn't believe it. The fleeting Pittsburgh spring had slipped through his fingers like sand. He hadn't seen Anita since their dinner in Squirrel Hill last month. He'd texted her few times since then, but she kept blaming her work schedule.

He wondered if she was making excuses to avoid seeing him. He'd heard some crazy ones over the years, like that pharmaceutical sales rep who, after two dates, told Simon she was "questioning her sexuality."

Either way, Simon figured he might be better off alone. Fewer complications, less emotional trauma. Besides, Anita could be a little pretentious. (On their first date, she'd bragged about using cloth bags when grocery shopping, and scolded him for not doing the same.) So, when she contacted him last week about getting together, it surprised him. Half joking, he suggested a river tour of the city: why not spend an hour cruising Pittsburgh's rivers on a slow boat? But she'd called his bluff, texting back: Sure, let's do something random!

As their riverboat, the Gateway Clipper, pushed off the Station Square and chugged upriver, they drank gin-and-tonics from the back deck. They traded highlights of their summers and apologized for not staying in touch. She wore a blue V-neck shirt and tight white shorts. From behind his shades, he admired her toned legs and round butt.

"So, how have you been?" he asked.

"I was a bridesmaid in my cousin's wedding last weekend. The wedding was a traditional Hindu ceremony. I had to wear a sari. I think I have some pictures. Wanna see?"

She handed him her phone. Her dress was long, flowing, and shiny: the color of maroon, with gold accents.

"Wow, it's beautiful." He twitched. "I mean, you're beautiful."

She laughed. "So, what have you been up to?"

"Nothing that exciting. I saw a band in Millburg a couple weeks ago." Simon paused. "You know something? Our hometown seems to get weirder every day. I ran into Jason Rockenstein. Remember him?"

"Yeah. Football player."

"Did you know he was gay?" Simon paused. "He tried to kiss me."

Her mouth fell open. "Shut up."

"Dead serious." He watched the shoreline as the boat crawled upriver. "By the way, I heard you on NPR last week. You're blowing up right now."

At least she wasn't lying about her schedule. With the expanding national debate over fracking– natural gas drilling had expanded to ten more states– Anita's expertise on the subject put her in demand. She'd been on cable news networks and had written for national magazines.

"They interviewed me. Typical stuff, the environmental dangers of fracking. Oh, and guess what else? Chesapeake Energy offered me a job. As their Public Relations Consultant. Could you see me as lobbyist for an oil and gas company?"

Simon imitated Darth Vader. "Anita, come to the dark side."

"I turned it down. I like being a pain in their ass too much."

He asked if she was still covering the mine accident.

She said no. "I thought it was over, anyway."

"The miners' families filed a complaint. Looks like there might be a trial."

"Did you ever talk to that guy who left you the crazy voicemail?"

Simon summarized his meeting with Ken, and how they were being followed.

"By whom?"

"George's private security. His goons. They were standing outside the restaurant. Freaked me out. I didn't tell you because I didn't want to scare you."

Their boat passed under a railroad trestle. The graffitied stanchion read: I LUV U BOBBI JO, with a heart around it.

"So, are you freelancing now?"

"I'm still with the Press, but I have more flexibility."

"Sounds like a sweet deal," he said.

"It's not bad, but I've become cynical about journalism."

"It's good to be skeptical. About the government. The economy. Everything."

They rounded Point State Park, and started up the Allegheny. As the clouds rolled in, the water turned from bright blue to metallic gray.

"I haven't trusted the government since Bush and Cheney fooled the world into believing Iraq was responsible for Nine-Eleven," Anita said. "But I've always had faith in journalism. I was proud of my field and my colleagues. Whether it was the Iraq War, GITMO, or the economy, there were passionate, intrepid reporters out there, trying to uncover the truth. And I don't mean that tabloid bullshit. I mean the embedded reporters, the ones who go deep to find a story."

"So you think journalism has changed?"

"Editors have lost their courage. They're afraid to send writers into dangerous places. And writers don't want to go. The whole industry has gotten soft."

Simon rubbed his chin. "You know how everyone says nine-eleven was the moment that changed the world? Well, I think our generation changed more profoundly in the summer of 1994 than 2001. First, there was Kurt Cobain's death, and then– "

"The OJ trial?"

"How'd you know I was going to say that?"

"I agree. Before the OJ trial, I believed in our legal system. But if you have money and fame, I guess it's true. You really can get away with murder."

"I turned eighteen in '94," Simon said. "I was trying to make sense of the world. Instead, it seemed to get more fucked up. And don't forget, Woodstock II also happened that summer. "

"Some of my Amherst friends went. They called it a giant frat party."

"It was a total shit show! The corporations finally got their hands on the outdoor music festival genre and turned into another revenue stream. Fucking capitalists."

"The revolution got sold," she said. "I remember one of my editors in Boston once told me the paper is not allowed to criticize capitalism."

"At least, not until the market crashes and banks collapse again, right?"

"One-third of America now lives in poverty, yet the market keeps climbing."

"Nobody's policing the system. No oversight of corporate law or accounting rules. Plus, most CEO's fill their board-of-director slots with cronies."

Simon pictured capitalism as one of those rogue agents in The Matrix. Even if you smashed it into little pieces, it turned into a gel substance and reformed.

"Technology has manipulated our desire," he continued. "We don't know how to rebel, anymore. We're told what to watch and consume. We're told what to like."

"And what to think."

"You ever read Ray Bradbury's Fahrenheit 451?"

She nodded.

"Just as he predicted, there are big screen televisions and video monitors everywhere. They spoon-feed us propaganda. Now, if you read a book in public, people glare at you."

"Hold on," she said. "You don't get arrested for reading in public."

"Not yet. But police can pull you over for a broken taillight, search your car, and take your money and valuables. They call it Civil Forfeiture. And the NSA has data on everyone. They can track our movements by our phones and credit cards. It's true, Big Brother is watching." He kept going. "You know, during France's Reign of Terror, The Committee of Public Safety guillotined anyone remotely suspected of treason. By the end, Committee members were beheading each other."

She scrunched her forehead. "I don't see the connection."

"Department of Homeland Security. Committee of Public Safety." He held out his hands like two even scales. "They sound similar. Think about it."

She tilted her head back and laughed. "Now, that sounds paranoid!"

"All I know is that capitalism is deranged. Consider all these mental health disorders people now have. ADD, autism, Tourette's, depression, social anxiety. Technology and information is not only distracting, it's making us sick."

She pushed her sunglasses up into her hair.

"Could you imagine bringing kids into this slaughterhouse of a world?"

"But what's the alternative? Sit and watch the world die?" She paused. "Besides, I'm not sure we ever leave this world when we die."

"Meaning what, that we're trapped in our bodies?"

"No, our souls. The Hindus believe in samsara, a cycle in which the soul is reborn as another living organism."

"Like reincarnation?" Simon asked.

"Karma, your deeds and actions. They all affect how your soul is reborn. And this cycle continues until your soul is liberated. That's called moksha."

"Makes more sense to me than heaven and hell."

"Somehow, I think we answer for our deeds, both good and bad." She paused. "My hope is the next generation can fix our mess."

He rolled his eyes. "Such an optimist."

"How did you become such a cynic?" she asked. "I bet it was a girl."

He knew this was coming: that moment where the conversation to past relationships and love gone sour. He faced her. "Go ahead. Ask me anything."

"Well, you never told me what happened with your busted engagement. I mean, calling off a wedding. That's pretty drastic, just saying."

Simon watched a four-man crew boat row past in perfect rhythm, the boat skimming the surface like a missile. "Lindsey cheated on me. With a teacher at her school. I found their texts."

She studied his face. "I'm sorry. That sucks."

"We were doomed from the start. I ignored all the red flags. I mean, she tried to control me. And her temper. Whoa. She once threw a dish at my head."

"My boyfriend in Boston was like that. So nice and charming on the surface. My friends and family loved him, but in private, he'd flip a switch. He said I didn't deserve to be with him. He once called me his token minority."

He shook his head. "Why are there so many shitty people in the world?"

"I just want someone who embraces my weirdness and makes me laugh."

He looked around. They just passed the Strip District and were approaching the Ketchup Factory. "Look, it's my loft."

"Too bad they can't drop us off here. How long until we get back onshore?"

"An hour, at least."

Just then, a wild idea crystallized in his head. The boat was only ten or fifteen yards from shore, and there was no railing off the back. He checked her clothes: she had on shorts and sandals. Like him.

"Do you have a phone in your pocket?" he asked.

"Nope. Just a twenty-dollar bill and my car keys. Why?"

He took her keys and put them in one of his zipper-lined pockets. "Can you swim?"

"Wait." She wagged her finger. "Hell no. We're not jumping off."

He grabbed her hand. "We've been talking about rebellion all day. Let's rebel!"

She pulled it back. "The current's too strong! We'd get sucked under the boat!"

"Not if we jump out far enough." He unclipped the rope railing.

"Simon, there's no way —"

Before he lost his nerve, he ran to the edge and jumped. He tucked his legs and cannonballed into the cold, murky water. When his head popped back up, and he looked back.

"C'mon!" he yelled, waving his hands, but she didn't move.

The top-deck passengers gasped and pointed at him. Treading water, he smelled mildew and dead fish. When his leg brushed against something, he imagined a dead body. (The Pittsburgh mafia, he'd heard, was alive and well.) The boat was pulling away. He'd gone too far this time. He'd not only be swimming to shore alone, he'd never see Anita again.

But, just then, she waved her hands and shouted. "Wait! I'm coming!"

She got a running start and jumped from the same spot. She squealed in the air before splashing. He swam over and grabbed her arm.

"Wow, that just happened!" he said, kissing her.

Simon waited in his kitchen — drenched in wet clothes, eating a peach — while she took a shower. He glanced around at his bachelor pad: the big glass windows, the brick walls, the exposed ceiling, the red ladder leading to his bed. A big space. Big enough for two.

After spending the day with Anita, the holes in his life became more visible. In her presence, he felt more relaxed. The nervous twitches disappeared, replaced by a quiet confidence. But he also felt stronger. She gave him the courage to leap off riverboats and defy corrupt, dangerous men.

She came out of the bathroom, her shiny black hair dripping wet, in a Spiderman towel.

"That was a baller move, jumping off that boat. And nice form on your cannonball."

"Thanks. I could use a shower, too. I reek of chemicals and dead fish."

She held her nose. "I can smell it."

When he returned, she was still draped in the towel.

"Can I borrow some clothes?" she asked.

He sifted through his clean t-shirts, then picked out his blue PITT LAW t-shirt— with the gold Panther logo underneath the letters— and a pair of running shorts. "I hope these fit."

She examined the shirt.

"The panther is my spirit animal," he said.

"No," she corrected him. "Karl Marx is your spirit animal."

She dropped the t-shirt and shorts, then loosened her towel. "On second thought, I don't think I need clothes." She let the towel drop, revealing her bellybutton ring, a tiny patch of black hair, and her glistening wet skin. "What do you think?"

His mouth half-open, he couldn't speak.

She walked up and kissed him. She removed his shirt and unbuttoned his shorts. Finally, she took his hand and led him to the couch. He didn't protest.

Afterward, he made pancakes and eggs on the electric griddle.

"Breakfast for dinner," he called it.

She picked up his Chia-Pet on the counter. She seemed puzzled.

"You don't remember Chia-Pets? What about The Clapper?" He clapped his hands twice and the lights went off. "Go ahead, try it."

She clapped her hands. The lights turned back on. "That's kind of awesome."

"After my breakup, I went through an Infomercial-product phase."

"I thought oppressed Asian women and children make all these products."

"It was just a phase," he said, winking at her.

"Hey, come check this out," she said, reading from his laptop. "Something about that miner who'd been in a coma."

"Luke Sadowski," Simon ran to the computer. "What does it say?"

"He just died. It's right here on the Associated Press page."

"Holy shit," he said, glancing at a photo. He scanned the article, but it provided no details. "This thing keeps getting more bizarre."

"I'd say so."

"Remember when I told you about meeting Ken, and how we were followed?" He paused. "Well, that wasn't the only time. A couple weeks ago, I broke into George's office. I was looking for some confidential files. Someone followed me."

"What happened?"

"Since I knew the back roads, I lost him."

She was silent for a minute. "What'd you find in George's office?"

"Nothing. Didn't have time to go through his files. But Ken has a storage unit full of boxes of confidential documents and emails. He gave me the unit number and locker combination. He said if anything happened to him, he wanted me to open it up."

"You need to get in there and see what he's got."

"I don't know. His security guys know my face."

"If you're that worried, I'll do it."

He removed his glasses and rubbed his tired eyes.

"Simon, eight miners died. Nine, counting Luke. We need to find out what really happened. And if they're trying to blame you, then you have to defend yourself."

He'd never considered it in those terms, but she was right.

Defend your honor. Build a strong fort. Protect your castle.

THE DEAD HOUR

Early Sunday morning, Denise checked her watch. Five o'clock. Two hours before the graveyard shift ended and the day shift began. Nurses called it the dead hour because it was the quietest of the day. She was off tomorrow for Memorial Day, and wouldn't be back until Tuesday.

She wore jeans and a gray hoodie. She pulled down the bill of her black Pirates cap, hiding her eyes. She entered the hospital through the back stairs, avoiding the front lobby. She heard footsteps above. Just the janitor. On the fifth floor, she crept down the hall.

Though she carefully plotted her mission, she hadn't expected to go through with it. But she couldn't keep living this way. The last straw had been George: learning he not only visited Luke, but told his doctors to keep him alive at any cost. His ego had no limit! But she wouldn't let him play God with her husband. He'd with the wrong woman.

The ICU nurse station was vacant. She looked around for Carla, scheduled behind the desk tonight, but she was nowhere in sight. Stepped away for a cigarette, maybe.

With no other staff in sight, Denise slipped into her Luke's room undetected. Morphine snaked into his arm through a long white tube. He looked peaceful: his head resting on the pillow, eyes closed, mouth ajar. Flower vases and gift baskets on the side table.

She walked behind the bank of life-support machines and followed their wires. Except for the battery-powered heart monitor, everything else was connected to one large power strip. *Amazing,* she thought. Some rooms in the Orthopedics wing were wired this way, but she figured the ICU rooms would have better safeguards.

When a patient's pulse flat-lined, it triggered an alarm at the nurse station. Reaction time depended on various factors: time of day, number of staff on duty. But with Carla downstairs and the other nurses occupied, there would never be a better moment.

Strangely, she didn't feel nervous or anxious. If anything, a calm resolve had overtaken her. She held Luke's hand and kissed his cold lips.

"I'm sorry we didn't make it." She looked into his cloudy blue eyes. "You were the only boy I ever loved."

She removed his ventilator, walked behind his bed and unplugged the power strip from the socket. The machines died. The alarm started beeping.

Finally, she ran down the hall and descended the back stairs, not passing anyone.

Except for the distant sound of the alarm, it felt like she'd never been there, like it was part of some crazy dream. But not her own.

GOLFING WITH THE ENEMY

On Wednesday morning, the first week of June, Simon found a quiet corner of the Seneca County Law Library and reread his motion to dismiss. He'd filed it with the Clerk of Court's office last week, in response to the civil lawsuit against Commonwealth Energy – and George and Richard Blount, as individuals – which had been filed by the dead miners' families. Their complaint averred negligence, malfeasance, and breach of fiduciary duty. Today, however, only the motion to dismiss would be argued before the judge. Though Simon drafted the motion, Mark Wentworth had come along for backup.

"Your motion looks solid," Mark said. "You lead. I'll chime in, if necessary."

Simon was fired up. "We're meeting in the main courtroom?"

"Judge's chambers. In small counties, pretrial motions are held there."

They entered Judge Novak's chamber. Simon shook hands with the short, pudgy man. As a former public defender, he had a reputation for fairness and equity. His office was spacious, and there was a framed print of Edward Hopper's Nighthawks on the back wall. The judge and Mark knew each other, and started talking about golf courses.

"I played Laurel Valley the other day," said the judge. "Beautiful out there."

"Heard good things, but I've never been."

"Where do you belong, again?"

"Field Club," Mark said. "And Oakmont."

"Oakmont? You ever need a playing partner, call me!"

When Eric Turner, the plaintiffs' lawyer, entered, they got quiet.

Turner was maybe thirty-five, around Simon's age, with a military haircut and a solid, athletic frame. He'd been a JAG attorney before starting his own firm. He looked like he could kill a guy with his bare hands.

"Morning everyone." The judge tapped his fingers on his oak desk. "The plaintiffs clearly have standing in this case, so the major question today is whether they have established a legitimate cause of action." The judge paused. "Mr. Turner, please state your claim."

"Your honor, as stated in my complaint, the tragic deaths of these miners was caused by an explosion resulting from the defendant's failure to maintain safe conditions, including defective equipment, improper training of the miners for emergencies, fines, and citations."

The judge glanced up at Simon. "Mr. Yoder, what's your response?"

"First, they can't prove the defendant's negligence or misconduct. The standard—"

Frowning, the judge interrupted him. "I know the standard. The plaintiffs don't need to prove their case, only that they have a legitimate claim. Further, MSHA's findings are not irrefutable. Therefore, motion denied. We're moving forward with the case. The trial date is set for October, but I certainly hope you can reach a settlement before then."

All three lawyers filed out of the judge's chamber.

"Mark," said Turner. "I've called you twice about settling this."

"Forty million in damages? Don't waste my time."

"Give me a fair number, then."

"Five million. That's a fair number."

"That's a joke."

"You're a commission guy," Mark said. "This is your lottery ticket, right? But think about your clients. You lose, they get nothing. And so do you."

"And I'm guessing you charge about four hundred bucks an hour, so you want to keep milking this cow, right?" Turner walked away. "Call me when you're serious."

"Wow," Simon said. "Did I just fuck that up?"

Mark shook his head. "We didn't stand a chance to get the case thrown out, and this young cowboy wants to make a name for himself. This puppy's going to trial."

"What should I tell George?" Simon was scheduled to play golf with him in two hours.

"Don't worry, I'll talk to him."

Five miles south of Millburg, Simon turned onto Country Club Lane, which paralleled the ninth hole of the club's golf course. He parked beside George's Tahoe, the one with the 'COAL-FIRED' vanity plate. Shouldering his golf bag, he approached the first tee. Two cougars in tennis outfits shuffled out of the clubhouse. Simon smiled and waved.

He joined George on the practice green. His boss wore plaid pants and a black sweater-vest with the COMMONWEALTH ENERGY logo.

Simon wasn't eager to spend four hours on a golf course with his boss, but because this was a Blount-sponsored charity event– with proceeds benefiting groups like the local United Way and American Red Cross chapters– he couldn't decline without a compelling reason. For years, George had given generously to local and regional charities and nonprofits, something his critics overlooked.

"We're the final twosome," said George. "Need any warm up?"

"Won't do much good."

The Millburg course tested a golfer's skill, even the best ones. Though not extremely long, the elevation changes, dog legs, and hazards – deep sand traps, water – kept you honest. Simon's father had played here. He'd loved golf more than life itself.

Simon felt confident on the first tee, until he duck-hooked his drive into some bushes. By the time they finished the front nine, he wanted to tear up the scorecard and get drunk.

"Forget about it," said George. "Clean slate."

The tenth hole was a long par-three over water. Simon pulled out a five-iron. He hit a high fade, making solid contact. The ball cleared the water but kept drifting to the right, landing in a greenside bunker.

"You're safe there," George said. "You've got a smooth swing."

"Hopefully, I can figure out my short game on the back nine."

George hit a six-iron. His ball started out fine, but in mid-flight a gust of wind knocked it down, and it landed twenty yards short of the green. "Where'd that wind come from?"

"Bad break."

They crossed the footbridge. A red-tailed hawk soared above the trees.

"I must be the only guy over fifty who doesn't ride a golf cart." George laughed. "Maybe when my knees and hips give out, I'll start using one."

They both carded bogies and shuffled to the next tee.

"A good walk spoiled," Simon said. "That's what my dad called it."

"We worked together at Armco. I had great respect for your father. He went too soon." George had a way of steering a conversation that kept people on their heels. "By the way, did he ever tell you the story of Fred?"

"Doesn't ring a bell."

"There was an old timer at the mill named Fred Zimmer. He became a mythic figure. This was back when they used the Bessemer process to make steel. One day, Fred's working on the top platform. His job is to monitor those big pots of coke and iron ore as they got dumped into the blast furnace, to make sure everything runs smooth. Tough job. The platform is narrow and it's hot as balls up there."

Although he loathed George, and what he stood for, Simon did enjoy his stories.

"So, one minute, Fred's walking around up there, doing his job. The next minute, we turn around and he's gone. Vanished. Never seen or heard from again."

Simon tilted his head. "He fell into the furnace?"

"You do the math. There's no other logical explanation. But since no one saw it, nobody knows if it was accidental or intentional."

"What a crazy way to go out."

"I know," said George. "But there's also something perfect about it."

Simon tried to pull a message from the fable, but like George himself, it was shrouded in ambiguity.

The eleventh hole at Millburg was a hidden gem. A short par-four that doglegged hard left. The reachable green tempted you like a siren. You could hit an iron to the middle of the fairway, or take a driver and hit a blind shot over a grove of tall pines. If he caught it just right, Simon thought he could reach the green.

George played it safe, hitting a four-iron.

But with nothing to lose, Simon teed his ball high and pulled out his driver.

"A gambler." George smiled. "Golf brings out your competitive side, I see."

Simon lined up the shot, playing the ball forward in his stance. He relaxed his grip and brought the club back past parallel, then uncoiled his hips and swung hard through impact. He'd struck the ball solidly. It started up the left side, along the tree line.

He looked for his ball in the left trees, but found nothing. He continued up to the green. Sure enough, his drive had reached the front edge, leaving a twenty-foot putt.

"Is that for an eagle?" George asked.

"Yep." Simon lined up the putt. It was straight and slightly uphill. Perfect for making an aggressive stroke. As the ball left his blade, he thought he'd pushed it, but it curled a tad left and back-doored into the cup.

George smirked. "Must be your day."

On the next hole, they passed the club's swimming pool, separated by a fence. Simon glanced over at the wives of leisure, rubbing suntan lotion on their arms, while their bratty kids splashed and shrieked.

"These kids today, they don't know how easy they've got it." George shook his head. "When I was their age, my swimming pool was a limestone quarry pond. Either that, or the polluted creek that ran through our hollow."

"Yeah, most of them take it for granted. I know, since I used to be one."

"But you're lucky," George said. "Your dad taught you the importance of work ethic, and the value of a dollar. He provided you with a good example."

"That's true." Simon nodded. "He made me work around the house for my allowance. I raked leaves, mowed the grass, shoveled snow. And I had my first real job at thirteen, delivering newspapers on my bike around the neighborhood."

"Exactly. Most people in the world don't even have indoor plumbing. They shit outside! And that's the problem. All the shit is piling up, metaphorically."

Simon nodded.

"Americans wonder why the world hates us. But they don't hate us as individuals. They hate how we live, the luxuries we enjoy. They want the same things. And if they can't have those things, they would rather destroy them."

As they came to the final hole, Simon glanced at his scorecard. If he made par on the last hole, he could break forty on the back nine, which would be a personal best.

"By the way, the judge denied our motion this morning."

George nodded. "I know, Mark called me." He didn't seem angry. He cut a fresh cigar and lit a match. "It's fine. The coal boom's over. I'm getting out of the mining business."

As George seemed ready to deliver a sermon, an idea boomeranged around Simon's head. If he could somehow record the conversation, George might slip, and say something to incriminate himself. In casual moments like this, his comments were often unpredictable.

When George walked back to his golf bag – changing clubs – Simon reached into his pocket and pulled his phone out. He clicked on the Voice Memo app, pushed the red "record" button, then he stuffed the phone back in his pocket.

"After this legal mess is over, I'm selling our mines." George walked back to his teed-up ball and took a few practice swings. "Dan Blackburn made me a good offer to buy two of them, including Sarver. Now, I need approval from our board. I think the explosion has convinced them." George locked eyes with Simon. "To run a good business, you need to turn mistakes into opportunities. We'll focus on natural gas. That's the future. Cleaner and safer. No more coal mine explosions for us. I'm tired of being the bad guy."

Simon wondered how long he and Blackburn had been negotiating the sale of Blount's coal mines. Obviously, an accident would reduce the sale price. But how would that favor George? Unless there was something he didn't know about their relationship.

"And I want you to stay on board, Simon. Don't abandon ship. Your first year has been rocky, but things will get better."

"What makes you think I'd leave?"

"I've been watching you. You're frustrated. You think the explosion was the company's fault. But when all the information comes out, you'll see. Lightning caused that explosion. Some people can't accept that. They see a crime and look for a criminal."

"You don't think it will go to trial?"

"The DA said he won't pursue any criminal charges, and the federal prosecutors won't touch it, either. Of course, the civil lawsuit is pending. But with that MSHA report coming out, and ruling in our favor, I think the families will try to settle."

George was right. The Mine Safety Agency published their final investigative report, and for the company, their conclusions were solid gold: they'd not only found lightning to be the probable cause, they believed Commonwealth complied with all major safety laws, adding that the high methane section was sealed, and the self-rescuers were not defective. In other words, the miners' deaths stemmed from their own failure to follow proper instructions, and their decision-making was compromised by stress and panic.

"So," George said. "Stop acting like a fool."

"Excuse me?"

"Cut the shit." George's voice had a sharper edge now. "I know you met with Ken Schultz. I know you broke into my office. I know you're dating a journalist named Anita. I could've fired you by now. So, don't test me any further."

Simon heard buzz of a low-flying plane overhead. "Well, I guess there's no point in keeping any more secrets."

George studied him. "Go on, please."

"Ken told me he was fired because he asked too many questions."

"Ken was smart and ambitious, but disloyal. He tried to subvert me."

George addressed his ball. Then, he hit a long drive that split the fairway. "Of course, my best drive of the day comes on the last hole!"

Walking down the fairway, Simon felt rain drops on his face. He stayed close enough to George, he hoped, for his phone to pick up the conversation.

"Another thing I learned about Ken," Simon said. "We're totally different."

George grunted. "That's for damn sure."

"So, why did you hire me to replace him?"

"You answered your own question. Because you were the anti-Ken."

"Meaning what?"

"You're not ambitious, which was perfect. I didn't want another moral crusader who'd try to change the office culture."

Simon kept walking, his mouth a tight line.

"Be honest, Simon. You're not an alpha male. You listen to music in the office. You're on Facebook and Twitter." George chuckled. "You have a Nerf hoop!"

"I get it now," Simon replied. "Several miners are killed in one of our mines, but you expect me to play dumb and not ask questions. Right?"

"Don't be so naïve. Mining's a dangerous job. That's why miners are well paid. In China, hundreds of miners die every year. Our coal mines are the safest in the world. By the same token, I'm not running a bookstore or bakery."

Simon stepped in front of him, forcing his boss to stop. "You know what, George? I'm not the right person for this job. I think I should tender my resignation, as of now."

"Fine. It's not the mafia. I won't keep you against your will. However, you need to stay until the legal issues are done. If it does go to trial, you can't leave."

"Why do you need me? I wasn't even involved with the Sarver Mine."

"Because your testimony, as legal compliance manager, is crucial. We need to show our house is in order. Also, your last name is respected in this town, which carries weight in a jury trial. And let's be honest, half the people of Millburg think I'm a snake."

"You won't lose in court. You said it yourself a minute ago."

"But there's always a chance. Some juries try to play God. They give the victims fifty million bucks, and bury the company." George wagged his finger. "I won't let it happen."

Simon considered this. "If I agree to stay, tell me the truth about one thing."

"Name it."

"The accident." He inched closer to George making sure his voice would be heard on the recording. "It was the company's fault. That lightning theory is bullshit. Right?"

"Of course." George sighed. "Look, some people cheat a little on their taxes, or buy the generic car tires, or don't replace the hot water tank until it floods the basement. They don't intend malice. They're not trying to hurt anyone. Sometimes, people take shortcuts because they have no other choice. Nobody's perfect all the time."

Simon's adrenaline was spiking. Having lost his concentration, he missed the par putt. Despite his stellar round, his mind was focused on bigger things.

He thanked George, saying he couldn't stay for the dinner reception. He grabbed his bag and ran to his car. On his phone, he played the first few seconds of the Voice Memo. Audible, crystal clear! He couldn't wait to get home and listen to the whole thing.

While backing out of his spot, his mind raced. He checked the rearview mirror. There was a car blocking him in. A full-size sedan. A Ford Crown Vic. Gray. Tinted windows.

The driver's window came down. Simon broke out in a cold sweat. Staring at the pale face and long blonde hair, he recognized the man from the coal mine, the one who claimed he was a state trooper. But this time, there was no uniform, and no badge.

The man lifted his Ray Bans. Simon looked straight into the man's glassy blue eyes, but– much like staring at the sun– he was forced to avert his gaze.

"Be more careful next time," the man said.

Simon nodded. He tried to speak, but no words came out.

Frozen, he watched the Crown Vic pull away.

SORRY FOR YOUR LOSS

By the end of Luke's evening viewing session, held at the Thompson Funeral Home, Denise's feet throbbed. She wanted to take her heels off, get out of her tight black dress, and order a pizza. The greeting line finally thinned out. As she waited to greet the last mourners, she turned around and peered into the open casket. Her first impression hadn't changed: thanks to the mortician's heavy makeup job, Luke's face resembled that of a sad clown.

Denise's mom tapped her shoulder. "I'm going home. You staying with me tonight?"

"I think so."

"There's some pasta and salad."

Denise had recovered from her mom's words this morning. "Oh honey," she'd said, trying to comfort her. "He didn't want to make you suffer anymore. That's why he chose to go now." The comment had stung like ten whip lashes.

The afternoon viewing session had been packed, with people coming out of the woodwork to pay their respects. Her friend Gina, and other miners' wives. Luke's relatives and miner friends. Her family. Old high school friends. Kathy and the nurses from Presby.

Larry had stayed with her all day, filling awkward silences and hanging up coats. Presently, he was talking to a miner buddy, and Denise found herself facing Luke's brother, Jed, who'd come from east Texas. He wore a plaid shirt, bolo tie, black jeans and cowboy boots.

"You still working on those offshore rigs in the Gulf?" she asked.

"I'm on paid sick leave. I had a minor stroke."

"Sorry, I had no idea."

"One day on the job, I passed out. Scary, but it made me change my diet. Cut the sugar and red meat. Went to a fat camp in Utah. Lost fifty pounds."

Her nurse-friend, Kathy, finished one of those survivalist obstacle races, where you climb up mud-slicked walls and crawled under barbed wire. "Well, you look great. By the way, is your dad coming?"

Jed rolled his eyes. "He's been dead to Luke and me for a long time."

"I knew Luke hadn't spoken to him in years, I wondered about other family."

Denise excused herself and walked toward the bathroom. She brushed past Luke's cousin, Brian, with the Hitler mustache. Earlier today, he'd asked her to invest fifty grand in his new restaurant specializing in gourmet tacos called El Camino. She'd declined the offer.

She paused in front of Luke's picture board. She loved his childhood photos, especially him riding a Big Wheel. Jean shorts, tube socks, curly hair. There had never been a cuter kid.

Before eight o'clock, George Blount walked in. Impossible to ignore, he was sporting a black double-breasted suit, black tie, Italian leather shoes, and a gold watch.

He made his way down the greeting line, talking to each of Luke's relatives— his brother, aunt, uncle, and a few cousins— until he reached Denise.

"So sorry for your loss," he said.

He hugged her, then kissed her on the cheek. Her body went rigid. He reeked of cologne.

"Thanks for coming." She tried to stay calm, but her skin was crawling.

"My heart sank when I heard the news. What a tragedy."

For the next few minutes, he laid it on thick: how much they'd all been suffering, how he'd visited Luke in the hospital, how he told the doctors to "spare no expense" taking care of him. She smiled and played along, but inside she was raging.

He pulled out a business card. "If you need anything, let me know and I'll take care of it for you." His cold hand caressed her forearm.

As he walked away, she rubbed her shoulder, trying to get the knot out. She felt the urge to take a bath or shower. She never wanted to see his face again. But she couldn't shake the feeling that she'd never outrun him.

Simon drove down Jefferson Street, past the funeral home. He'd read the notice in the paper for Luke's viewing. He considered stopping, but chickened out at the last minute, not sure if he'd be welcome and not wanting to cause further grief. Besides, he was running late for his mother's birthday dinner.

He drove up Institute Hill. He passed Memorial Park, where he and the neighborhood kids used to play Capture-the-Flag. As a kid, Simon often stayed in his room. After finishing homework, he watched MTV, listened to albums, or played Atari. But in the summer, he and his friends played outside all day. No computers. No internet. No Instagram or Snapchat.

He turned onto Belmont Street, past his former babysitter Paula's old house. She'd worked at the National Record Mart at Clearview Mall, and would give Simon the employee discount on tapes and albums. Paula had been Simon's first music teacher, introducing him to new wave, post-punk bands like Joy Division, The Smiths, Missing Persons, The Cure, New Order.

Simon's boyhood home stood at the end of a cul-de-sac. A white Cape Cod with dark green shutters. Belmont Street had more curb appeal back in the eighties, with manicured lawns and healthy gardens. The door was unlocked. He walked through the living room, past family photos above the fireplace. His mom was in flannel pajamas and slippers, holding a coffee mug. Her shoulders were stooped. She looked like a frail bird.

"John!" his mother said with a half-smile, the only person who still called him by his first name. "What a nice surprise."

"How're you feeling, mom?"

"A little foggy, but that means the drugs are working."

His mother loved his father more than anything else, and more than he deserved. When he died, something in her died. Her vitality drained. Her doctor put her on some new depression medication. But she skipped her pills, thinking she was healthy enough to cope, and the disease continued to trap her. Simon could tell by her flat monotone, and because she never played golf or worked in the garden, her two favorite hobbies. One night last month, he found her asleep, with an empty bottle of Ambien on the nightstand. He took her to the ER, where they pumped out her stomach.

"Someone should be checking on you every day."

"Betty and Judy come by a lot," she said. "And I have you."

"Did you forget about dinner tonight?" For her birthday he was taking her to Giordano's, Millburg's oldest Italian restaurant.

"Of course not," she said, grinning. "Give me a minute to get dressed."

Giordano's hadn't changed in twenty years. The main dining room had a low ceiling and dark red walls, adorned with photos of the old country. Rome, Venice, Naples. He looked around. Some families, several old couples. A few people waved to his mother. Every Saturday night the owner, Bruno, played the piano. He finished his set and approached their table.

"Hello Judy," he said, kissing her cheek. "You look as beautiful as ever." He was tall, handsome, and dark-featured, probably in his seventies. He loved flirting with older women.

She touched his arm. "Thanks Bruno, that's very kind."

"I know it's been awhile, but I'm so sorry about Jack's death."

"It was a big shock for us."

"Is this your son?" Bruno held his hand waist-high. "I remember when he just a tiny boy! Hey, let me pick out a bottle of wine for you tonight. How about a chianti?"

Simon entered the conversation. "Pinot noir."

"My pleasure."

Simon's mother watched him leave. "He used to flirt harder. I must look bad."

"Are you kidding? He was shameless."

"Honey, are you okay? You're doing that eye twitch thing again."

Simon looked away. "Work stress."

"I wish your dad was here to give you some advice."

He rolled his eyes.

"He wasn't the greatest father, I admit. But he loved you in his own way."

"Why couldn't he love me the normal way?"

She ignored the comment. "Did you hear about your brother? They sold their Brooklyn condo and bought a house in Greenwich. With a growing family, I guess they needed more space."

That's lovely, Simon thought. There was nothing like hearing about his perfect brother, and his perfect family, to cheer him up.

"So, tell me more about that girl, Anita. You're still going with her, right?"

"I think *going out* is the correct phrase," Simon said, shaking his head.

"Since the breakup with Lindsey, you act like a soccer player faking an injury."

"Great metaphor, Mom." He smiled. "Yes, Anita's a friend. Nothing serious."

"Where did you meet her? Is this another girl from the Internet?"

"She's from Millburg. Her last name is Sekran. Her father is a doctor."

When Simon's mother realized that Anita might be Indian, she got quiet.

He pivoted the conversation. "Still taking your meds?"

She nodded. "Some days are better than others."

As he dropped her off, Simon asked about her golf game. Athletic and competitive, she used to love golf. "Haven't played much this year," she said.

"Let's play sometime. Just nine holes."

She kissed him and stepped out of the car. "I want more details about the girl."

At home, Simon checked the Pittsburgh Press website and clicked on the Obituary section. He'd always been fascinated by obituaries, by the facts and details that defined a life. He searched for Luke McCurdy, but his eye landed on a different name: KEN SCHULTZ.

Shocked and horrified, he studied the photo. Widow's peak. Eye patch. He scanned the obit: born and raised in East Brady. Graduated from Pitt Law, worked at Commonwealth Energy. There was no mention of a family, and no description of the cause of death.

LET'S GO BOWLING

Denise curled up on the couch with the lights off. She ate from a carton of moose tracks and planned to binge on the first season of Breaking Bad. Having endured two days of platitudes and fake smiles at the viewings and the memorial service, she'd intended to stay home all weekend and avoid humanity. And when her phone buzzed, she tried to ignore it, but she gave in. Seeing Larry's name, she answered.

He asked how she was holding up.

"Tired. I still can't believe George showed up. I wanted to spit in his face!"

Larry guffawed. He had such a goofy, hillbilly laugh.

"Hey, let's do something fun tonight," he said. "Like bowling."

"Well, it beats a church or funeral home, I guess."

"You find out anymore from the hospital about Luke's death?"

"Only that it happened between five and six, before the day shift. I guess they tried to revive him, but it was too late."

Of course, she hadn't told him yet. He wasn't ready to hear it, nobody was. The strange thing was that her memory of the act had nearly vanished, as if her cortex had blocked it out. Later, she'd been interviewed by the hospital administrator. He said they would conduct a full investigation, but she made it easier by quitting. And she had a valid reason: to keep returning to the site of her husband's death would cause emotional distress.

Upstairs, she wrestled into her lucky jeans– with fake rhinestones on the back pockets– and turquoise cowboy boots. She sprayed perfume on her chest and threw on a black V-neck.

At first, she'd viewed Larry with a narrow lens. She needed a father figure, and he needed to feel like a father again. But soon, she began to notice his different layers. Larry was like a piece of coal: a hard mineral formed by organic matter.

They met at Sherwood Lanes, near the high school. He said their floors had the best wood patterns, whatever that meant. He was on a middle lane, rolling with his black ball. His gray hair was pulled back. First, she had to rent shoes.

"What size?" asked the acne-faced kid behind the counter, staring at her tits.

"36C," she said, watching his cheeks turn red. "Oh, my shoe size? Seven."

She waved to Larry, walking over. He looked so much better. He'd put on weight, and the color had returned to his rugged, weathered face. He had on a black t-shirt and jeans.

"You look like the Johnny Cash of Bowling."

He kissed her cheek. "Nice boots," he said. "You should bowl in those."

"I'd break my ankles."

"Let me pick you out a good ball."

"Anything but pink."

He picked out a turquoise ball with swirls. "Matches your boots."

The pin-setting machine dropped down, cleared the lane, and reset their pins.

Larry went first. He lined up the shot, took a few steps, and slid into his roll, finishing with his right hand extended. The ball curled right to left and smacked the center pin, setting off a massive collision that ended in a strike.

"Nice roll," she said. "Any tips for me?"

As she gripped the ball, he guided her right arm through the whole motion. "Turn your wrist at the end. That gives you the spin. And follow through."

"You got strong hands," she said.

She never mastered the spin. After three gutter balls, she reverted back to her old method: the two-handed, between-the-legs, push.

"Don't laugh," she said.

"Whatever works. I won't judge."

They rolled a second game. Once again, Larry was throwing strikes and picking up spares. The bartender came over with another pitcher. Since there was no music playing, Denise walked over to the jukebox, and along the way she could sense the other men watching her, their eyes running up and down her jeans, so tight they looked painted on— so tight she had trouble getting change from her front pocket— but none of it mattered because tonight she felt bold and alive, because tonight she was not Denise, just a sexy, carefree girl that looked like Denise, and once that Stone Temple Pilots song came on the place was hers, she owned it, and as she walked back to her lane, she strutted and swayed— highlighting every curve— and winked at every panting, salivating animal in her path.

By the end of two games, she had a good buzz going. Not hammered, but over the limit. Since her DUI some years ago, she'd been a lot more careful.

"If you want," Larry said. "You can stay in my guest room, and we'll get your car tomorrow morning."

She didn't argue with his logic.

On the ride home, she had dozed off.

Quietly, she followed him inside. While he put clean sheets on the guest bed, she drank a glass of water and took some aspirin.

"Just let me know if you need anything else," he said.

She tried to suppress her sexual urge, her desire to feel his strong hands on her skin. But she left her bedroom door open, just a crack, letting him know he had a green light, if he wanted to take it. At one point, in the middle of the night, she heard him walk into the kitchen. She almost called out his name when he passed outside her door, but she resisted. Maybe she needed a friend more than a lover right now. Maybe he did, too. She felt herself getting wet. *Why deny it,* she thought. She caressed her nipples and slid her hand under the elastic of her undies, running her fingers down the front. Then, she opened her legs. A little wider.

In the morning, Larry's dog greeted her with licks to the face. She laughed and pushed him off. She opened the chest of drawers and threw on his Neil Young t-shirt.

Larry was in the kitchen fixing eggs, skinny legs poking through plaid boxers.

"Did Fred bother you?"

"He was sweet. Like his owner."

As they rode back to the bowling alley for Denise's car, she informed him that she'd quit her job. "Couldn't keep going back there every day. Too much happened there."

"I don't blame you," he said.

"And I joined the lawsuit."

"I understand that, too. Your situation has changed."

As for immediate plans, she'd be spending the coming days at her brother's lake house. Alone. She hoped the solitude would help her find some clarity.

STASH

On a mild Sunday night in June, Simon sat in the passenger seat of Anita's car and glanced beyond the Allegheny River, admiring the quaint village of Oakmont. Anita had offered to drive to Slate Lick and keep lookout while he'd search Ken's storage unit.

After reading the obituary, Simon was now convinced of two things: First, George was not only crazy, but dangerous. Second, Ken was murdered. Anita believed Ken's death gave them a better chance to search the storage unit, but Simon didn't share her confidence.

"He's dead. No longer a threat." She stared at the road. "He's off their radar."

"But I'm still on their radar. And that guy who impersonated the cop at the mine entrance. Whoever he was, he saw me with Ken."

"Okay, fine. How does that change anything?"

Simon laughed. "You know, when I first started at Blount, I thought George was the decent one, and Richard was the asshole. But George is a goddamn lunatic. He's an evil puppet master, pulling strings when he wants people to move. And cutting strings when he wants them to stop moving."

"Are you too scared to do this? You want to turn around and go home? I mean, you have that recording of George from the golf course, where he basically makes a confession. Maybe we don't need to take any more risks."

"No. We still need supporting evidence. Documents, email threads, and whatever else is hiding in that storage unit. Let's get it over with."

"I'll search it," Anita said. "Give me the lock combination."

Simon shook his head. "You don't know what to look for. It would take longer."

They parked at a gas station down the road from the Bob's Self Storage.

"Keep your phone on," Anita said. "And be careful."

Simon pulled the handgun from his backpack and checked the safety.

"What are you doing with a gun?" she asked.

"Being careful."

He left the car and started walking along the shoulder, toward the BOB'S SELF-STORAGE sign. There were no street lamps. The Sunday evening traffic was light, just a few pickups rolling past. Some acres of forest stood between Denny's and the storage facility.

His handgun, a nine-millimeter, weighed down the pocket of his green army jacket. Although he hadn't shot a gun in years, he hoped it was like riding a bike.

A six-foot chain fence, no barbed wire, surrounded the storage units. There was a code-operated access gate, but he squeezed his body around it.

He walked down the second row, to Unit 13. Checking the numbers Ken gave him, he turned the combination lock, stopping at all three numbers. It opened on the first try. He lifted the stall door and turned on his Maglite. Banker boxes were stacked high against the walls.

He checked his watch. 8:30. Assuming the worst, he had fifteen minutes to get in and out. Since that wasn't time enough to read inspect each file, he started pulling any file that might be relevant – Sarver Mine citations, Bauer Foam Blocks, Self-Rescuer Devices – and stashing them in his backpack.

When his bag was almost full, he received Anita's first text: CROWN VIC APPROACHING. GET OUT!

It was 8:42. *How the fuck,* he wondered, *had they tracked me so fast?*

A minute later, the sound of tires on gravel. He closed his backpack, pulled down the stall door, and locked it. He sprinted into woods, behind the last row of storage units. His Maglite guided him along a narrow footpath, but he tripped on a tree root and snagged his pants on jagged thorns. He heard the sound of a tractor-trailer shifting gears, remembering that the woods connected to the highway.

Behind him, some branches crackled. Maybe a deer, but they came out to feed at twilight. Then he noticed a flashlight beam, darting around.

He ducked behind a large tree trunk. The footsteps grew louder, the beam of light brighter. Squinting, he glimpsed the outline of a tall man. When he stepped into a patch of moonlight, Simon noticed the long, blonde hair: George's goon, the cop impersonator.

Simon picked up a small rock. With a strong toss, maybe, he could throw him off his path. What if the rock hit a branch and landed in front of him? He'd be fucked. In the end, what saved him was the rustling of a squirrel or raccoon. Hearing the noise, the goon veered left and ran toward it, farther away from Simon.

He waited another minute, then backtracked. Like a gazelle, he bolted back to the storage unit. He surveyed the gray Crown Vic. He tried to open a door. They were all locked. So, he pulled out his hunting knife and slashed the two right-side tires.

He hopped the fence and sprinted down the dark road toward Anita's car.

When he heard a noise in the woods, he glanced right and saw the flash of a gun. The bullet grazed his ear, but missed. He jumped into the drainage ditch and crouched low, and pulled out his handgun. He raised his head.

The goon was emerging from tree line, about thirty yards back.

Simon fired.

The goon stumbled, grabbing his right leg.

Simon rose from the ditch and ran like hell.

He was only a hundred yards away from Anita's car, when another shot hit the pavement, near his feet. He swerved left into the parking lot and jumped in.

Anita pulled onto the road. A bullet took out their back windshield.

She screamed "Oh my God, we're going to die!"

"Keep driving!" he yelled.

They merged onto the highway. She drove like Danica Patrick.

"Who chased you?" she asked. "Did you get a look at his face?"

"The cop impersonator." Simon said, breathing hard. "It must be one of George's guys, because he's not a fucking cop."

"Too late to worry about it now." She glanced at his backpack. "What'd you find?"

He kept his eyes locked on the road. "We'll know in a few minutes."

Back at the Ketchup Factory, they spread out the folders on Simon's coffee table, not unlike kids inspecting their stash of Halloween candy. He checked the first label - RE: Oxygen, Self-Rescuers. Inside was a thread of emails from Ken Schultz to Richard and George.

"Okay, what's this?" she asked.

He summarized the first email: the Sarver Mine site manager requested new oxygen canisters because, after conducting some tests, he found that over half the cans had broken seals, and the oxygen leaked out. Some were defective in other ways, like missing parts.

"Here is George's reply email." Anita read it aloud: *The new cans are way too expensive. We have to make do with the ones that do work. We bought new ones for the Fayette County mines because they were totally out of juice. But the Sarver Mine doesn't make enough money to justify the cost.*

She laughed. "This language is so conceited. It's perfect!"

"That's what I hate most about them," he said. "The arrogance. If you make a mistake, that's one thing. But to cover it up, that's a different animal."

"What else do we have?"

He mentioned a letter from MSHA, stating that the foam blocks violated a federal statute that required concrete blocks to separate high methane areas. The letter, which came with a fine, also warned that if Blount didn't change within six months, they could shut the mine down.

"Look at the date," Anita said. "The letter's more than two years old."

"Yep. And check out this email from George Blount to Ralph Bauer, CEO of the company that makes the foam blocks."

She took a minute to read it. "Really? George is on their Board of Directors?"

"And he has stock worth nearly a million!"

"Hey," she said. "Can we listen to George's voice memo again?"

He grabbed his phone and played back the voice recording labeled Conversation with George. Then he leaned back and watched Anita's expression change, from amusement to shock.

"Wow," she said. "I can't believe you got him to say all that."

"I just I started asking questions."

"I love how he says everyone cheats on their taxes!"

Simon smiled.

Anita started walking in circles around the table. "Do you realize what this means? Between the recording and the documents, we've got a smoking gun. It's enough to nail the company for civil damages, and maybe even convict George and Richard, criminally."

"There are no criminal charges."

"Not yet." Anita rubbed her chin. "But what if some new evidence came up during the civil trial?" She held up Simon's phone. "Like a confession."

"That's a good point." He paused. "I have an idea. A law school friend of mine works in the state Attorney General's office. In fact, I think he works in the White Collar Crime Unit. He'll be a good resource. Meantime, what should do we do with this stuff?"

"Let's take it to the court of public opinion. If I post these documents online, I'm confident they'd get picked up by national media outlets. And, if we wait before the trial begins, they won't have time to react."

He shook his head. "They'll trace it to you. And back to me."

"Fuck them," she said. "They can't prove that you're my source."

"Hold on." Simon lowered his voice. "We're getting into some deep shit, here. I mean, if these guys killed Ken, how do we know they'll stop there?"

"We can't go back now. It's too late."

Wow, he thought, *she's incredibly ballsy, or she's fucking crazy.*

"C'mon, big man." She unzipped his jeans. "Don't go soft on me now."

Either way, she knew how to persuade him.

PART FOUR

EASY GAS

On a cold November afternoon, Simon stepped inside the Harp & Fiddle, an Irish bar in the Strip District. Glancing around, he spotted Henry at a corner booth.

Simon's life, in recent weeks, finally slowed to a normal and steady pace. Mentally, he had quarantined the mine accident, and all related issues. At work, he focused his energy on other projects. And he hadn't spoken a word about the new evidence with anyone, except Anita.

They were still dating, and Simon was ready to make a serious commitment. He wanted to ask her to move in but hadn't found the courage. He wasn't certain of her answer. Since her work schedule remained hectic— she'd spent two months researching natural gas wells in Colorado and Wyoming— he couldn't get a good handle on their relationship, and how invested she was.

But now, with Thanksgiving two weeks away, and the trial scheduled for the first week of December, Simon needed to make some big decisions. Would he walk the company line and destroy the evidence? Or would he try to expose George? If he chose the latter, how could he succeed without risking his career, and his life?

Under the weight of this stress, he'd called his law school friend, Henry. They'd arranged to meet for a drink the next time he was in town. He'd always admired Henry. Born in Korea but raised near Philly, Henry had served as Pitt's Law Review Editor and finished in top five percent of the class, and yet he'd studied less than Simon. When it came to memorizing case law and understanding complex ideas, Henry's mind was a sponge. He had easy gas, like those freak major-league pitchers who'd go out and throw hundred-mile-an-hour strikes without warming up. Simon thought he was destined for politics. After law school, he took a job a with well-connected law firm in D.C. But something about the job or the lifestyle didn't suit him, so he returned home to his native Bucks County. Years later, he was elected district attorney, and

Simon figured he'd become a judge one day, but then he was recruited by the state attorney general, to run the white collar crime division of their office in Harrisburg.

As Simon approached, Henry stood up and gave him a quick bro-hug. He wore a turquoise Polo shirt and khaki pants. Preppy, his customary style.

"Good to see you, Simon."

"You haven't changed a bit."

"Nice getting back to the 'burgh'."

"What are you drinking?" Simon asked.

"Guinness, I suppose."

"First round's on me."

Simon walked up and ordered two pints from the cute red-haired bartender. The Pogues played on the stereo. Two Irishmen watched a rugby game on television.

"Old stomping grounds," Simon said, returning with two pints.

"We used to get so shit-canned here," Henry said.

Simon nodded. "Remember finals week, when you jumped on the bar and started river-dancing with Amy Shapiro?"

Henry smiled and raised his glass "To Amy!"

"I still have the photos. When you run for governor, I might try to bribe you."

Henry chuckled. "Your 401k plan."

"I know you're on the fast track. How's the new job, by the way?"

"Beats racking up DUI's and convicting meth addicts. It's fun going up against smarter criminals. Investment bankers and CEO's. So, where are you these days?"

"Have you heard of George Blount?"

Henry laughed. "I heard you'd been working for him. So, the rumors are true?"

Simon nodded. "In-house counsel for Commonwealth Energy."

"I never would've guessed," Henry said. "How do you like it?"

"Do you really need to ask?" Simon said. "It sucks."

Henry leaned in and lowered his voice. "I've been trying to nail George Blount for years. He and Dan Blackburn, back when they worked together, did some ugly shit."

"Really? Like what?"

"Not reporting accidents or environmental damage."

"How do you get away with that?"

"Set up shell companies. Bribe local politicians. There are ways. "

Simon felt light-headed. He swilled his beer.

"Blount is more polished than Blackburn, who's a total redneck. But those coal guys are a different breed, as you've probably discovered."

Simon nodded. "Indeed, I have."

Henry paused. "So what's your angle here? Why did you call me?"

"I'm weighing my options. There's a pending civil suit. I have evidence that could change the outcome, stuff that incriminates George. But I have some questions first."

Henry sat upright, like an eager schoolboy. "Commonwealth's coal mining business has been corrupt for years. Not with their mine safety standards, but corporate fraud. Shady accounting methods, embezzling funds."

"At first I ignored it," Simon said. "But I've had that feeling for a while."

"After the accident, we considered launching a criminal investigation. But we didn't think we had enough to prosecute the top brass, like George and Richard. Once we heard about the miners' lawsuit, we decided to put our project on hold. Wait and see what happens."

"Can you still press criminal charges, even after a civil case?"

"First, we'd need a guilty verdict against the company. Second, there must be evidence of willful or intentional misconduct that has a direct causal link to the miners' deaths."

"That's a higher standard than simple negligence or malfeasance, right?"

"Yes," Henry said.

"What if Blount and the plaintiffs settle out of court?"

"If Blount does not have to admit liability, it doesn't matter how much money they pay out. We can't launch a criminal case."

"That clears things up," Simon, "But I'm still not sure how to proceed."

"If you scratched my back, I'd scratch yours."

"How, exactly?"

"Perhaps a government job in Harrisburg or D.C. I know people on Capitol Hill."

"Okay. What about whistle blower protection?"

"You'd be covered by several federal statutes, not just Whistleblower Act. Worker injury and death comes under OSHA and the Mine Safety Act. Environmental damage comes under the Clean Air and Water Act. And since Blount is a publicly traded corporation, the Sarbanes-Oxley Act would apply, if Blount lied to shareholders and investors."

"But whistle blower rights only cover the loss of my job?" Simon said.

"Essentially, that's correct. If you expose them in court, or in the media, Blount could not retaliate by firing you. And if they did, you could sue for lost wages and back pay."

"What about a financial reward? I remember that case in Mississippi after Katrina. Two sisters, worked for State Farm as adjusters. They had documents showing State Farm wasn't paying claims for wind-damaged houses. They won three-hundred grand in damages."

"Different case," Henry said. "It came under the False Claims Act, which only applies to federal money. State Farm got federal money to pay claims and help rebuild those homes."

"So, there's no reward for the good guys?" Simon asked.

"If you blow the whistle, you're going down a hard road. I mean, look at Edward Snowden. He's still living in a Russian hotel."

"Good point."

"I have to ask. What kind of evidence are you holding?"

Simon paused. "A verbal confession from George. A voice recording."

"Wow. That is a game-changer."

"What about physical protection? Like hiring a security guard."

"You really think George Blount would try to physically harm you?"

"Henry, they've tried to kill me." Simon lowered his voice. "One of his goons followed me one night. He chased me through the woods, and fired a couple shots."

"Well, I know some good private security firms. If it ever came to that."

Henry finished his pint. They stood up and shook hands.

"Keep in touch," Henry said. "And be careful."

"Why is everybody telling me that?"

"People like you, Simon. You're one of the good ones."

CONSPIRATORS

When Denise received the text from Simon– "I have good news," it read–
she didn't know how to respond. At first, she ignored it, but Larry said they
ought to hear him out.

They had agreed to meet at the North Hills Eat n Park, a local diner serving
comfort food.

"Bright in here." Denise pointed to the orange wallpaper.

Cakes and cookies spun around in a glass case beside the register.

Larry told the hostess they were meeting two people. "Young couple. Tall
guy, with an Indian woman."

The hostess led them through the dining room. The after-church crowd had
swarmed the place. Denise caught glares from a blue-haired lady at the salad bar.
Though she'd never met Anita, Denise recognized her face. She wedged herself
into the booth beside Larry.

"Thanks for coming," Simon said. "And Denise, I'm sorry about Luke."

It had been over five months, but Denise's emotions were still raw.

Anita spoke up. "I covered the mine explosion for the Pittsburgh Press.
I've written about the misconduct and corruption of George Blount and Commonwealth Coal. And, I went to Millburg High School."

"She's on your side," Simon added. "We both are. Denise, remember that
day at the hospital, when you said I need to pick a side? Well, that's what I'm
doing."

"What's in it for you?"

"For starters, it's my job. When lawyers see their client or company en-
gaging in illegal behavior, they have an ethical duty to report it. But I'm also
protecting myself, in case Blount and his lawyers try to blame the explosion on
me during the trial."

"How could they blame you?"

"As Compliance Manager, I'm normally in charge of safety issues. But I had only been there six months, and they kept me in the dark about the Sarver Mine."

Denise frowned. "There needs to be a bigger reason."

"They've tried to kill me once already," Simon replied. "Is that a good reason?"

Denise and Larry shared a nervous glance. She wanted to know more details, but Simon seemed too reluctant to elaborate.

"You said the miners could never win in court," Larry said. "What's changed?"

"Judge Novak has a liberal streak, as a former public defender. Also, we discovered some new evidence. I can't share it now, but it's enough to prove guilt."

"You sandbagger!" Larry smiled, punching Simon's arm.

"One thing against us is MSHA's investigation report, which came out in support of Blount, and their lightning theory."

Denise shook her head. "That is such bullshit!"

"Two Mine Safety guys came to my house and interviewed me," Larry said. "I told 'em the truth, that Blount is a corrupt company with dangerous mines. Guess they ignored it."

Denise fixed her eyes on Anita. "What's your role in all of this?"

Anita smiled. "I've been helping Simon investigate. And, I'll use my connections to attract national media coverage of the trial."

Denise respected Anita's intellect, but she seemed cold and arrogant. "I don't trust reporters. They exploit people. Remember the media coverage of the explosion?"

"I'm not a television reporter," Anita said. "And I'm not a tabloid journalist."

Denise gave her the benefit of the doubt, for now. "Where do we come in?"

Simon gestured to Larry. "You're a key witness. Your testimony could support our evidence against the company. Like the oxygen cans. I found some documents and emails confirming they didn't work. But we have to keep this secret. These guys are dangerous."

"We've been followed." Anita paused. "And Simon was shot at."

"Nothing leaves this table," Larry said.

Denise still questioned this alliance. It felt like the Americans and Russians joining forces during World War Two. She didn't know if they could be trusted. But, since she'd joined the lawsuit, she favored anything giving the plaintiffs a better chance.

"What about George?" she asked. "Will he go to jail?"

"There'd have to be a separate criminal prosecution, which is possible, but not likely."

"Great. So, nothing changes."

"Not necessarily. If the jury give the plaintiffs a large enough monetary award, it could force the company to fold, or file for bankruptcy."

Larry raised a hand. "If the miners' families win, how much money do you think they'd get?"

Simon shrugged. "My guess? Perhaps ten or twenty million, total."

Denise did the math in her head. As much as two million per family. She tried to picture two million dollars. She wondered if it would fit in a carry-on bag.

RIDE THE RIVER

Larry Jenkins climbed the icy steps of the Seneca County Courthouse, hugging the side rail. After a week of jury selection, the trial began, and Larry was the first witnesses on the docket. Swarmed by reporters and cameras, he kept repeating "no comment." As Anita had predicted, the trial was attracting national media attention.

Walking down the main hallway, he glanced at portraits of former Seneca County judges: an endless row of old white dudes in black robes. He passed two juveniles in orange jumpsuits, handcuffed and escorted by a deputy sheriff. Then, he emptied his pockets— car keys, loose change— before going through the scanner.

The trial's venue was one of those of traditional, patriarchal courtrooms with high, wooden bench seats and ornate balconies. Like a church, Larry thought, but more austere. He sat up front, behind Mr. Turner, the miners' lawyer, who wore a gray suit and solid red tie. Combined with his Army-style haircut, he looked intense. The two Blount attorneys wore pinstriped suits and gold watches.

Larry turned his head and watched the courtroom fill up. He smiled and waved at Denise, sitting in the back row because she didn't want to make him nervous.

At ten o'clock, the bailiff called everyone to order. "Court is now is session," he said. "Please rise for the Honorable Judge Harold Novak."

The chubby, black-robed judge waddled through a side door and climbed into his chair. He had a white beard and wire-rimmed glasses. From the opposite side, the jury entered.

Larry scanned the jury box, but he didn't recognize any faces.

The judge warned everyone that, despite the media attention, this was not a circus, but a court of law. "No talking beyond a whisper, cell phones off, no photography, and no video."

To Larry the whole thing felt staged, like a scene from Law & Order.

Turner, the plaintiffs' lawyer, made his opening statement first. "Ladies and gentlemen of the jury," he said, "the defendants will try to complicate things. They'll try to confuse you with complex theories and hypotheses of what caused the accident. They'll say lightning, if it hits a grounded cable in the right spot, could cause an electric fire in a high-methane pocket, which could cause an explosion. They'll say this explosion was an act of God." His tone was deliberate, and his manner precise. "But the facts and the law of this case are simple. The actions of the company, and their failure to maintain safe working conditions, caused this tragic explosion, an accident that could have been prevented. A methane explosion that kills nine miners is not natural occurrence. Commonwealth Coal's defective safety equipment and the dangerous condition of their mine are the reasons we're here today. Thank you very much."

Larry admired Turner's style. Direct and to the point, no bullshit.

The defense lawyer, the tall one, stood up and buttoned his suit, then approached the jury box.

"Folks, as you know, coal mining is a dangerous occupation. Fires, roof collapses, explosions. Some accidents can be prevented. But others cannot. That's the nature of the industry. Ladies and gentlemen, after weighing all the facts of this case, the only reasonable conclusion is that the Sarver Mine explosion was an accident caused by forces of nature beyond our control. In other words, even the most vigilant and comprehensive safety methods and equipment could not have prevented this accident."

This guy was polished and relaxed— in a southern country lawyer kind of way— but Larry wondered if that style would appeal to a Rustbelt-town jury.

"On the first of April, a severe thunderstorm hit the area near the Sarver Coal Mine," he continued. "Experts who investigated the accident will explain how lightning hit a grounded electric cable that ran inside the mine, how the voltage caused a massive spark, perhaps even a fire in a high methane section, and how that caused an explosion. And despite the company's best efforts to seal off that section, a strong enough blast would have destroyed any wall, and carbon monoxide would have penetrated any coal mine." Commonwealth's lawyer paused. "Folks, I come from a mining family. My grandfather mined coal in eastern Kentucky, so I understand the dangers. And I know some companies operate unsafe mines. But Commonwealth Coal has been an industry leader in safety for years. They treat their workers with respect. Ladies and gentleman, this was an accident, a sad reminder of the dangers of mining. The legal term is force majeure. This is an emotional case, but you must base your decision on facts, logic, and law, rather than emotions."

A few moments later, Turner pointed to Larry.

"Your honor," he said. "I call my first witness, Larry Jenkins."

Larry climbed into the witness box, feeling stiff in his starched button-down and khaki pants and paisley tie, the only one he owned. He'd spent an hour trying to tie a Windsor knot. He also cut his hair; chopped off the ponytail.

"Good morning," said Turner. "As the only survivor of the explosion, can you tell us what happened that day? Just walk us through it, step by step."

For the hundredth time, Larry described the first moments. "It felt like a small earthquake. I never felt no earthquake, but you get the idea." His comment drew laughter.

Larry's chest felt tight, like a belt was wrapped around it. He hated being in the hot glare of the spotlight, always had.

"Then what?" Turner asked, now looking at the jury.

"We started walking toward the entrance. The smoke got thicker the farther along we went. Then, a collapsed roof made us turn back."

"Can you explain a collapsed roof?"

Larry shifted his weight in the hard, unforgiving chair. "The tunnel's roof caved in from the blasting. A big pile of rock and debris blocked the way. We didn't have time to dig through it. So, we decided to retreat to the back of the tunnel."

Turner rubbed his chain. "What did your safety training suggest you do?"

"Same thing." He'd practiced his answers in the mirror, but it was tougher now. "We're taught to find a remote section of the tunnel, with good air, and build a curtain. So, we did."

"By curtain, what do you mean?"

"You take pieces of rock and debris and build an airtight wall. It was our best chance to survive, keeping the smoke and carbon monoxide out. The bad air, we call it."

"What did you guys do behind the wall, and how long were you down there?"

Larry scratched his head. "Several hours. At first, everybody seemed chill. We played cards and talked about stuff we'd do when we got out, like go hunting or take a vacation."

Turner tried to keep Larry on track, knowing his answers could drift off and follow tangents. "When did people start using their oxygen canisters?" he asked

"At some point the bad air started seeping through the cracks. It was gradual."

"Your honor, I'd like to submit this as evidence." Turner held one up. It looked like a soup can connected by a tube to a small breathing mask. "Larry, how does it work?"

Larry grabbed it. "You put the mask on like this, and turn the switch on the can here. Problem was, they're pretty damn old, and some didn't work."

"How much oxygen do they hold?"

"An hour or so, I think. But if you take small hits every couple minutes, you can stretch them out longer. We tried to share, but it got ugly near the end."

The other defense lawyer – short, lizard-faced – objected. "He's not an expert. He can't speak to how they worked, or whether the other miners used them properly."

"Overruled." The judge sat upright in his chair. "He may not be an expert, but he can describe his experience using them, and what he observed."

"Please continue, Larry. What did you see around you?"

Larry straightened his tie. "Guys were coughing and wheezing real bad. I kept a handkerchief over my mouth. After a few hours, guys started passing out. I was feeling dizzy and lightheaded, too. Luke walked around and checked all the oxygen cans, and a couple were still half full. That gave us another hour or so."

"So, you and Luke worked together?"

"Luke is the reason I'm alive. He kept me awake, until the rescuers came."

In back, Denise stood up and left the room, as if she needed oxygen, too.

"What's the next thing you remember after that?"

"Waking up in the hospital, where I stayed for about two weeks."

"Did they diagnose you with anything?"

"No. They did a bunch of tests on my lungs and heart. They ran a tube down my throat to suck out the excess fluid. I have bad lungs, so they kept me there for precaution."

"Bad lungs?" Turner asked. "Can you be more specific?"

"I smoked for several years, but I also inhaled a lot of coal dust over the years. It scars the airways, then gradually destroys lung tissue and blood vessels. I don't have cancer or nothing, but I got these things called precancerous lesions, they tell me. "

Turner spun and faced the jury. "How do you know Denise McCurdy?"

"She's Luke's widow, and she was also a nurse at Presby. She worked in Orthopedics. She visited me every day and gave me updates on Luke. She helped me recover."

"Did you ever see Luke at the hospital?"

"Once, some days before I left. He looked half-dead. I can't describe it, but he wasn't the same guy I remembered."

Turner looked at the judge. "No further questions."

Thinking he was finished, Larry stood up, but the judge told him to wait. "The other side needs to ask you some questions."

He glanced into the jury box, wondering what they thought of him. There was a bright-eyed woman in a red sweater, smiling at him. He remembered what Turner said: avoid eye contact with jurors. He felt like a goddamn zoo animal.

The company's lawyer stood. "I have some questions, Mr. Jenkins."

"Fire away," Larry said, fidgeting with his hands.

"You were never diagnosed with black lung disease, or lung cancer, correct?"

"That's right."

"Okay. Now, returning to the accident. Your oxygen can worked fine, right?"

Larry nodded. The judge reminded him to give verbal answers.

"Yes. It lasted longer than I thought."

"And you guys were stuck down there about fourteen hours?"

"That sounds about right," Larry said.

"But some of the other guys used up their cans faster, correct?"

"Yes."

The company lawyer gestured with his hands. "Even if all the cans worked perfectly, most would have still run out long before the rescue team arrived. So, isn't it logical to conclude the outcome would not have changed, and therefore, the cans were not the cause of death?"

"Some cans didn't work." Larry glared back. "That's my logical conclusion."

In the corner, the court reporter hammered away on her typing machine.

"Moving on," said the company lawyer. "You're not part of this lawsuit, right? In other words, you have not filed a lawsuit, and you don't intend to sue the company in the future?"

"That's correct." Larry's skin crawled. He was done the bullshit.

The company lawyer walked back to his table and picked up a piece of paper. "Please confirm that this is the agreement you signed with the company."

Larry checked his signature. "Yes."

"By signing, you agreed the company was not responsible for the accident?" "Yes."

"And your signature was not forced, coerced, or signed under duress?" "Excuse me?"

"In other words, you freely chose to sign the contract?"

"I had bills to pay. I couldn't afford to wait around for a million bucks that I might not ever see. That's why I signed it."

"Last question." The company lawyer paused. "Did you spend any time in prison, for the manufacture or possession of marijuana?"

Larry was raging inside. "Thirty days in Mississippi. So what?"

"Nothing further, your honor."

The judge checked his watch. "Okay, let's take a ten-minute break."

Larry's shirt was drenched in sweat as he walked to his truck. He removed his tie, then opened the glove compartment. He pulled out a thick wad of hundred-dollar bills, from the settlement check he'd cashed. He fingered the bills, and considered his options: *I could leave now and drive south, back to the Gulf Coast. Better yet, I'll buy a boat and cruise down the Ohio and Mississippi Rivers, ride the current down to the Big Easy. I did my job and testified. I've paid my debts. Fuck this place, and fuck those goddamn lawyers.*

He drove to Millburg's East End. He passed Tree's house. The FOR SALE sign was still posted. He cruised through Alameda City Park and stopped near a bench.

A skinny white kid in a Yankees cap sauntered up to his truck. "What you need, old man?"

"Eight ball. And some Oxy."

Larry held up a wad of money, and they made the exchange.

He left Millburg and jumped on I-79 South. Twenty miles later, he took the McKee's Rocks exit. The Steel Horse Gentlemen's Club looked the same as he'd remembered it ten years ago. Outside Pittsburgh city limits, there were fewer rules and restrictions than the city clubs, but the girls were hotter than the ones in the redneck strip joints.

There were a few cars in the lot. Before going in, he snorted a couple lines.

The place was quiet, as if they'd just opened. Girls in bikinis smiled as they walked by. Three men sat on velvet chairs near the stage, which had a long runway and a brass pole.

He went to the bar and ordered a Wild Turkey-and-Coke. A short Asian girl approached him. "Hey big boy," she said. "You want buy me drink? You want dance?"

He declined. Never take the first offer, the best ones always came later.

He took a seat and watched the girls dance. They played the same music they had a decade ago: Guns N Roses, Motley Crue, STP. The curvy black woman on stage was dancing to "Round and Round," by Ratt.

The biggest difference was the girls. More variety now. All shapes, sizes, colors. *The United Nations of Strippers,* he thought. And they danced better now. Instead of a couple twirls around the pole, they'd climb halfway up and do gymnastic tricks.

The next dancer, a cute brunette, grabbed his attention. She danced to "Closer" by Nine Inch Nails. She performed a Naughty Nurse routine, as if she'd read his mind. She ripped off her nurse outfit, revealing red lace bra and panties, a garter, and fishnets. Small breasts, nice round ass. She climbed halfway up the pole and did things with her legs that shocked him, like some contortionist at a perverted magic show.

When she finished her routine, she emerged from the dressing room and walked over. "I saw you watching me," she said. "What's your name?"

"Larry."

"You seem like a sweet one. How about a private dance?"

He cracked a smile. "Can you play that naughty nurse again?"

She winked. "I'll be whatever you want."

PLAY LAND

Thursday: Day Three of the trial, Simon's day on the hot seat. Yesterday, from the back of the courtroom, he listened to a member of the rescue team describe how they found Luke and Larry and brought them out safely. Then, a senior MSHA official, who led the independent investigation, explained his conclusion that lightning was the most likely cause. Using graphs and charts, he tried to show how an electrical charge ran through the mine by electrical wires, and how sparks combusted with high-methane air to produce the blast.

Eating a bagel on the couch, Simon picked up yesterday's paper from the coffee table and reread the headline of Anita's front page story: BLOUNT TRIED TO CONCEAL EVIDENCE LINKING EXPLOSION TO COMPANY'S SAEFTY VIOLATIONS AND DEFECTIVE EQUIPMENT.

He wondered if it was too late to turn back. If he kept his mouth shut and said nothing controversial on the stand, would George forgive him? *Fuck no,* he thought. The only remaining question was whether George's voice recording would be admitted as evidence. Last week he sent an anonymous copy to Turner, the plaintiffs' lawyer.

He crossed the South Main Street Bridge and rolled past the Seneca County courthouse. The packed front steps reminded him of Obama's campaign rally here, when he talked about reviving the rust belt, like every presidential candidate for the past thirty years. Of course, there has been no revival: only more rust.

Simon parked five blocks away, hoping the walk would relax him before testifying. He'd practiced his answers, yet his anxiety was still brewing. Needing positive energy, he inserted his earbuds and scrolled through the music on his phone. Tool or Fugazi could do the job, but he chose Metallica. In a tight jam, no one delivered like Metallica.

Inside, he found the bathroom. Standing before the mirror, he tightened the knot of his royal blue tie and buttoned his gray suit. He splashed cold water on his face and wiped it off with a paper towel. His heart palpitated. I can't do this. He felt great a minute ago. Now, he wanted to get in his car and leave the state.

He walked out and looked for an EXIT sign.

Rounding a corner, he bumped into Anita.

"Hey," she said, kissing him. "You look pale."

"I can't go through with this."

"Yes, you can." She squeezed his hand. "This is your moment. Own it."

"Are you coming in?"

"I'll watch from the back, but I have to leave early. I'll call you tonight, okay?"

"Great, that makes me feel so much better." Simon couldn't hide his sarcasm.

"Relax. You've got this."

Simon sat several rows behind the Blount brothers. The goons were nowhere to be found. Neither was Larry. The other day, he'd done such a great job testifying. He wondered about Larry's future, and what he'd do with his settlement money.

After the judge and jury entered, Mark Wentworth stood up.

"Your honor, we call John Yoder to the stand."

Simon felt the hot glare as he walked down the center aisle and stepped into the elevated box, beside the judge. Stay calm. No twitching.

Today, Mark wore a plaid blazer with dark gray slacks. Perhaps he thought the casual, country-lawyer appearance would endear him to a Seneca County jury.

"Can you explain what you do for Commonwealth Energy?" Mark said.

"I'm the Legal Compliance Manager. I draw up business contracts, draft safety and training policies, and generally deal with the legal regulations of coal mining."

"Could you give us an example?"

"When you drill or mine in a new area, you have to complete an environmental impact statement and get a permit. I oversee that process."

"What's your background?"

"Born and raised in Millburg. College at Penn State. Pitt Law. A one-year judicial clerkship in Scranton, then two years at Rooney & Paine."

"And Commonwealth Energy was one of your clients at Rooney?"

"Yes."

Simon studied the jury box. He counted seven women, five men. Except for one Latino man, they were all white. He scanned the rest of the room. Family members of the dead miners sat behind Turner, snarling, like they wanted to hurl stones.

"How long have you been at Commonwealth?"

"About a year. I started six months before the Sarver accident."

"Why did you accept the job?"

Simon drank from his Styrofoam cup of water. "Rooney was a great experience, but I didn't like the big firm culture. I was familiar with George Blount. It felt right."

"Regarding the Sarver Mine, did MSHA send you any citation notices or fines stemming from safety violations?"

"My first month there, we received a citation and major fine. The letter said our use of dense foam blocks violated federal law. It was a repeat violation."

"How did you respond?"

Simon's wooden seat groaned as he shifted his weight. "Richard took the letter. He said any documents related to the Sarver Mine should go to him."

"Did he tell you anything else?"

So far, all the questions were standard. Nothing unexpected.

"Richard explained that most mines, by nature, have a few pockets of high methane. They need to be sealed off. And he said we used dense foam blocks, instead of concrete."

"Did he say why?"

Simon felt beads of sweat on his forehead. "They were cheaper, but could withstand as much pressure as concrete. He also talked about negotiating with MSHA for some kind of exception. It made sense to me."

"What other citations have you received, and how do you respond to them?"

"We got one for inadequate safety training. So, we added a day of training for new miners. Now, we make them undergo three days of safety instruction before starting."

"Skipping ahead to day of the accident," Mark said. "What do you remember?"

"Chaos. Around lunchtime, the corporate staff got word of the explosion. All day, I was trying to get information from coworkers. And the internet."

"Where did you go that afternoon?"

Simon stole a glance at George and Richard. Arms crossed, they looked anxious.

"After lunch, Richard told me to report to the accident scene, and find George."

"For what purpose?"

"In an advisory role, in case any legal questions came up. I stayed with George, as he talked to reporters and family members, but he seemed to be in control of things and didn't seek my advice. A few hours later, I went home. I ate dinner and watched the news. When I fell asleep, CNN was reporting the miners alive. But the next morning, at work, I learned the whole story. Richard told us that bad weather might have caused the explosion."

"Can you be more specific?"

"His theory was that lightning hit a grounded cable running into the mine, the cable threw up sparks, something caught fire, and it triggered a blast."

"Nothing further." Mark smiled at him before sitting down.

Simon's eye twitched. His anxiety level began to spike. The moment of rebellion had arrived. Ladies and gentleman, fasten your seatbelts, we expect turbulence.

Turner, the miners' attorney, approached him. He'd brought his game face.

"Good morning, Mr. Yoder." Turner smiled. "I'm unclear about something you said earlier. After that first citation, did you receive any more safety fines or violations regarding the foam blocks?"

"A few months later, we got fined for the same issue. In the letter they called it a violation notice, not just a citation. When I asked Richard, he said there was a mistake."

Mark and Seth exchanged a nervous glance.

Simon smiled. *Welcome to my world, you fuckers!*

"Do you know the difference?"

"A violation is more severe. For example, a repeated problem."

"Did this raise any red flags in your head?"

"Yes. The problem was being ignored."

From his desk, Turner picked up a square gray object. "Can you identify this?"

"A dense foam block. Like the ones they used in the Sarver Mine."

He handed it to Simon. "How does it feel?"

Simon examined it. "Not substantial. Lighter than a concrete or cement block."

"Could it withstand the pressure and force of an explosion?"

"I doubt it."

Wentworth objected. "The witness is no engineer."

The judge agreed.

Turner continued. "Did you see any of these studies Richard mentioned, showing the foam blocks being as strong as concrete?"

"Never."

"When you discussed possible causes of the explosion with coworkers, were there any other ideas mentioned?"

"Defective oxygen cans," Simon replied. "That made logical sense to me. When I first started the job, the Sarver Mine site manager told me those self-rescue devices were his biggest safety concern. He said they needed to be replaced."

Turner faced the jury box. "And what about the lightning theory? Was that ever talked about around the corporate office?"

"Honestly, aside from Richard, nobody else gave it much credibility."

"So, do you think the lightning theory was a hoax?"

Simon nodded. "Yes. That's my feeling."

"Objection!" yelled Seth. "Pure speculation!"

The judge sustained it, but the jury clearly heard Simon's answer.

"Based on your legal experience, do you think the senior officers and executives of Commonwealth breached their duty of care?"

Simon fidgeted. "In corporate law, the basic rule is that officers and directors must act on behalf of employees and shareholders, using the best information available. Thus, if George and Richard and the directors had knowledge of the defective oxygen cans and foam blocks, and failed to act in the best interests of the miners, then yes, they're negligent."

The jurors traded shocked glances. Whispers issued from the audience.

Turner returned to his table, where his paralegal handed him a device that looked like a small tape recorder. "Have you ever spoken to George about the accident outside the office, for example, at a cocktail party or on the golf course?"

"Yes." Simon briefly described their golf outing at Millburg Country Club.

"Did you discuss whether the company was legally responsible for the accident?"

Simon nodded. "Yes, it came up a few times."

"And did you happen to record any part of this conversation?"

"Yes."

Turner held up the device. He played the conversation: loud and clear enough for everyone to understand the words and recognize the voices of Simon and George.

The judge pounded his gavel. Wentworth stood up. "You honor, is this a joke? This is the first time we've heard of his. And the authenticity of that recording is not verified."

Turner picked up a document from his table. "This letter, signed by an independent voice expert, confirms that it's the voice of George Blount."

The crow buzzed. The judge remained quiet for what seemed like a minute.

Finally, he overruled the objection, explaining that, because the content is relevant to the central issue of the case, the defendant's liability, the voice recording should be allowed.

Simon looked around, in shock.

Turner continued. "Was that the first you'd heard about Dan Blackburn or Blackburn Coal buying up Commonwealth's coal mines?"

"Yes. George mentioned, a couple times, that coal was dying, and his long-term goal was to focus on natural gas. But I had never heard of a deal with Blackburn."

"What was your impression of that comment?"

"It didn't make sense. I mean, why would Blackburn come in and buy our distressed assets, unless he was getting a great value for them?"

"Last question," Turner said. "Regarding the tone of that conversation on the golf course. Did it seem clear that George was admitting fault for the accident?"

"Yes, that was my interpretation."

"Why do you think he would confess something like that?"

"Maybe he was tired of the bullshit," Simon said. "He'd built his company from scratch. He was tired of defending his actions and how he ran things."

The judge permitted a redirect by the defendants. Now Seth, that little jackhole, would take center stage and ask the questions.

Simon tried to buoy his own confidence. Last mile of the marathon.

Seth buttoned his suit and approached him. "As the company's only lawyer and compliance officer, isn't it your job to deal with safety violations?"

"Yes, but since the foam-block issue predated me, Richard handled it."

"Richard is the CFO. He's not a lawyer or compliance manager."

Simon's eye twitched. "As head of the corporate office, he manages various things, including my work. And he's my boss, so I do what I'm told."

"Didn't you graduate in the bottom quarter of your class at Pitt?"

"Pitt's an excellent law school. I'm not ashamed of that."

"And you failed the bar exam?"

"By two points." Simon couldn't believe the question. "Pennsylvania has one of the hardest exams. I passed the second time, with flying colors."

"And weren't you fired from your previous job at Rooney & Paine? I have your employment file here. It says you failed to meet your billable hour requirements."

Simon turned to the jury, speaking directly to them. "The big firms make you bill fifty hours a week, which amounts to seventy or eighty hours total. Even working night and weekends, it's nearly impossible to meet every week. Also, many big-firm lawyers pad their hours. They overcharge clients." Simon pointed to Seth. "For example, I'm sure this guy has been overcharging Blount for years!"

Laughter spread around the audience.

"Didn't you suffer a nervous breakdown at work?" Seth asked.

"I have nervous tics. They flare up when I'm stressed. Along with the job pressure, my fiancée was cheating on me. I called off our wedding. A few months later, my dad died. So yes, I suffered severe anxiety. I'm not perfect, like you."

Seth winked at him, as if mocking his eye twitch. "Moving on, why did you record that conversation with George?"

"Because I thought he might say something important about the case."

"What made you think that? Had you been talking about the case all day?"

"Like I said before, it came up a few times."

"Weren't you trying to get a confession out of George, in order to cover your ass?"

"Fuck you," Simon yelled. "Asshole."

"Nothing further." Seth returned to his seat.

The judge called for a recess, then told both attorneys to meet in his chambers.

Simon staggered off the stand and walked outside. He checked his watch— 11:30. He wondered how long it would take to get fired. His testimony had sealed his fate. Throughout this odyssey, his main goal had been to do the right thing, to expose corruption and fraud. But even if Blount went bankrupt, another mining company would replace them. The demand for energy would never stop. The capitalist machine would plow ahead.

He felt like an unmoored boat, unsure where the current would steer him. He noticed George descending the front courthouse steps, and walking toward him. His first impulse was to run, but he stood his ground. "Hey George. How can I help you?"

George grabbed his arm, tight, and pulled him into a dark, narrow alley.

"If you scream, I'll kill you." He stopped beside a dumpster. "I can't believe you went through with it!" George laughed like a hyena. "You got some big balls!"

For some reason, Simon started laughing, too.

"You piece of shit," George said. He lifted him up by his suit coat. Then, he shoved him backward, slamming his head into the brick wall.

Woozy, Simon rubbed the back of his head. There was blood on his finger.

"You're fucking with the wrong person. You've put my company in jeopardy." George was shaking like a strung out junkie. "Your legal career is over."

"Whatever," Simon gasped. "You'll survive it."

"You know what? I don't want to see your tired ass again." George pulled his checkbook out of his inside pocket. "You will take this check. And then you'll fucking disappear, and never say another word about this case to anybody. You understand me?"

Simon nodded.

George filled out the check and handed it to him. "Take it."

Simon's eyes bulged as he read the amount: five-hundred thousand dollars. And it was signed by George.

"You have until tomorrow to clean out your desk. After that, if I see you again– "

"You won't," he promised.

Simon pocketed the check and sprinted down Main Street, all the way to his car.

He drove north of town and weighed his options. The afternoon was free. He could see a matinee at the Clearview Mall Cinema. Get day-drunk at the Chester Hotel. Go roller skating at the Skate Castle. He drove with no specific direction or destination, but once he passed the McDonald's – the one with the huge Playland – he slowed down and pulled a U-turn. Could there be anything better than diving into a pool of plastic balls, then feasting on chemically-engineered burgers and nuggets? The perfect capitalist metaphor! He turned the car around and parked right under the Golden Arches.

In the restroom, he wiped the blood from his head. Then, he walked toward the Playland area. He watched a small boy– maybe two or three– in denim overalls, climbing a ladder to the top of a slide. The boy shrieked with joy as he shot down the slide and launched into the pool of plastic balls. He grinned at Simon, like they were teammates in a secret game. Simon examined the slide, wondering if he'd break it.

"Should I do it?" he asked the boy. The boy giggled.

Luckily, no other kids were around. At the top of the ladder, Simon laid his feet down first and pushed off. Picking up speed, he lowered his head and torso, shooting through the tunnel. Then, he sailed through the air. The pool of balls made a popping sound as he plunged in. He remained under the surface for a while. *A poetic ending,* he thought, *to a strange life.*

He floated to the surface and swam to the edge. He smiled at the boy, who was now holding his mother's hand. When Simon glanced at his mother's face, his mouth fell open.

It was Lindsey. His ex-fiancée.

"Hello, Simon," she said, frowning. Her arms were crossed over her small breasts. She wore a floral-pattern dress revealing her toned legs. He noticed the big rock on her finger.

The only other time he'd ran into her since the breakup, shopping at Target, he twitched like a madman. But now, his anxiety remained dormant.

"You looked funny going down that slide!" said the boy.

"Tyler, honey, don't talk to this crazy man."

Simon felt no spite or ill will. "How are you, Lindsey? Still teaching?"

"I took a year sabbatical when Tyler was born. But now I'm back."

She looked the same – thin, blonde hair – but her eyes looked tired.

Simon smiled. "He seems like a great kid."

"Thanks." She looked at her watch. "We need to go. C'mon Tyler."

It felt like watching a parallel universe, or some alternate version of his life.

On the way home, he called Anita and asked if she'd heard his testimony.

"Masterful," she said. "You fried those fuckers today!"

"But Seth was pretty harsh."

"You did major damage," she said. "George testified today. He claimed ignorance about the safety violations, and everything else. He tried to blame you and Ken, but the jury knew he was full of shit. Then, some meteorologist hired by Blount went through the whole lightning theory thing. But Turner made it sound like science fiction."

"That guy's a pit bull," Simon said. "I'm hiring him if I ever get sued."

"Closing statements are tomorrow," she said. "I think they might settle."

"Keep me posted."

FRIEND OF THE DEVIL

Sitting at the counter of Morgan's Diner, Denise dribbled hot sauce on her eggs. She thought about the trial, which had gone faster than expected. It was only Friday, and yet people were saying it might conclude by the end of the day.

"Where were you yesterday?" she asked Larry. "You weren't in court."

"I was sick, stomach bug." He sipped his coffee. "My nerves caught up with me."

"Simon was incredible. He outwitted those big-city lawyers."

"You talk to your lawyer today?"

He called this morning, asking everyone to meet at his office before court. "Good news. That's all he said."

She made Larry drive her car because she was too nervous. From the passenger seat, she lit a cigarette and cracked a window.

"I don't need that smoke in my face," he said.

"Tough shit, it's my car."

He laughed. "So, you think they made an offer?"

"Trial's going bad for them. They don't want to risk a guilty verdict, because it could lead to criminal charges against George and the other top dogs."

"I wonder how much."

"Whatever they give me," Denise said "You're getting part of it."

Larry smiled. "I appreciate it, but I'm okay."

"You can't say no. You've been my rock through this. And that settlement you got from the company is not enough. You deserve more."

She leaned over and kissed him. He looked dazed, his cheeks glowing.

They walked into Turner's office, on Jefferson Street. Larry waited in the lobby, as a paralegal led Denise into the conference room, where she joined the other family members. For Denise, it felt like a strange homecoming.

Turner stood up. "Thanks for coming on short notice. First, a quick summary of the trial. As you know, the national media coverage really helped our cause." Denise thought about Anita. Her reporting prior to the trial – exposing company violations – had a big impact. She admired Anita's tenacity. "But Simon Yoder's testimony, and the new evidence we introduced, was the crucial factor. After that, the defense's case fell like a house of cards."

Everyone at the table clapped and cheered.

"So, here's the good news." Turner paused. "The senior defense attorney, Mark Wentworth, called me this morning. He wants to negotiate a settlement."

"How much?" someone asked.

"Right now, their standing offer is twenty million, total." The room fell silent. "That's about two million per family. It's a great offer, and I recommend we accept, but I want the whole group to vote on it together."

He looked around, waiting for them to process it.

"I don't need to think it over," said Ron's wife. "I'm ready to vote."

"Hold up," Denise said. "What happens to George Blount, and the company?"

Turner addressed her concerns. "First, twenty million is a major hit to their bottom line. My guess is that Commonwealth will survive, but get out of the coal mining business. Second, with the new voice recording evidence, it's possible George will face criminal charges."

"That's all we can hope for, I guess."

"So, are we ready to vote?" asked Turner.

Everyone nodded.

"Okay. Whoever wants to accept the offer, raise your hand."

They all did, including Denise. It was time to get her life back.

People hooted and hollered.

Gina came over and gave Denise a big hug.

"I'm so sorry about Luke," Gina said.

"Thanks girl."

"Listen, I'm having all the families over for a cookout next weekend."

"I'll stop by," Denise said. "Can I bring Larry?"

"We'd love to see both of you."

❧

Waiting for his coffee to brew, Simon checked his phone. Maybe all those horror movies he saw as a kid had brainwashed him, but the weirdest things always seemed to happen on Friday-the-thirteenth. He considered not going back to the office, but he wanted to box up his things and say goodbye to Julie and Jim.

From the car, he called Anita. "Any news?"

"Big news. They settled! Denise just called me."

"What are the terms?"

"Get ready." She paused. "Twenty million, total. Over two million per family."

Distracted, he nearly drove into the car ahead of him. He jammed the brakes at the last second, stopping inches short of the car's rear fender.

"Where are you?" she asked.

"Heading to work."

"They didn't fire you yet?"

"Not officially," he said. "I'm just going to clean out my desk."

"You shouldn't be going back. Not after George assaulted you like that."

If either George's Tahoe or Richard's BMW were in the parking lot, Simon had planned to turn around and leave. Both of their spaces, however, were empty. Simon entered through the side door, trying to avoid Deb. As Richard's chief informant, she reported everything – information, facts, gossip – that she heard around the office. And she flaunted her position. She could be careless and rude because Richard favored her.

He walked straight into Julie's office and closed the door.

Julie covered her mouth. "I can't believe you showed up today!" She paused. "George was here a few minutes ago. And he was pissed."

"I defected. I'm done here."

"At least someone had the guts to speak out. But I'm worried. They might come after you."

Simon winked. "I know plenty of good lawyers."

Julie hugged him. "Take care of yourself, Simon."

He grabbed a cardboard box from the storage closet and filled it with legal textbooks, files, folders, office supplies, and his law school diploma. He discovered an old photo of Lindsey, taken during their trip to St. Croix. She was on the beach in a green bikini, holding an umbrella drink.

Hippie Jim walked in, wearing his trademark Hawaiian shirt.

"So counselor, I guess this is it?" Jim smiled.

"Guess so." They shook hands, which led to an awkward-white-male hug.

Jim smiled. "A friend of the devil is a friend of mine."

It was a game they used to play. During boring office meetings, they'd exchange Grateful Dead lyrics by hiding them in conversation.

"I may be going to hell in a bucket," Simon said. "But at least I'm enjoying the ride!"

One last time, Simon closed his office door. He walked the main row of cubicles, carrying his banker's box of personal junk.

Passing Deb on his way out, he tried to sound cheerful. "Take care, Deb. Nice working with you. By the way, is George coming back today?"

She cut her eyes. "I always knew there was something rotten about you."

He set the box down. "I'm sorry you feel that way."

"You betrayed us. Watch your step. I'd be real careful if I were you."

Outside, he shielded his face from a gust of wind. He opened his trunk and set the box beside his golf clubs. Just then, Richard's BMW pulled beside him.

Richard looked like shit: his tie loosened and hair disheveled. "Didn't think you'd have the balls to come back."

"How did closing arguments go?" Simon asked, playing possum.

"You're fired. But I guess you knew that already."

"Yes, but I'm curious. What's the exact reason?"

Richard snorted. He pulled a tan folder from his briefcase and handed it to Simon. He opened the folder, which contained professional eight-by-ten photographs. There were a few black-and-whites of Anita and Simon on their first date: dinner at the Squirrel Cage. Those did not surprise Simon, since he remembered seeing a man taking pictures from the street. But the photographs of them standing on the Gateway Clipper boat – and a few with Larry and Denise at Eat N Park – made him nervous.

"Nice camera," Simon said.

"You've been lying to us for months." Richard shot back. "But testifying against us in court, and taping George on the golf course – that's where you crossed the line."

"You've been lying to me even longer. Starting with your cop-impersonating goon. By the way, what happened to the real Ken? How did you kill him?"

"Excuse me?"

"Don't deny it."

"Ken took his own life. But his death is the least of your problems. You're not only fired, we'll bar your license. You'll never practice law again."

Simon pulled his attorney ID card from his wallet and ripped it to shreds. "I hate being a lawyer nearly much as I hate your company."

Richard shook his head. "Your little stunt in court might bankrupt us. When we have to lay off the whole corporate office, they can thank you for it."

Simon laughed. "You're such a sad bastard."

"We trusted you, and you betrayed us."

Simon peeled out of the parking lot, his heart pounding like a hammer.

BOLERO

An hour before the football game was scheduled to kick off, Simon and Anita traversed the Clemente Bridge. They passed vendors selling Steelers jerseys, hats, and t-shirts. Simon stopped to buy a yellow towel.

"What's that?" Anita asked.

"The Terrible Towel," he said, indulging his yinzer accent. "Everybody waves them when the Steelers score. Myron Cope, a local broadcaster, started the movement."

With Christmas three days away, there was an inch of snow on the ground, and the forecast called for more tonight. They passed office buildings adorned with red and green lights, and nativity scenes in front of churches. They passed the Warhol Museum and the baseball stadium.

Heinz Field stood at the far end of a vast sea of parking lots, like some treasure-filled pirate ship. They passed throngs of tailgaters, grilling burgers and dogs, drinking Iron City cans. A father played catch with his young sons, reminding Simon of his dad and brother decades ago.

Anita asked Simon why his jersey looked different from the rest. He was wearing a throwback seventies jersey, with Jack Lambert's number '58' stitched in fat block numbers. The hardest-hitting linebacker, back when the Steelers won four Super Bowls, Lambert had been the soul of the Steel Curtain Defense. While several players from those teams – Bradshaw, Swann, Harris – became celebrities, Lambert remained a recluse. The Thomas Pynchon of the NFL.

They looked around for Denise. The tickets had been her gift. They found her in a back corner of the lot, surrounded by tailgaters, most of whom looked more country than city. They were standing near a new Ford F150, black with a yellow stripe down the center of the hood. Maybe Larry made an impulse buy, Simon thought.

Denise waved them over. She wore a black jersey over a gray hoodie.

"You didn't have to do this," Simon said.

"A doctor I know had extra tickets. He gets 'em from pharmaceutical reps."

Denise was now a nurse at Pittsburgh Children's Hospital, and she loved her new job.

Simon salivated at the table of ribs, burgers, dogs, and wings, all fresh off the grill. There was a beef stew roasting in the crockpot. Simon piled his plate with wings and ribs, the tender meat falling off the bone.

"Where's Larry?"

"Bathroom." Denise pointed him out, walking back from a port-a-john.

Larry – jeans, boots, Carhartt jacket, red Santa cap – smiled and waved.

"Nice hat," Simon said. "Great spread here."

Anita and Denise started talking to a group of other women.

"Simon, follow me," Larry said. "I want you meet Joey, Hank's son."

"Hank, the miner who died?"

"Yeah. His boy's a miner, too."

They approached two guys playing horseshoes. The big hillbilly gave Simon a firm handshake. "I heard you testify in court. You were badass, man!"

Simon didn't know how to respond. "Just tried to do my part," he stuttered.

"We all appreciate what you did," Larry said. "You need anything, let me know."

Their seats were near midfield, about thirty rows up, and exposed to the elements. But football was meant to be played in the wind, rain, and snow. A few rows away, a group of belligerent Ravens fans barked at Steelers fans around them.

"Your quarterback's a rapist!" one guy yelled.

"Your running back beats his wife!" a Steelers fan shouted back.

"That just reminded me why I don't watch football," Anita whispered.

Simon knew that a disturbing number of NFL players were shaky role models and bad citizens. While he didn't come to the games to judge morals, as a fan he'd been embarrassed and offended by the unethical, even criminal, behavior of players he once admired. Even worse, neurologists had shown a causal link between concussions and brain damage among many former players. Mike Webster, the Steelers' Hall-of-Fame center died homeless and demented, living under a bridge. Another former Steelers lineman killed himself by driving the wrong way along the New York Turnpike and colliding with a tractor-trailer. But the NFL still denied it.

On the second play of the game, Pittsburgh's running back gained twenty yards up the middle. Then the quarterback, Roethlisberger, connected with his tight end on a shallow crossing route, but he was tackled short of the first-down marker, so Pittsburgh was forced to punt.

When the Ravens quarterback got sacked, Simon jumped up and waved his towel.

"Who sacked him?" she asked.

"Harrison."

"Right, the crazy one." He'd coached her up on players to watch.

On the next play, the Ravens quarterback delivered a perfect pass to his running back on a wheel route – just over the linebacker's shoulder – for a thirty yard gain.

"Who's the better team?" Anita asked.

"Pittsburgh and Baltimore, each year, are two of the best teams in the league," Simon explained. "But we have six Super Bowls. More than any other team."

He remembered the Steelers' magical playoff run in 2004. During the conference championship game against the Colts, no one gave them a chance. But their defense smothered the Colts' quarterback all day. With a minute left, they were ahead by a field goal and appeared ready to score a victory-sealing touchdown. From the one-yard line, Jerome Bettis ran behind his left tackle, but before crossing the goal line, he fumbled. A Colts player picked up the ball and ran the other way. He had only one man to beat, but the Steelers' quarterback stuck his arm out and tripped the guy – Pittsburgh's version of the Hand of God – to preserve the win. A few weeks later, the Steelers won the Super Bowl. Despite the sub-zero cold in Pittsburgh that night, Simon drove to the South Side and watched chaos unfold.

"Now that Blount is in your rearview mirror, what's the next chapter?"

"Spend more time with family," Simon said, mocking the cliché football coaches used when they got fired. "Not sure. Maybe a job in the Attorney General's office."

"Is that what you want?"

"Not really." Simon shook his head. "I don't want to go back to the law."

The best Steelers wide receiver got loose and streaked down the sideline. The quarterback fired a cannon, but the ball sailed long. The crowd groaned.

"I might have a job for you," Anita said. "I'm writing a nonfiction book about the dangers of fracking. Just signed the contract with a New York publisher."

"Wow!" he said. "Congrats, that's awesome."

"I need a research assistant. Someone who knows the subject matter. But how do you feel about working for a female boss?"

"Would you sexually harass me?"

She removed her glove and grabbed his crotch. "Only if you want me to."

He considered her proposal. "It's tempting. Of course, with that check from George, I can afford to do nothing for a while."

"Have you deposited it?"

"Went to the bank yesterday. They put a five-day hold on it."

"It might not be a real account," she said. "Don't count your chickens yet."

In the second half, the snow fell harder. He looked around at the empty seats, shocked that so many Steelers fans would leave early.

"Not everyone cares as much as you," Anita reminded him.

"I'll bet it comes down a field goal. And the wind is gusting hard off the river."

"Does the wind really make a difference?"

"It does in this stadium," he said. "Kickers have tough jobs. They have to come off the bench and make high-pressure kicks at the end of games. And they have no job security. Most have one-year contracts. A lot of them have drug and alcohol problems, actually."

She frowned. "Sorry, but I don't feel much sympathy."

On a key third-down play, the Ravens running back was stopped for no gain. Their kicker ran onto the field. He'd be attempting a fifty-yarder, into the wind.

"Let's test your theory," Anita said. "I bet he makes it."

"No, he'll come up short. Look, see how he's throwing grass in the air and taking more time to set up? He's got no confidence."

"Winner buys the first round," she said.

The kicker struck it well, but as the ball sailed through the air, it hit a gust of wind. The ball plunged like a dying duck, falling two yards short of the crossbar.

"What can I say?" Simon lightly punched her arm. "I know football."

Late in the fourth quarter, Pittsburgh's running back bounced outside and ran sixty yards down the sideline, diving into the end zone. But the Ravens came back, mounting a long drive. They needed a touchdown to win. On fourth-and-goal from the six-yard line, the Steelers quarterback anticipated a screen pass. He jumped the route and intercepted the ball, icing the win.

"Great game," Anita said, leaving the stadium. "But I still prefer hockey."

"Blasphemy. High treason."

"We should do something to thank Larry and Denise. By the way, what's their deal? Are they just friends? Friends with benefits? Boyfriend and girlfriend?"

"Here's another good question," he said, pausing. "What's our deal?"

She squeezed his hand. "What do you mean?"

"Are we just friends, or something more?"

She leaned in and kissed him.

"You remember that day I ran into you at Curry Favor? I lied about one thing."

She raised an eyebrow.

"The French Club trip to Montreal. You don't remember this, but one night in the hotel, I bumped into you, coming out of your room in a white t-shirt and spandex shorts. I wanted to tell you how I felt that night, but I froze. I thought I'd missed my chance, yet here we are."

"Guess what?" she said. "I lied, too. I did remember that night."

At some point, they'd made a wrong turn. Simon knew they were on the North Side, but he hadn't been up here in years. The streets were empty, the sky was dark, and there were no street lamps.

"This doesn't feel right. Let's head back to the stadium. We'll figure it out."

When a black Chevy Tahoe with tinted windows rolled by, Simon tensed up. And for good reason: there were plenty of black Tahoes in Pittsburgh, but only one with a 'COAL-FIRED' vanity plate.

"Anita" He balled his hands into fists. "Let's turn around."

The vehicle stopped at the intersection, then made a sharp U-turn and drove back, gathering speed. When it jumped the curb, Simon knew he was the target.

He grabbed Anita's hand and ran toward the nearest parking lot.

They ducked behind a row of cars.

"What the fuck is going on?" she asked, panting.

"It's George and his goon squad. This is bad."

The Tahoe had stopped in the middle of the road.

"Anita, run back toward the stadium. Just beyond the overpass, there's a crowded sports bars called Hi-Tops. Go inside. Wait there. Stay away from the door."

"What about you?"

Simon pointed to the city park across the road. "I'm running the other way. Let's meet at Hi-Tops in ten minutes. Once I lose these guys."

"I'm not leaving you," she said.

"You have to. If I don't show up, call Larry. He'll find me before the cops do."

He kissed her hard. "I love you."

He took off, running behind the Tahoe. He heard the door open, and the sound of boots on pavement, but he kept running across the park, toward the darkest section. He stayed in the shadows, near a grove of trees. He thought he was free and clear. Then, he heard footsteps from behind. Someone tackled him, driving his shoulder into the ground.

He looked up and saw a familiar face.

"We should stop meeting like this," Simon said. "People might talk."

The creepy blonde-haired goon pushed his knee into Simon's back, pinning him down. Simon felt a prick in his arm. The guy was holding some kind of needle.

"What the fuck did you inject me with?" Simon yelled.

The goon flashed a smile, exposing his yellow teeth. Simon's arm and shoulder throbbed in pain. He tied Simon's hands with rope, then yanked him toward the vehicle.

"Where's your girlfriend?" she asked.

"I'm alone."

"Bullshit," the goon said.

He shoved Simon into the Tahoe and sat beside him.

George was in front, looking amused. "Magnus, where's the girl?"

"Lost her," said Magnus.

George sneered. "Idiots. Why do I even pay you?"

The other goon – a short Italian guy named Frankie – drove slowly along Stadium Drive, past the row of sports bars. Luckily, there was no sign of Anita.

Simon stared at the rope around his wrists.

"Your girlfriend might outlive you by a few hours," George said. "But this is so much fun, why do it all at once? By the way, I like to save the dirty jobs for Steeler Sundays, when everybody is glued to the game; even the cops."

Aren't you a genius, he thought. "Why are you doing this?"

"C'mon Simon. After spending all summer trying to fuck me, did you really think I'd just hand you a check and let you go free?"

They merged onto the parkway, heading north.

๑~๑

The roads were coated with an inch of snow by the time Denise and Larry left the game.

"You sure about driving home?" she asked. "You could stay at my apartment."

"I like driving in snow. Been doing it since I was fourteen. " Larry grinned. "My old man let me start a couple years early. He had a '58 Chevy. God, I miss that car."

She wasn't sure if he was being polite, or he couldn't take a hint. "What'd you think of Simon and Anita? They looked cute together, don't you think?"

"He's lucky. He'd better hold onto her." Larry turned onto Boulevard of the Allies.

"You know, there's something I never told you." Denise paused. "I'd been waiting for the right time. It's about how Luke died. I wasn't honest. What I'm trying to say is –"

"Denise, I know the truth."

"What?" Her eyes grew wide. "How could you know?"

"Luke died the same way we all die. Natural causes. An act of God."

Their eyes locked. She knew that he understood. All of it.

"I'm a hot mess," she said, wiping her face with a tissue. "Mascara's running."

"We've both had a tough year. We should have some fun."

"I have an idea. Let's take a road trip. Down south. Your old stomping grounds. We could go to Memphis, Mississippi, even New Orleans."

His gray eyes shined. "That's the best plan I've heard in a long while."

As Denise pictured colorful shotgun houses – peach, yellow, coral – in the French Quarter, her phone rang. It was Anita calling.

"Hey!" she answered. "Did you guys enjoy the game?"

"Simon's in trouble." Anita sounded scared. "Is Larry with you?"

"Hold on." Denise put the phone on speaker. "Go ahead."

"They took Simon!" Anita's breath was shallow and quick. "Some tall, blonde-haired guy. I think it's one of George's thugs. They're driving a black Chevy Tahoe. Simon told me to call Larry before I call the police."

"Hold up," Larry said. "Where did this happen?"

"The North Side. I was there, but I slipped away. I'm downtown, at my office. One of the tech guys is helping me track Simon's phone. They were heading north, but the signal cut out."

Larry pulled over and stopped the car. "You said a black Tahoe?"

"With tinted windows." Anita started crying. "Please help him, Larry."

"Keep tracking his phone. I'm heading up there now."

Stunned, Denise hung up the phone. "Holy shit."

"I'll drop you off at my house," Larry said.

"No way." Denise shook her head. "If you go, I go."

"Too dangerous."

"Larry, they might have three or four guys. You need me. I can shoot."

He held his tongue. They both knew he couldn't talk her out of it.

Simon's phone was tucked away in the back left pocket of his jeans. But his hands were tied. He looked out the tinted window as they passed familiar landmarks – Giant Eagle, North Park Lounge, Conley's Golf Course. They were heading north. Back to Seneca County, maybe. Simon noticed George was decked out in hunting gear: camo jacket, pants, and boots. He glanced into the cargo space behind his seat: two rifles, some rope, a bag of lime, and a chainsaw.

"Are we cutting timber?" Simon asked.

"A little comic relief," George said. "I admire that."

"Where are you taking me?"

George lowered his window. "I love the first snow of the season."

Simon repeated his question.

"Back to where it all began. The perfect ending. You'll see."

Where it all began? What the fuck does that mean? "You don't need to do this. I won't cause any more trouble. I'll leave the state. You'll never see me again."

"Too late for all that." George tuned the satellite radio to a classical station. "Bolero, by Maurice Ravel. Hey Magnus, do you know this one?"

Magnus shook his head.

Simon glared at the tall goon beside him. "I thought you were a state trooper."

George laughed. "I almost forgot! When did you figure it out?"

"At the golf course. Why were your thugs following me, George?"

"You can never be too careful. I had to test your loyalty, and you failed. For some reason, I gave you another chance. My mistake." George turned up the radio volume. "Simon, I bet you listen to classical music. Do you know this piece, Bolero? There's something I love about it. How would you describe it?"

Simon had taken a music theory class in college. "It's neither a traditional symphony nor a sonata," he said. "The simple melody belies its sophistication. It repeats, getting louder and faster. Controlled, yet chaotic."

"Outstanding!" George smiled. "Indeed, it's a rebellious composition. Ravel was not French, he was a Basque. He had no country of his own. Like you."

The pale, dim light faded in the western sky. The clouds had cleared, giving way to the bright new moon. They turned onto Dinnerbell Road, heading into coal country.

The Sarver Mine, he thought.

Even with his hands tied, if he could he pluck the phone from his pocket without being noticed, maybe he could dial Anita's number. Magnus was busy cleaning his gun, and George seemed preoccupied with his phone, although the driver kept glancing at him through the mirror.

Simon inched his butt to the right, directly behind the driver's seat. He rotated his torso to the right, so his hands could reach the phone. Using the index and middle finger of his left hand, he tried to chopstick the phone from his pocket, but it was jammed in tight. He tried again, but as he glanced up, he and the driver locked eyes through the mirror.

Shit, he saw me.

"Hey Magnus, check the kid," Frankie said. "He's squirming around back there, like he's digging for something."

Magnus reached over and grabbed the yellow-covered iPhone.

"Slipped out," Simon said.

"Give it to me." George took the phone and scrolled through Simon's contact list. "Anita Sekran, there you are! I'll keep this number." He transferred her contact information into his phone. Then he lowered his window and hurled the phone over a bridge.

"I always knew you were fucking crazy."

"What a vulgar thing to say." George frowned. "I gave you a great opportunity, but you tried to bite the hand that feeds you. Was it your sense of morality? Did Anita talk you into it? Did you want to show her the kind of man you are? She's attractive. That olive skin. Those dark, seductive eyes. I get it, Simon, I really do."

"Stay away from her, you fucking sadist."

"Why did you testify against me? Why did you betray me?"

"You're the worst kind of criminal. You sacrifice lives for money and power."

"You're nothing but a little maggot. You never had to struggle or fight. Your parents gave you every chance to succeed. Like my own kids. But instead of working hard and paying your dues, you try to stir up chaos."

Simon clenched his jaw. "No wonder everyone fucking hates you."

George continued. "You thought you could bring me down, but you failed."

"Oh really? You owe the miners' families twenty million, and you could be facing criminal charges. I think I did some damage." Simon laughed. "I hope you spend your retirement in federal prison and share a cell with a serial rapist looking for a new girlfriend!"

George motioned to his goon. "Tape his mouth. I've heard enough."

Magnus grabbed a roll of duct tape and slapped two pieces over his mouth.

George pulled a handgun from the glove box. "So here's the deal. My friends and I are hunting you tonight. And we made a bet. Whoever catches you first you gets a free steak dinner at the Saxonburg Hotel."

"Best steaks in town," Frankie said. "Grilled to perfection."

Simon wasn't sure how much time had passed as they drove along the Sarver Mine access road. Frankie slowed down, pulled onto the shoulder, and cut the engine.

Magnus pushed Simon out of the vehicle. He fell in the snow.

"Get up." Magnus ripped the duct tape from his mouth.

"Make him walk to the edge," said George.

"Go." Magnus poked him with his rifle. "Straight ahead."

With his hands still tied behind his back, Simon followed the order. He walked the narrow path into the woods. He was groggy and his legs felt heavy. The snow made it worse.

He came to a plateau that overlooked the valley. His breath left vapor trails. He looked around, searching for the best escape route. The moon was bright. He could see in all directions. To the left, the ground dropped into a deep ravine.

"Since I'm a true sportsman, I'll make this hunt a legitimate challenge." George motioned to Frankie. "Untie his hands."

Frankie came over and cut the rope around Simon's wrists. Then, he pressed the blade to his neck. His face looked like a wad of wet dough. "When I catch you, I'm going to skin you," he whispered in Simon's ear. "But when I find your girlfriend, I'll take my time with her."

"Here's the deal." George took out a stopwatch. "I'm offering you two options, and you must choose one. The first option: you get a thirty-second head start."

"And the second?" Simon asked.

"You get a two-minute head start. But it comes with a hidden condition."

"What's the condition?"

"Let's just call it a minor physical restriction."

Simon assumed they would tie his hands back together. *Not a problem,* he thought. He could easily free himself. "I'll take the two minutes."

"Excellent choice." George chuckled. "Frankie and Magnus, go ahead."

"Get on the ground," Frankie said. "Lie on your stomach."

Simon did as he was told. Frankie grabbed his hands, but he felt another hand on his right ankle. Were they tying up his legs?

When he felt something sharp cut against skin, he turned his head to get a better look.

"What the fuck?" Simon screamed. He kicked his legs, but he couldn't move.

Frankie held his right leg down, while Magnus started cutting behind the ankle.

"It's what slave drivers did," George announced. "If a slave was caught trying to escape, they'd cut both of his Achilles tendons."

"Please, God, no!" Simon begged. "Don't do this!"

"We're only cutting one heel, so you'll have at least one good leg. Like I said, I'm a sportsman. I'm giving you a fighting chance, here."

Magnus drove the knife deeper into the back of his leg, above the ankle. For a moment time stopped, and Simon felt nothing. But a few seconds later, as blood started gushing out of the back of his leg, the pain receptors in his brain clicked on.

"Motherfucker!" he howled.

The goons backed away.

"It may hurt a bit, but it won't kill you." George said. "Remember, you have two minutes of lead time." He held up his stopwatch. "Three, two, one... Go!!"

Simon stood up on his left leg, the good one. He tried putting weight on his right foot. It not only hurt like hell, but his foot wouldn't push off the ground. It was useless – he'd have to drag the foot – and blood was still pouring out of the cut.

He hobbled to the edge of the ravine. He studied the steep pitch and picked a good place to slide. Then he jumped, using his good leg, and landed on his ass. He slid down the wet snow to the bottom and landing beside a shallow creek. He grunted and groaned, from the pain.

He looked down at the ankle. Still bleeding. He needed a tourniquet, so he dug into his pocket for his car keychain, and then he used the mini-Swiss Army Knife to cut a piece of his Steelers jersey. He wrapped it around the ankle and tied it off. Glancing back up the hill, he didn't see anyone.

There was a shallow creek running along the valley floor. Instead of walking in the snow, he jumped into the creekbed and followed it, so they couldn't track his boot prints or trail of blood. He splashed his way through, dragging his right foot like a gimp.

Since he could not outrun them, he looked around for a hiding spot. There were a few large boulders to his left. He climbed out of the stream and crouched behind them.

He examined his ankle. It throbbed, but the bleeding had stopped. He poked his head up and looked back up at the plateau. With a clear sky and bright moon, Simon could see two figures at the edge of the ravine he'd slid down.

The two goons sidestepped their way down the ravine, guns in their hands, but Frankie tripped. He kept yelling "Shit!" as he rolled down steep pitch.

"Get up, fat ass," yelled Magnus. "Look for his tracks in the snow. You take the right side. I'll follow the stream."

Simon tucked his knees into his chest. Magnus blew right past him, thank God. He followed the creek down the hill, and soon he disappeared.

For a few minutes Simon sat motionless, gazing at the moonlit trees. Snow-covered spruces and firs. He thought about his dad, and how, each year, they'd go out to Schramm's Tree Farm and cut down a Christmas tree. A Norway Spruce or Frasier Fir, his mom's favorites.

He glanced around. He considered backtracking, going inside the coal mine. It seemed the last place they'd look, perfect hiding spot. He wished Larry was here. He'd know what to do, where to go. He heard two ATVs in the distance. But he couldn't walk that far. No fucking way.

When it felt safe enough, he got up. He hobbled toward the western ridge, but he kept stumbling. The pain was throwing him off balance, and he felt groggy. He wondered if he ate or drank anything in the truck. Then, he remembered when Magnus first captured him, injecting him with some kind of sedative.

He'd made it about twenty yards, when he felt a gun barrel press into his back.

"Steak dinner, boys!" George shouted into the cold thin air.

Larry raced north toward Slate Lick, but the snow and football game traffic slowed him up. On the highway, he weaved through all three lanes of traffic. He wanted to go alone, but Denise insisted. He knew she could shoot, she'd grown up hunting with her dad, but these were dangerous people. He wanted to help Simon, but his main concern was protecting Denise. His hunting gear – his Mossberg thirty-thirty, a box of shells, his Red Wing boots, and a flashlight – was in the truck. At least he wouldn't have to stop home.

"What kind of gun do you want? I have both a twelve-gauge shotgun and a nine-millimeter handgun here in the truck."

"What are you going to use?"

"My hunting rifle, a thirty-thirty."

"I'll take handgun," she said. "It's lighter. Easier to run with."

"Good. Now, let's think about gear."

"I got jeans and hiking boots on."

"And I have an extra camo jacket in the backseat."

Denise checked her new text message. "It's Anita. She couldn't track Simon's phone any further. The signal dropped. But she did call the cops."

"His phone's either dead or destroyed. Cops can't do much without a location."

"So what should we do, just drive around?"

Larry nodded. "My gut tells me they're somewhere near the Sarver Mine. Blount owns the woods behind it, and there are no houses back there."

He drove east along Route 422, then turned onto Ridge Road. The snow was deeper here, and the road wasn't plowed. He slowed down. "Tire tracks. Looks like a truck or SUV."

They came to a fork in the road. Larry turned his headlights off. He pointed to the black Tahoe straight ahead, parked just off the road. He killed the engine. "Let's get out here and check the vehicle."

He changed into his boots. He stashed his flashlight into one coat pocket and his hunting knife in the other. Denise took off her Steelers jersey and zipped up the camo jacket.

He pulled the handgun out of the glove compartment, then he checked the cartridge and the safety. "Be careful. It's loaded." He handed her the gun. Finally, he grabbed his Mossberg and loaded the magazine.

They approached the Tahoe and peeked inside the rear window. Empty.

He looked down at the markings in the snow. "These boot prints are fresh. I'll go on ahead and follow them. Stay here, unless you see something. But don't go far."

She nodded.

He pointed above the tree line "Use the coal tipple for a landmark, in case you get lost or disoriented."

"I'll be fine," she said. "You go on ahead."

Larry felt a sense of calm wash over him as he entered the forest. It seemed he was meant to be here, as if he'd been guided some vision that came to him in a dream. He always felt better in the woods. He followed the boot prints to the end of a ledge. A light mist filtered through the trees. Below him, the narrow creek ran like a bloody gash through the chest of the land.

Farther down the valley, he heard the crackle of branches underfoot. His eyes followed the creek until he noticed a stocky man in black, stumbling through the snow. Larry crouched and watched the man, as he stopped and sat on a tree stump. The man seemed to be eating a candy bar he'd pulled from his pocket. He resembled a black bear.

It had to be one the goons, Larry thought. *Sunday night, in a remote part of the woods, who else could it be?* The man finished his snack. Then he stood and cupped his hands around his mouth, like a megaphone. "Simon!" he yelled. "Come out, come out, wherever you are!"

That was all the confirmation Larry needed. He descended the hill with short steps, keeping his feet quiet, and tracked the bear. His target was about hundred yards away, but Larry didn't trust the shot because it was through the trees. He kept going, each step well-placed, using the spruce and fir trees as cover. He crouched behind the wide trunk of an oak tree and sized up his target: about fifty yards now, with a clear angle. He turned the safety off, brought the rifle to his shoulder, and lined it up with his left eye.

When his prey stood up again, Larry fired, feeling the slight kick against his shoulder. The bullet caught its target below the right shoulder. He went down.

He hopped across the stream, his rifled aimed and ready to fire. He reached the big mound of flesh and stood over him. He kicked away the handgun. He made grunting sounds, trying to slither away. Larry shot him in the leg, above the knee.

"Fuuuck!" he screamed.

"How many others are here?" Larry said. "And where are they?"

"Go fuck yourself, old man!"

Larry pulled out his knife, not wasting another bullet. He planted his knee on the goon's chest. Then, he made a long cut from the bottom of the throat to the stomach. Intestinal slag and blood spilled out, blackening the snow. He waited until he stopped moving, until the life drained out of the man's eyes.

Larry stood up and looked around. Suddenly, he hated himself for letting Denise come along. Spending the last month with her had given him reason to live again. She'd offered him hope, salvation, redemption.

He followed the creek, looking for footprints on either side. Clouds blocked out the moon, cutting visibility. Overhead, a raven cawed. Off to his right, two shapes moved among the trees. He skirted the left edge of the tree line. Two voices, somewhere up ahead. He crouched behind another wide trunk. When the moonlight reappeared, he could distinguish the shapes: Simon was in front, limping and dragging and his right foot. George was poking his back with a rifle or shotgun barrel, yelling at him to walk faster. They were heading toward a clearing. When they arrived, a third man – tall, with white hair – appeared.

Larry stayed out of their sightline. The tall guy began tying Simon's hands with rope. George stood at the far side of the clearing and faced them. Larry overheard their discussion.

"What happened to Frankie?" said George. "I heard a couple shots."

"The fat ass probably took a lunch break."

"I'm fuckin' hungry myself. Let's finish this off."

"What should we do with him?"

"The original plan. Bury him inside the mine." George turned to Simon. "How does that sound? Nobody will find you for a hundred years!"

"They'll find you and lock your crazy ass up!" Simon yelled.

"Who, the police? Your girlfriend, that intrepid reporter?"

"I swear to God, if you lay a fucking hand on her – "

"Chivalry to the bitter end." George laughed. "So romantic."

Larry considered his options. The tall guy had a handgun or semi-automatic. George had a rifle or shotgun, maybe a twelve-gauge. It would take longer for George to fire, so he should take out the tall guy first. He raised his rifle. He wanted to get closer, but there was no more time. He had to move now.

Simon found himself in the middle of a clearing, kneeling before Magnus. There was a handgun was pressed against his temple. Simon considered making a final plea for his life. He was too weak to speak more than a few words. The wind snaked through the trees, whipping up a snowdrift. The picture resembled a snow globe: the perfect metaphor for Simon's life, his thirty-six years on earth. Yes, there had been a few moments of grace and joy and love, but those moments were fleeting. The rest of his life, it seemed, he'd been confined to a room filled with fear and pain and regret, and each time he tried to escape, he ran into a glass wall.

George stood some twenty yards away. He was shouting at Simon, telling him how they were going to bury him deep inside the coal mine, where nobody would find him for a hundred years. Blah, blah, blah. He yelled something back, not even sure what words came out. He pictured George, tied to a large bonfire pit, burning alive.

The cold metal of Magnus's gun against his temple brought him back to reality. He heard the first shot, from the woods behind him. His body twitched. He opened his eyes. Magnus was rolling on the ground: eyes wide, gasping for air. Blood spilled from his head, forming a dark pool.

Behind him, Larry was running out of the woods. His body was exposed.

"Get down!" Simon yelled, but too late.

The buckshot shell from George's shotgun caught Larry's left arm, ripping it open.

They fired shots at each other, until George retreated into the woods.

Larry ran over to Simon, knelt down, and freed his hands.

"What happened to your ankle?"

"They cut my Achilles tendon."

"Are you fuckin' kidding me?"

"Long story," Simon said, slurring his words. "What about your arm?"

"I'll survive." Larry examined his bicep, punctured with little holes. "Where'd George go?"

Simon pointed to where he'd entered the woods. "How'd you find me?"

"Anita called us."

That news gave Simon a warm feeling. "Is Denise here?"

Larry nodded. "We should split up. We need to find her."

"Where's the other goon?" Simon asked. "The fat one."

"Dead." Larry rubbed snow on his arm. "I want you to stay here, and keep an eye out for Denise. I'm going after George."

Simon watched him disappear into the thicket.

Denise waited by the truck for a few minutes before getting antsy. She didn't come all the way up here to stay on the sidelines and let the men handle everything. She'd tried that before. She'd been doing that her whole life. It didn't work. Time for a new plan.

She entered the woods. She climbed a knoll and kept to the high ground. She knew these woods because she'd gone hunting with her dad back here, but navigating in the dark posed a greater challenge, and the snow deadened the sound of footsteps. The land sloped downward toward the creek. She passed a crumbling wooden shed. Beside the shed lay a stained mattress and a rusted tricycle, half buried in snow.

Faint voices echoed from the valley floor. She followed a narrow path through a grove of fir and spruce trees. The wind whistled through the branches.

When she approached a clearing, the voices became more distinct. She hid behind a thicket of bushes. Three men stood in the clearing. George – closest to her, with his back turned – was holding a rifle or shotgun. Simon and the tall, white-haired guy were at the far end. Simon appeared to be kneeling beside the tall guy. No sign of Larry.

She had a clear shot at George's head. She considered taking it, but then she heard a shot from the trees, off to her left. The tall dude went down. She crouched lower.

From where the first shot issued, Larry ran into the clearing. He and George fired a couple rounds at each other. Larry went down, but she couldn't tell where he'd been hit. Meanwhile, George turned and vanished into the woods.

She wanted to check on Larry, but what if another goon was nearby, lying in wait? She couldn't reveal her position. She trusted Larry knew how to survive. He'd proven it, time and again. She'd come back, but first she had to finish the job.

It was the reason she was here.

She followed George's path, deeper into the woods, knifing through the skinny walnut and maple trees. The bright moon illuminated the woods, as if Luke was holding a spotlight overhead.

Her hands were cold, but she kept a firm grip on her gun. As she moved uphill, following George's boot prints, she noticed droplets of blood. She ran along a plateau, just below the ridgetop. She was gaining ground.

When the trees thinned out, she spotted him. He wore jeans and a dark green jacket. He was breathing hard and loud. He ran toward the end of the ridge, where it dropped into a gorge.

When George reached the edge, he stopped and turned. Their eyes met.

"Don't move," she yelled. "Drop the gun."

He raised his shotgun and fired, hitting the tree beside her. He sprinted left, and she pursued. He struggled to climb a steep pitch leading to the spine of the ridge.

She unlocked the safety of her handgun. Then, she fired.

The bullet caught George in the back, below the left shoulder. He rolled back down the hill, grunting in pain, and came to rest near her feet. She grabbed his shotgun and threw it behind her. She circled him, her gun leveled at his head.

"Hello again," she said. Her hands trembled.

He didn't move. Slowly, he looked up at her. His eyes were empty.

"Remember the night of the accident, in church?" She wiped snot from her nose. "You told us the miners were dead. Then that woman, she tried to punch you. Remember that?"

"I'm sorry," he pleaded. "For everything. Please don't do this."

"Shut the fuck up," she said. "Too late for mercy."

She pressed the gun against the side of his head. "I'm going to make it hurt. The way you hurt Luke. The way you hurt me. The way you hurt everyone."

She backed a few yards away. "I don't want your blood and brain splattering me." She found herself laughing at this.

She regained her poise. She aimed the gun at his chest.

Before squeezing the trigger, she heard something behind her.

ஒஒ

Larry climbed the hill, but he stopped twice to catch his breath. The second time, he coughed up flecks of blood. When he reached the top, the trees thinned out. He followed a narrow trail below the ridgetop.

As he neared the edge, two figures emerged.

Denise was standing over George, her gun pointed at him.

In the distance: police sirens.

Denise spun around. "Larry?"

"Denise!" he shouted. "Don't shoot him, it's not worth it!"

He kept running until he reached her. She dropped her gun and opened her arms.

"It's over," he whispered, caressing the back of her head.

George was crawling, trying to reach his shotgun in the snow. Larry noticed. He brought his boot down on George's arm, and then picked up the gun.

The ridge was quiet. In the valley below, the sirens grew louder.

SOUTHERN DRIFT

They drove through the Mississippi Delta, passing tin roof shacks and cotton fields ready for harvest. Denise thought the budding bolls looked like powdered sugar sprinkled over the rich, black soil. Above, clouds billowed and mushroomed.

Larry asked her opinion of Graceland, referring to their morning tour.

"Too much velvet," she said.

Yesterday at dawn, they left Pennsylvania and drove south, through the rugged terrain of West Virginia and eastern Kentucky. Larry looked around for bald mountaintops, but only saw one. He explained how mountaintop removal mining was done several miles from interstate highways. "Out of sight, out of mind."

Along the Bluegrass Highway, they passed horse farms and white picket fences. She'd counted three 'HELL IS REAL' billboards before leaving the state. They skirted Nashville and drove west on I-40. They spent last night in Memphis: eating ribs and chicken at Gus's, getting drunk on Beale Street.

Now, they were entering Clarksdale, heart of the Mississippi Delta. When he lived on the gulf coast, he came here to watch old blues legends, like T-Model Ford and RL Burnside, play. He pointed out the famous CROSSROADS intersection.

"That's where Robert Johnson sold his soul to the devil."

"What'd he get in return?" Denise asked.

"Mean guitar skills."

She laughed. "Lousy deal."

They wandered around the quiet streets An old smoker and frayed couch sat on the porch outside a juke joint. In a record store, she flipped through a stack of blues albums, while a tailless cat slept on the stack beside her. There was a mannequin in the window of a black men's clothing store, decked out in a purple zoot suit and white fedora.

The abandoned buildings reminded her of Rustbelt towns, like Millburg.

"A hundred years ago," Larry said. "The Delta was the hub of the cotton trade."

"You're just like my dad. Full of weird facts."

After a beef brisket lunch at Abe's Barbeque, they left the Delta and drove south on the interstate. Kudzu covered the trees and bushes like ornate curtains.

They reached the coast, Bay St. Louis, by early evening. She lowered her window, feeling the warm gulf breeze as they drove down the beach road. The bayside houses were on stilts: most were new construction, but some were older, bearing the scars of Katrina. Gazing at the white sand and glistening water, she wondered how anything bad could have happened down here. But she remembered the images on television: families stuck on roofs, bodies floating through streets.

They parked outside a surf shop and walked down to the beach. The sky was clear, and the water glimmered in the setting sun. The tide was going out. She took her sandals off and gathered seashells. They sat down in the sand and listened to the gentle break of the surf.

"You ever see dolphins down here?"

"Sometimes," Larry said. "They like to come out and play at dusk."

Resting her head on his chest, Denise closed her eyes.

ACKNOWLEDGMENTS

I'm grateful for the support of many people. Thank you to the editors at *Prairie Schooner, Texas Review, Word Riot, Burnt Bridge, Binnacle, Facets, Monongahela Review, Northern New England Review, Pine Hills Review,* who published my fiction, nonfiction, and poetry, with special thanks to Jeremy Chamberlin at *Fiction Writers Review* and Matthew Pitt at *Descant*.

Thanks to the Virginia Center for the Creative Arts, where much of the novel's first draft was written. I'd like to thank my Pittsburgh and Butler friends who encouraged my writing habit. To my teachers, classmates, and friends in Oxford – including Barry Hannah, John Brandon, Jesmyn Ward, Ann Fisher-Wirth, Gary Short, Chris Offutt, Gary Sheppard, Travis Blankenship, Bill Boyle, Anya Groner, Meredith Hayes, Jimmy Cajoleas, Square Books, Lucky Tucker, and Michael Gaunt – I say thanks y'all. Likewise, to friends at Nebraska, like Tim Schaffert, Sean Doolittle, Ted Kooser, Jordan Farmer, Gabe Houck, Nick White, and Raul Palma, and Jonis Agee. To my early readers, like Randy Steinberg and Ellen Wertman, and to Sharon Pelletier for believing in this book. At Penn State, thanks to Steve Sherrill, Lee Petersen, and Erin Murphy. And a special debt of gratitude to Tom Franklin and Beth Ann Fennelly for being great mentors and friends.

At Stephen F. Austin State University Press, thanks to my editors, Josh Hines and Kimberly Verhines. Thanks to Stewart and Trudy O'Nan, for your generosity. And to Jody and Jenny Offstein, my oldest friends. To my extended family, the New York Bennitts, as well as the McDougalds and Cranfords (my Mississippi outlaws.) To my father, Fred, for your patience and support, and my mother, who died of cancer five years ago, for your belief. And finally, to my son, Hal, and my wife, Rebecca, for everything.

Born and raised in western Pennsylvania, Tom Bennitt earned an MFA (Fiction) from the University of Mississippi and a PhD (English) from the University of Nebraska. His work has appeared in several literary journals, including *Texas Review*, *Prairie Schooner*, *Word Riot* and *Descant*. The 2017 Emerging Writer-in-Residence at Penn State-Altoona, he now resides in State College with his family. For more information, visit: tombennitt.wordpress.com.